CAROLINE and JULIA

CAROLINE
and JULIA

— Clare Darcy —

WALKER AND COMPANY
NEW YORK

First published in the United States of America in 1982 by the Walker Publishing Company, Inc.

Published simultaneously in Canada by John Wiley & Sons Canada, Limited, Rexdale, Ontario.

ISBN: 0-8027-0694-0

Library of Congress Catalog Card Number: 81-51969

Printed in the United States of America

10 9 8 7 6 5 4 3 2 1

CAROLINE and JULIA

= 1 =

THE LEAFLESS BRANCHES of the elms lining the weed-choked carriage way jostled and shoved one another awkwardly in the stiff, October wind, as though, denuded of their green crinolines to give them grace, they felt shame at this rude exposure.

They blurred in Caroline's vision and she bit her lip sharply and turned away. I will not feel sorry for myself, she thought. Mama always said it was not an emotion that ever succeeded in accomplishing anything, and something has *got* to be accomplished. Immediately!

Barely sixteen years old, Caroline Deveraux was in the direst possible straits. Her mother's death two weeks before had left her completely alone in the crumbling family mansion which she was no longer entitled to call home. It was empty of everything that had made it at one time the country seat of a gentleman; her father had sold off most of the furnishings over the years, after selling every acre of the estate except for the small park in which the house stood to pay off his more pressing creditors. Just before his death three years before he'd managed to sell the house itself, though he had not seen fit to inform his long-suffering wife of the fact. That staggering blow had been dealt her in a letter from a London solicitor, who also communicated to her the more welcome news that the purchaser, having no immediate plans for the property, offered the widow the use of the house until she could arrange for other accommodations. Mrs. Devereaux had perforce accepted the offer, having no other home to go to, nor means to make a new one for herself. She and Caroline had closed off all the empty, echoing rooms where the bare walls were splotched with damp stains and pale, symmetrical patches from which the painted visages of several centuries' worth of Devereaux had once surveyed their kingdom with a simpering smile or a haughty eye.

The former housekeeper's room had most recently served as Mrs. Devereaux's boudoir, and a maid's room next to it was Caroline's. Their drawing room was the kitchen where they had, for the past two years, lived very cosily and comparatively happily.

Compared, that is, to what had gone before, for Jack Devereaux had been a brutal husband and an indifferent father, hard drinking, gambling, and riding to hounds his only interests in life. The gay, laughing girl who had come to him with her loving heart and three thousand pounds in dowry found after only a few weeks that the first commodity had no value for him as long as she performed her wifely duties, and the second soon melted away on the gaming tables of London. Its disappearance had not, however, halted Jack in his ruinous career. He borrowed heavily on the expectations of inheriting from his uncle, Chandos Devereaux, whose closest living relative he had been. This uncle had never encouraged these expectations in any way; quite the reverse, indeed. He had despised the nephew as a wastrel and made no bones about telling him so. Jack had, nonetheless, remained confident that the old man would never leave his money away from the family, and since he was the eldest of the remaining relatives, it was, he was certain, bound to be his one day.

In the meantime, carriages, stables, servants, and silverware had melted away over the years, though their loss had never discommoded Jack very much, since he spent so much of his time away from home. The birth of a daughter had not moved him to return home before the baby was some three months old, and then he'd shown only irritation if she cried or anger if she inconvenienced him by demanding her mother's attention when he had need of his wife's services.

He had knocked his wife about quite savagely when he had been drinking, and after several vicious swipes at the toddling Caroline, Mrs. Devereaux had taken great care to keep the child out of his sight, cautioning her to play quietly until Mama could come back. Caroline, docile and intelligent, had learned the wisdom of this injunction by the age of two and could amuse herself for hours together without fretting, knowing her mother would return when she could.

When Jack was away from home they took up again the quiet, happy skein of their lives. Their isolation from the world made them all-and-all to each other. Lavinia Devereaux, *née* Crofton, had been an orphan, raised by a spinster aunt who had managed to send the girl to school for a few years and eke out a small dowry for her. At seventeen Lavinia had met and fallen desperately in love with dashing, handsome Jack Devereaux, and had married him in spite of her aunt's reservations. Lavinia's joy in the union was short-lived, but the aunt having died within weeks after the wedding, Lavinia had no other relatives to turn to for help in her unhappiness. She had never met any of Jack's relations and the few families in the neighbourhood who had called on the new bride had, within a year, fallen away. Lavinia had not been able to return their calls, as Jack refused to keep a carriage, and she could not entertain them properly in her own home. She had been too proud to allow them to know of her distress in any case, and had as a consequence earned the reputation of an eccentric. The neighbours had been relieved to drop her, as Jack was not a man they cared to entertain in their drawing rooms.

In the absence of friends for the elder and playmates for the younger, therefore, mother and daughter became those things for each other. Mrs. Devereaux would enter Caroline's world of "pretend" with all the seriousness of a six-year-old girl, sipping tea from an acorn teacup while gravely inquiring after the health of Caroline's doll children and complimenting her on their looks. In return Caroline would listen carefully as her mother read aloud to her from books far beyond the child's understanding, and beg her mother to sing and play the pianoforte—when it was still in their possession.

They worked together in the kitchen garden, tending their rows of beans and carrots, and went for long, rambling walks, each carrying a basket to hold the first wild strawberries, and later currants, blackberries, walnuts, and apples—everything that could eke out their meager diet, in fact, since unless Jack were in residence, the larder was distressingly bare.

When he came home for the last time, he arrived in Squire Grantley's farm cart, flat on his back, his gelding trailing along behind. The Squire, red-faced and inarticulate, clumsily tried to console the new widow.

"Couldn't have felt a thing, madame, not for a moment. Horse balked at a jump, over Jack went right onto his head, and there was an end to it, quick as a wink."

He made her an offer of thirty pounds for Jack's horse, she calmly requested seventy, they settled on fifty, and he took his departure thinking her a cold-hearted woman to be wife to Jack Devereaux, as red-blooded a man as ever lived, by God!

Mrs. Devereaux and Caroline, however, were indifferent to Squire Grantley's opinion. Jack's death was a happy release for both of them. They had fifty pounds and another thirty found in his pockets, more money than they'd ever seen, and were free of his violence for the first time in their lives with him. Fear and revulsion were the only emotions he'd ever engendered in either of them while alive and relief was the only one they felt at his death.

For two years they had lived happily in their snug apartment at the back of the house, while the rest of the mansion slowly fell into disrepair around them. They spent their store of money only on the barest necessities, managing to live quite healthily on the products of their garden and the woods and fields around them. From time to time they found a jug of fresh milk, a piece of fresh-killed pork, or a basket of new-laid eggs on their doorstep, left there by their nearest neighbour, one of Jack Devereaux's former tenant farmers, a kindly man who worried about the two females all alone in that great barn of a house with no one to turn to.

The work of providing for themselves was, however, too time-consuming for them to spare a thought for the truly terrible destitution of their lives. They had expanded their garden, there was the continuous chore of providing firewood, and there was the need to refurbish their wardrobes, which they managed for the most part from the great trunks in the attic filled with garments stored away for several generations. There were also the hours Mrs. Devereaux devoted to Caroline's education, mostly during the winter, when bad weather held them indoors. For entertainment they read aloud and sang, or Mrs. Devereaux told stories of her happy childhood and of the glorious years she had spent in Miss Kentish's School for Young Gentlewomen, where she met her dearest friend, Julia Coke, now a very successful actress on the London stage under the name of Mrs. Daventry. They speculated endlessly on this fascinating woman and the exciting life she must lead.

On rare excursions to the village for some item they could not do without they saw outdated newspapers with articles about various productions in which Mrs. Daventry was playing the lead role, read them avidly, and treasured the occasional hastily scrawled letter Mrs. Devereaux received from her.

Now, however, those busy, shared days were over. Two weeks before, Mrs. Devereaux had suddenly stood up from her chair by the fire, her sewing falling unheeded from her lap, and pressing her hand to her breast said, with quiet surprise, "Oh!" and collapsed to the floor.

Caroline had dropped to her knees beside the still body, for a moment so paralysed by fear she could not move or speak. Then she had tried frantically to revive her mother, to no avail. Caroline remained for two hours on her knees beside her, holding the cold hand, the tears slipping silently down her cheeks in seemingly endless supply.

She had finally risen stiffly to her feet and fetched a blanket and pillow for her mother, as she could not lift her to the bed. She then washed her own face, put on her cloak and stout boots, and set off across the fields to fetch the farmer.

The services for Mrs. Devereaux had been perfunctorily performed by the curate from the next village, since the Vicar, with two other, much grander livings, rarely made an appearance in this poor, sparsely settled parish. Mrs. Devereaux was conveyed to her place in the Devereaux family plot in the farmer's cart and mourned only by her daughter and the farmer and his wife. Afterward these good people attempted to persuade Caroline to come home with them, but she, never having spent a night away from home in her life, firmly but courteously refused their invitation.

She had written immediately to her father's Uncle Chandos, but now two weeks had passed and he had not replied. Remembering the cold brevity of his condolence note to her mother after her father died, she could not really be shocked at his neglect, though she had not asked him for monetary assistance, nor even hinted at the possibility that she was in need of anything other than the names of any families of his acquaintance who might be in need of a governess. She had told him of her proficiency in all the genteel arts, due to her mother's good training, and her belief that though young she was well qualified to serve as a governess to young female children. However, it appeared that even this small request was more than he was willing to accede to, so she must think of another way.

She could offer lessons on the pianoforte, but her father had sold the instrument long before, and it was therefore many years since she had played herself. Apart from this, there was the problem of finding pupils, there being few of the proper age in the neighbourhood with parents able to pay. This last proved to be the negative answer for any of her other skills: fancy needlework, watercolour painting, and the use of the globes.

It was clear that if she were to become a teacher or a governess she would have to do it someplace other than here. The nearest town of size was Norwich. She had never been there, but her mother's description years before of the magnificent cathedral had left her with a mental image of cold grandeur that she now found daunting when coupled with the fact that she would not know a soul there.

I will be a stranger wherever I go, she thought. Where is there in all the world anyone I *do* know? Can there be another girl in England so friendless as I? I don't *know* Great-Uncle Chandos except as a name. My papa had a brother and there was a son, my Cousin Neville, but I don't even know where he is. I know the curate and the Vicar, and of course Farmer Caxton and his wife—and—and Mrs. Daventry! She heard her mother's sweet, admiring voice pronouncing this name, and looked around, almost expecting to see her mother behind her.

She turned abruptly back to her cheerless view of the elms, misty now as the tears filled her eyes. She dashed them away angrily, refusing to give way again. Now, Mrs. Daventry, she thought. Why haven't I thought of her before? She will be acquainted with a great number of people, no doubt; mostly in London, naturally, but if I must go away from here in any case, London will do as well as Norwich. Excitement mounting, she rushed to her mother's desk and pulled a sheet of paper before her, and after a moment's thought, dipped her pen and wrote rapidly, explaining her situation and her need briefly, and asking if she came to London could she hope for Mrs. Daventry's assistance in seeking employment? She signed and sealed it and turned it over to address it. But where to send it? She didn't have Mrs. Daventry's direction, but surely it could be sent to the last theatre Caroline and her mother had read of in which Mrs. Daventry was playing. If she was no longer there the letter would be sent to her home or another theatre.

She sat imagining the possible progress of the letter, its eventually reaching its destination, various reactions of surprise, sorrow, dismay—annoyance?—an answer being penned, and the progress of that answer back to herself. All of this could take as long as two weeks, possibly longer. In the meantime her rapidly dwindling funds might leave her without the means of making her way to London, even if Mrs. Daventry's response was an enthusiastic and urgent invitation to come at once. Even now she could only manage by taking an outside seat on the public stage.

No, she thought decisively, I cannot wait for her answer. Besides, what is there to wait for? I don't need permission to go, and if she will help me with introductions and references, she can do it just as well if I am there. If she cannot help me I can surely help myself better there than here.

She threw the letter on the fire and watched it burn. When the last feathery ash rose and floated out of sight up the chimney, she turned away with the feeling that a bridge had been burnt and there could be no turning back now. She went to her bedroom and began packing her box. Tomorrow she would walk to the village and try to arrange transportation, if necessary by farmer's cart, into Norwich to catch the stage for London.

2

JULIA DAVENTRY LEANED toward the glass for a serious inspection of her make-up, patting away the dampness of perspiration. The heat from the packed audience rising in waves from the pits and over the footlights, combined with the heavy costume and wig, had caused the make-up to run unbecomingly. She quickly creamed it off. Then with an impatient "Pah!" pulled off the tall, elaborately curled white wig and shook her head, causing hairpins to fly in all directions as her long, riotous dark curls tumbled exuberantly down her back.

"Tch! Really, Miss Julia, now what have you done? We shall have to dress your own hair again, and there's His Grace waiting in the Green Room this age!" exclaimed Mrs. Dainty, picking up the wig and carefully arranging it on the wig stand.

"Since I did not request His Grace to wait, I have no reason to hurry on his account."

"There now, such disrespect, Miss Julia! I'm sure I don't know where you learned such pertness. Sit down now, you can't dress till I've done your hair."

Julia recognized a tone of firmness long familiar to her and plumped resignedly back into the chair before her glass. Mrs. Dainty, formerly Nurse Dainty, had been with Julia from birth, and rarely remembered to call her former charge Mrs. Daventry. She would always be her darling Miss Julia, married or not. Mrs. Dainty was now in her early sixties, but so round, robust, and red-cheeked a little body was she, that she easily passed for many years younger. Though small of stature she was stern of aspect, and of an uncompromising respectability.

Let any say what they would of actresses in general, none could say one word about her Miss Julia, though she did disport herself on a London stage for all the world to gawp at. Mrs. Dainty devoted her every thought to making sure Julia's reputation remained untainted by the least hint of scandal.

Julia was content to remain the captive of this small-scale dragon, for though she enjoyed company and entertainment very well she had no inclination for dalliance even now, five years after darling Edward's death. The extreme pain of her early grief and rage that he had been taken from her had dimmed to a gentle sorrow and regret for the lost happiness, but she had not yet experienced any inclination to relinquish that part of her past in favour of a new love. When she thought of it at all, she presumed that someday she would marry again, for she had enjoyed the married state. No man had yet appeared, however, to stir her emotions sufficiently to create a desire for change. Such a man would have a great deal to live up to, for Edward had been a paragon of manly virtues: forceful, confident, and optimistic, with a mesmerizing quality of charm added to tall, lean good looks.

Rapturously in love, they had married when she was but nineteen and he twenty-one, a dashing lieutenant in the Light Bobs, of good family but no expectations beyond what he could make for himself. Everyone who knew him, however, agreed that his rapid advancement was assured.

When he went gaily off to Spain with Wellington after five perfect years, Julia returned to her parents. Her father, the Reverend Coke, would hear of no other arrangement, nor could Julia have taken a house on her own on Edward's small pittance. She proudly handed this money over to her father as her contribution to the household expenses, and Mr. Coke accepted it gratefully, for three younger sons had astonished their parents by appearing smartly within the space of four years after Julia was twelve years old, and long past the time when either Mr. or Mrs. Coke any longer entertained the hope of increasing their family.

The shattering news of Edward's death in action in the mountains of Spain had been devastating for all the family, who had adored him, and for a time her parents feared that Julia might never recover from such a blow. But after a year her youthful resiliency and common sense finally asserted themselves and she began to take stock of her situation. She still had the hundred and twenty pounds Edward's commanding officer had sent to her as Edward's back pay. She had tried to give it to her father but he would not take it.

Julia knew she could remain in the parsonage, a grieving widow, for the rest of her days without a word of reproach ever spoken or even thought by her loving parents. But that it would be a burden on their slender means she knew only too well. Even now the oldest of her little brothers was nearing the age when a school must be found for him and the means to pay for it were as remote as ever. It therefore behooved her to think of some means of not only lifting the burden of her own keep from their shoulders, but of making a positive contribution to their exchequer.

She brushed aside the thought of teaching or governessing for she knew she had no talent for it, nor skill in spite of the expensive education she had received at Miss Kentish's Academy for Young Gentlewomen, provided by her godmother, Lady Fremont. She felt that she could fill the post of companion to a young woman, or an old one, come to that, for she was ordinarily of a cheerful, happy disposition. She had discussed this possibility with her mother and it was Mrs. Coke who had directed Julia's thoughts of a career in such a wildly unlikely direction.

"Ah, my love," sighed Mrs. Coke, "I cannot bear to think of you in such a position. Women, young or old, who need a companion are generally too ill-natured to have friends, or are sickly, in which case they are cross-grained and treat their companions like servants. You're still sore with grief, but you'll regain your spirits soon. You've always been so gay-spirited. I remember you and the boys putting on those charades and plays for Papa and me. You were such a treat to watch! No matter how down in spirits I might feel, you always lifted my heart. You'd such a way of flashing your eyes, such drollery. Oh, dear, how I miss it all."

And I, too, thought Julia wistfully, a lump rising in her throat as she remembered those happy days.

The next morning as she opened her eyes the idea popped full-blown into her mind as though it had been forming as she slept. I will take my hundred pounds and go to London, she decided, sitting up and staring wide-eyed into space. I will go to every theatre and audition until someone hires me. I know I am a good actress, and though not a beauty, not so ill-looking either. She jumped up hastily, pulling on a morning robe, and ran downstairs to her father's study for his volume of Shakespeare's plays. She spent the next week memorising all the best speeches of Juliet, Viola, and Ophelia, practising them before her bemused parents.

Her plan had, naturally, not immediately appealed to the elder Cokes, but her determination to go could not be damped by any of their expostulations. At last Mrs. Coke gave way and began refurbishing Julia's wardrobe. Mr. Coke conceded defeat by insisting that Nurse Dainty be approached to accompany Julia. If she consented to come out of retirement and move to London with Julia he would say no more.

And all had worked just as Julia planned. She and Dainty had taken rooms in a modest hotel and for a week Julia had gone, accompanied by a grim Dainty, from theatre to theatre. There was interest expressed several times, but not until the sixth day was there a positive response. Mr. Montague Quinn of the Regent's Lane Theatre had been caught by the great liquid dark eyes and the elegant carriage and asked Julia to go onto the stage and recite for him. She gave him a speech of Rosalind's from *As You Like It*, and he was entirely captivated by her exhilarating enthusiasm and her real, if untutored, talent. And if her oval face was a trifle too long in the chin for true beauty, her large, well-shaped mouth and perfect white teeth more than compensated for the flaw.

He had hired her immediately, and began training her in small roles at once. Her first leading role was as Portia in *The Merchant of Venice*, and she became overnight the rage of London, and had remained so for the past five years. Other theatres had attempted to woo her away, but she remained faithful to Mr. Quinn, and he to her. She now commanded a salary that not only enabled her to send gratifying sums home to her parents, but left her with enough to live, if not in luxury, at least in a great deal of comfort with a cook, maid and butler, and her own carriage—and of course her own dear Dainty, who stood behind her now attempting to brush some order into Julia's thick tresses.

"If you don't sit still, missy, we will be here for hours," Mrs. Dainty chided as Julia twitched impatiently beneath her ministrations, picking up and discarding several posies from admirers, which cluttered her dressing table as tributes did every night she performed.

"Oh, do stop fussing, Dainty, that will do very well!" she finally exclaimed, slipping from Dainty's hands and crossing the room for her dark blue merino gown, dropping the simple cambric robe she always wore when she had removed her costume. "Come help me with these buttons, please. I'm so famished I feel quite faint and I must get home as quickly as possible."

"What! And what of His Grace waiting this long time for you, I'd like to know?"

"Oh, bother His Grace! He must surely be one of the greatest bores of London and I've no intention of letting him keep me from my supper."

"If you have some caper-witted notion in your head of not greeting His Grace of Malby, you may forget it. I would not dream of allowing you to display such a want of conduct!" Mrs. Dainty set her mouth in a grim line and stared coldly at Julia, whose eyes flashed rebelliously. For a long moment they confronted one another, and then, as was usual in these moments, Julia gave way.

"Oh, very *well*, though if you are entertaining visions of embroidering strawberries onto my undergarments you can rid yourself of the notion, for I've no ambitions to be a duchess. At least, not his!" Tossing her head defiantly, she sailed out the door.

"Impertinence!" called Mrs. Dainty at her departing back, having, as always, the last word.

Julia swept into the Green Room calling out, "Good evening, gentlemen," from the doorway. The dozen or so men standing about in groups chatting desultorily instantly sprang into action, descending upon her in a rush.

The pack was led by Montgomery, Duke of Malby, a short, stout young man with fair hair and bulging blue eyes set rather too close together in a florid face. Close on his heels were the Honourable "Bertie" Buckthorpe, thin to emaciation, whose beaky nose sloped back to forehead and chin to form a profile resembling a nearly perfect triangle, and Mr. Bartle à Court, a Dandy devoted to being the first in Fashion, and who, since Julia was the Fashion, had perforce declared his undying devotion. Trailing these was Lord Redvers Wrexham, whose careless Byronic locks and die-away air sat oddly on his tall, well-muscled body and healthily red-cheeked face. He wrote reams of dreadful poetry, all dedicated to "The Divine," Mrs. Daventry.

Behind them were a clutch of less prominent citizens, consisting mostly of tongue-tied and bashful youths, infatuated not only with the beautiful Mrs. Daventry, but with theatre in general, and awed to find themselves in company with these well-known Tulips of the *Ton* whose manners and dress they aped assiduously.

The Duke reached to take Julia's hand. "Madam—" he began, but got no further. Lord Redvers forstalled him by lithely stepping around everyone and dropping to one knee before Julia. He took her outheld hand and pressed it to his lips reverently.

His Grace, unable to check the impetus of his forward movement, nearly fell over his kneeling friend, only saved from ignominy by the Honorable Bertie, who instinctively grabbed his shoulder and pulled him back. Completely unaware of this diversion behind him, Lord Redvers breathed, "Divinity!" while gazing soulfully up at Julia. His Grace of Malby pulled down his waistcoat irritably and glowered at the back of Lord Redvers's head.

"Rudest thing I ever saw, Wrexham, pushing yourself in like that! What do you mean by it, sir?"

The Honourable Bertie laughed at the Duke's discomfiture. "Cut you right out, Monty, be demmed if he didn't. Never saw anything neater!"

"You've always been cursed with a rather bizarre sense of humour, Bertie," replied His Grace in a huff.

"Better than being cursed with none at all, old sprat," replied Bertie breezily.

"Gentlemen, it is charming to see all of you but—Lord Redvers, do get up!—but I am famished and must go away at once."

The air was immediately filled with a clamour of protest.

"But I've ordered a small collation—"

"You will allow me to—"

"Do me the honour, dear lady, I pray—"

She laughed, her dark eyes flashing and her white teeth sparkling, causing Lord Redvers to gasp and drop to his knees again.

"Oh! Brightest Star, to outshine the very Queen of Heaven! Say you will allow me to accompany you home. I've a new verse for you and you shall hear it as you dine."

"You will oblige me by standing up, sir," she commanded, "and I intend to become quite cross with you if you persist in such a ridiculous posture. As for reading to me while I dine, I thank you but it is out of the question. One cannot seriously address one's food while one's teeth and eyelashes are being rhapsodised. One becomes self-conscious and one's digestion is seriously interfered with.''

Undismayed he rose to his feet and clasped her hand in both his own. ''Then I shall unhitch your team and draw your carriage home myself,'' he declared feverently.

''I have no doubt of your ability to do so, Lord Redvers,'' she said smiling as she eyed the broad shoulders and well-muscled thighs, ''but I wish you will not be so ridiculous.''

''Yes, Wrexy, you're becoming a bore,'' drawled Mr. Bartle à Court, flicking an imaginary speck from an impeccable sleeve, ''just as your hero is a bore.''

''Lord Byron a *bore!*'' gasped Lord Redvers in accents of horror. ''The man who wrote *The Corsair—The Giaour—The—*''

''I was speaking of his conduct, not his writing, Wrexy. You must learn to discriminate.''

''The man is a degenerate bounder, unfit to enter a respectable drawing room. No woman is safe from his attentions,'' contributed Bertie.

''Actually, it's he who's unsafe from *their* attentions, Bartle,'' offered His Grace with a significant chortle.

''You're right, Malby, I don't know when I've seen so many perfectly unexceptionable women behaving so disgracefully over one man. And such a man! All those affected costumes and the carefully disarrayed curls. Why the man doesn't even look clean!'' Bertie exclaimed indignantly.

''D'you suppose it's the limp? Bringing out the maternal in the tender-hearted sex?'' queried His Grace. ''Takes 'em in, don't you know, then has his way before they know what's afoot.''

''Sir!'' warned Julia, feeling they were in danger of becoming bawdy.

''Really, Monty, you forget yourself! You insult our fair one by speaking so in her presence and you insult the genius of our age by speculating about his private life!'' protested Lord Redvers.

''Remind me to fill you in on his private life, infant, when we are next alone together,'' replied Mr. à Court with a leer.

''I appeal to you, Goddess,'' Lord Redvers said, turning back to Julia and almost reduced to tears, ''can the man who wrote *Childe Harold's Progress* be other than pure of heart?''

''Well,'' temporised Julia, having heard the rumours now flying about London regarding Lord Byron and his half-sister Augusta, more shocking even than his highly visible affair with Caroline Lamb, "I don't believe genius is necessarily a guarantee of good morals."

"But we agreed—" began Lord Redvers.

"We agreed to his genius, but I fear it is only too true that his private life could not bear close scrutiny without creating disgust in anyone of sensibility," replied Julia, softening the blow by speaking gently.

Lord Redvers looked so completely crushed that she reached out to pat his arm consolingly, and even Mr. à Court took pity.

"Never mind, infant. I won't tell you the grisly details. On thinking it over, you are much too young to hear them anyway."

"I am one-and-twenty, sir," Lord Redvers replied with cold dignity.

"No, you ain't, Wrexy," said Bertie pedantically. "You were twenty last birthday, because your mama told me so, and that was but a month ago. I remember it perfectly because it was at the ball your mama gave for you to celebrate and—"

Julia interrupted impatiently, "Dear friends, I am truly fascinated by our conversation, but I must tear myself away or Dainty will be extremely vexed with me and put me to bed without my supper."

There followed another chorus of protests and invitations, which she smilingly ignored, holding out her hand to each in turn to be kissed, and then firmly turning away to the door.

But she stopped with a gasp of astonishment, and behind her all the clamour ceased abruptly. In the silence could be heard several indrawn breaths and then, "Good God!" from Lord Redvers in a disbelieving whisper.

In the doorway, valise on the floor by her side, stood a young girl of such ravishing beauty as to seem unreal. She was small, but slender and well proportioned. Her dark green eyes shone like jewels from the pure cameo of her face, whose skin of translucent white was touched on each cheek with the faintest tint of pink. Her perfectly carved lips were a deeper rose, slightly parted now to reveal the small pearls of her teeth. Framing this exquisiteness were curls of rich auburn peeping from beneath her bonnet and falling in thick waves over her shoulders and down her back.

In the brief instant as they all gaped at her speechlessly, a flush rose slowly up her throat and spread over her face to the very roots of her hair. She dropped her eyes in confusion, displaying to advantage the long fringe of dark lashes.

" 'She walks in beauty, like the night / Of cloudless climes and starry skies; / And all—' " began Lord Redvers on a sigh, as though involuntarily.

Julia started at the sound of his voice and pulled herself together enough to ask dazedly, "Can I—er—help you?"

The green eyes came up shyly. "Mrs.—Mrs. Daventry?"

"Yes," said Julia encouragingly.

"I am—Caroline Devereaux."

"Caroline Devereaux," Julia parroted uncomprehendingly.

"Yes. The daughter of Lavinia Crofton Devereaux. But perhaps you've forgotten." Caroline blushed again even more furiously than before and bowed her head to study her shoe tops, obviously unable to sustain the riveted stares of so many people at once. "I beg your pardon," she whispered. "I should not have—I should have—"

"Lavinia! Lavinia Crofton's daughter! Good Lord!" Julia rushed forward, hands outstretched. "Forgive me, child, for being such a slow-top. We will blame it on the lateness of the hour." She took the small clasped hands in her own and leaned forward to kiss the satiny young cheek. "Is your mama with you, my dear?"

"No, Mrs. Daventry. She—she is dead—so I came to you."

Julia was jolted back into her usual good sense. In a flash she took in the shabby pelisse and bonnet, the old-fashioned valise on the floor, and the worn toes of the shoes peeping from beneath the gown. She also saw the tears beginning to form in the corners of the jewel-like eyes, and the brave tilt of the chin in an effort to hold them back. At the same moment she became aware of the fascinated silence behind her. The child must be gotten away at once.

"Of course you did, my dear. And now, not another word. We're going to go straight home and let Dainty coddle us. Good night gentlemen," she sang out, and picking up the valise she swept Caroline out of the room before anyone could speak.

Calling out to Mrs. Dainty to come along, she continued across the gloom of the backstage to the stage door where her carriage waited. Mrs. Dainty came panting after them and in less than a minute the carriage was bowling away.

3

CAROLINE'S STORY WAS heard in a horrified silence by Julia and Mrs. Dainty on the carriage ride home. When she came to the part about her trip to London on the outside of the mail coach, Mrs. Dainty, whose flinty exterior encased a heart as soft as eiderdown, lost the last of the defensiveness she had exhibited when first introduced to Caroline in the carriage. Her reaction had been occasioned by her fear of anyone imposing on her Miss Julia. By the time Caroline's history was unfolded, however, told with a lack of drama and self-pity which made it all the more affecting, Mrs. Dainty had turned about in her feelings completely, so that when they reached the door of Julia's elegant little town house Mrs. Dainty had taken charge of the situation. She bundled Caroline into the house, bossily calling out to the butler to carry up Miss's case and then take word to Cook that a basin of hot gruel was required at once, and ordering the wide-eyed maid to run upstairs and build a good fire and warm the sheets in the guest room quick as quick.

Julia was left to alight from the carriage and trail after them into the house, amused to note that she felt somewhat like the proverbial stepchild. She shrugged and requested that when Mrs. Dainty's needs had been met, her own supper be served in the back drawing room, and retired there at once. She removed her dainty velvet half boots and propped her feet on a large ottoman near the fire, sinking back into the soft cushions of her favorite wing chair with a sigh of contentment. This was always a delicious moment: a satisfying performance behind her, a good supper to come, and the warmth and solitude of her own home to soothe and enfold her. It had become so necessary a part of her routine that she made it a rule never to accept a social engagement after a performance.

Tomorrow night would be her last performance as Lady Townley in *The Provoked Husband* and then she would have a week's hiatus before they began again. She realized that week was a very fortunate thing as it turned out, for she would now have time to take the child about and show her the sights of London. There was the Liverpool Museum with a thirty-five-foot boa constrictor and a sixteen-foot giraffe. That would surely be suitable. Then she might like to see Mrs. Salmon's Waxwork Museum.

Belding, her butler, presently brought her a supper tray and she fell ravenously on the tenderones of veal with truffles and fresh peas. When she had scraped up the last bit of a charlotte of apples she sat back with a sigh of repletion and sipped her glass of claret. She always took a glass of wine with her meal after a performance. It helped to relax her after an emotionally charged evening.

Actually, she thought, staring into the flames, the child's entrance into my life might turn out to be a very good thing, for there is no denying I've become as settled in my ways as a spinster of fifty, becoming cross if anything disrupts my routine or keeps me waiting for my meals. I suppose I shall grow quite stout when I stop working.

She picked up a copy of *The Doubtful Son*, her next play, and begin silently mouthing the words of the Marchioness of Lerida, the role she would be playing. Presently the warmth of the fire and the good meal she had eaten caused the print to swim before her eyes.

"There now! Falling asleep already," came Dainty's accusing voice, causing Julia to start. She stretched lazily and smiled.

"I made sure you'd forgotten me, Dainty, now you have a real child to attend to."

"I'll see that, missy. Come along to your bed now before you catch your death sleeping here with nothing to cover you," scolded the nurse, pulling Julia to her feet and leading her out of the room. "As for the girl, she's no child. Full grown, she is, and as neat a figure as you'll ever see. Not that a person could tell with the clothes she has. Her mother's things, no doubt, all cobbled up to fit her. Only two gowns in that valise and they threadbare and most unsuitable. She'd not a stitch of mourning on her. You'll have to get her something proper."

"Oh, Dainty! *Not* mourning. She's far too young, and after all she's been through she should be helped to forget—"

"You're never saying the child shouldn't mourn her mother, and her not dead a month yet!" Mrs. Dainty was clearly scandalized. "Of course she will mourn her mother. We could not prevent that even if we wanted to. They were too close for her not to grieve. But she need not be smothered in black nor confined to the house with nothing to do but contemplate her misery. I will buy her some pretty gowns and take her about to help take her mind off it."

"It's most improper! What will people think if—"

"Let them think what they will," Julia replied, tossing her head defiantly, "her mother was my friend. If positions were reversed I wouldn't want my daughter forced to wallow in her sorrow. I should be grateful if Lavinia did her best to help my child to go on with her life. And that is what I shall do for hers, for I know she would want it."

Mrs. Dainty sniffed disapprovingly, but contented herself with ordering Julia into her bed and binding her down by tucking in the covers as tightly as possible, saying only, "Well, in any case, she'll not leave her bed for several days. I'll see to that."

She was unable, however, to carry out her threat, for after sleeping twelve hours, Caroline, with the resiliency of youth, bounded from her bed, green eyes sparkling, cheeks blooming with color, and desperately hungry. She splashed water onto her face, brushed ruthlessly at the tangled auburn curls, and dressed hurriedly. By the height of the sun in the sky she guessed it must be close to ten in the morning. *Ten*, she thought with amazement. She'd never slept so late! In the country, she and her mother had retired to bed almost as soon as darkness fell, not only to save candles, but because their hard work in the open air made them too exhausted to stay awake. As a consequence they were used to waking at dawn.

She halted in her scramble, standing still in the middle of the room, remembering with a vivid stab of pain that there would be no more of those mornings. Her eyes filled with tears that she allowed to run unchecked down her cheeks. When the pain had eased she turned quickly to the wash stand, dashed more water into her eyes and dried them, and left the room at a run, as though to escape her memories. She scampered down the stairs and was brought up sharply by Belding, who stood in the hallway watching her descent with interest.

"Oh! I'm—is Mrs. Daventry—" Caroline faltered, much flustered.

"In the breakfast parlour, miss. Just through that door."

At the word "breakfast" she smiled sunnily at him, and he smiled back encouragingly, as though he knew her problem. When she entered the room Julia, still drinking her hot chocolate, put down her cup, eyebrows rising in surprise. Caroline interpreted the look as one of censure for her lateness and immediately began an apology.

"No, no, dear child, you are not late in the least. I never come down early after a performance. I am only surprised that *you* are down at all. Mrs. Dainty told me you'd be in your bed for several days."

"But why?" Caroline looked greatly bewildered.

"She expected you'd require it after your ordeal."

"Oh, no," Caroline replied, scornfully shrugging aside over twelve hours on top of the mail coach in the sharp cold of early spring. She eyed the toast on a plate before Julia. Julia correctly interpreted the look.

"Would you like your breakfast now?"

"Oh, *yes*," Caroline breathed fervently.

Julia rang for Belding. "Bring Miss Devereaux—er—a large breakfast," she ordered when he appeared. In a very short time she was watching with amusement as Caroline finished off a plate of buttered eggs, several thick slices of ham, four muffins, and three cups of chocolate. The child might look like a porcelain doll but was obviously made of much less fragile material.

Mrs. Dainty, red-faced and panting, came bustling into the room. "Well! Belding told me just now he'd served you breakfast and I couldn't believe my ears. *What* are you doing out of bed, young lady?"

Caroline quickly set down her chocolate cup and looked guiltily up at Mrs. Dainty. Julia laughed.

"Now don't try your browbeating, Dainty. I know how disappointed you are to be deprived of your patient, but even you must admit that the child looks excessively healthy—not so much as a sniffle, and I can testify that she has just eaten an unusually hearty breakfast."

"I—was very hungry—" Caroline faltered, hanging her head in shame.

"Of course you were! And why shouldn't you be?" exclaimed

Mrs. Dainty, firing up in defense of her newest charge. She had never allowed anyone but herself to criticise one of her children.

"Caroline, darling, nothing could have reassured me more that you've suffered no ill effects from your journey. I had quite made up my mind I would have to live with my frustration patiently for several days before I could do all the things I have planned."

"Planned," Caroline parroted blankly.

"Why, yes. We must get you some new gowns and I want to take you to the Liverpool Museum and—oh, ever so many wonderful sights to see."

"Well," Caroline said doubtfully, "it is very kind of you, Mrs. Daventry, but I think I must set about finding employment at once. As for clothes, they must wait. I've very little money left to—"

"Darling child, you will please allow me to give you a few things. I would be—"

"Forgive me, dear Mrs. Daventry, but I could not allow—"

"For your mother's sake, as I know she would want me to—"

"I am really in no need, you see. I have two gowns besides this one, and—"

This exchange went on until Mrs. Dainty interrupted to state very firmly that Caroline would not be taken to the theatre to see Miss Julia perform unless she had a decent gown to wear that wouldn't put Miss Julia to the blush before her friends.

Since this was the dearest wish of Caroline's heart, confided sleepily to Mrs. Dainty the night before as she was being put to bed, she stared in dismay at Mrs. Dainty, unable to think of a reply to this dire threat.

"As for employment," Julia rushed in, taking advantage of the girl's confusion, "that is something I will not discuss with you at the present. You need a complete rest and will remain here as my guest for—as long as it may require."

"As long as what may require?" Caroline asked simply.

"Er—your recovery. Never mind, darling. If you've finished, run up and fetch your bonnet and pelisse. There are ever so many things we must do."

In a short time Caroline found herself staring saucer-eyed out the windows of the landaulet as they bowled over the cobblestones of London. They stopped at Bruton Street where Julia turned her over to the ministrations of Madame Colette, Julia's modiste, who surveyed Caroline's neat figure and astonishing colouring with exclamations of delight, while discreetly turning shocked eyes away from the drab costume.

Talking volubly in French, Madame Colette led a protesting Caroline away and returned with her, speechless, sometime later wearing an amber cambric walking dress vandyked at the hem, with a matching pelisse in velvet trimmed at neck and wrist with narrow bands of chinchilla.

"*Voila, madame! Ravissant, n'est pas?*"

"Genius! Sheer genius, madame! Do you like it Caroline? Caroline?"

"Yes, ma'am?" Caroline replied, dragging dazzled eyes from her image in the glass.

"Do you like the gown, my dear?"

"Oh!" was the only answer Caroline seemed capable of, but Julia took her meaning. She nodded to Madame Colette.

"But—but"—Caroline turned back as Madame Colette began to lead her away—"will not this do for the theatre—?"

"*Mais non!*" Madame raised horrified eyebrows. "Nevair, mademoiselle! One does not wear such an ensemble to the theatre! Come." She firmly led Caroline away.

The thin edge of the wedge having been inserted, morning gowns, round gowns, pelisses, and evening gowns followed in dizzying procession. After Madame Colette had relinquished the two, they proceeded to Pall Mall where a visit to Harding and Howell produced gloves, bonnets, sandals, and half-boots, and a stop at the Burlington Arcade was necessary to procure more intimate garments.

Home again, Caroline sat dazedly in her room while Mrs. Dainty bustled about unpacking the piles of bandboxes and stowing away their treasures.

"You'd best look sharp, my girl, if you want to see Miss Julia tonight in her play. Your bath water will be here in a minute and you still in that gown. Get out of it quickly. After your bath you'll have your dinner—"

"Oh, I couldn't eat, Mrs Dainty!"

"—you'll have your dinner," continued Mrs. Dainty inexorably, "and then I'll do your hair."

The bath was taken, the dinner was eaten to the last scrap,

and the hair was dressed just as Mrs. Dainty had prophesied. She then sat Caroline down beside the fire in her dressing robe, cautioning her not to move until she returned, and hurried away to change her own gown. Though much torn by the choice, Mrs. Dainty had elected to accompany Caroline to the theatre, assigning the maid to accompany Julia there and help her with her costumes. They had left some time before and the carriage was to be sent back for Caroline and Mrs. Dainty.

Presently Mrs. Dainty came rustling back in her best black silk, and standing Caroline before the glass, carefully lowered a gown of palest shell-pink gauze over her head, careful not to disarrange the auburn hair dressed *à la Anglais*, an artlessly simple arrangement suitable for a young girl.

Caroline stared awestruck at the most beautiful gown she had ever beheld. The square neckline was cut modestly low, the sleeves short and puffed. The high waist and long straight line of the skirt gave her more inches than she really possessed. The gown's only trimming was the rose-coloured velvet riband circling just below the bosom and hanging in long streamers to the hem where pale pink satin slippers showed. There were elbow-length white kid gloves and pearl earrings donated by Julia from her jewelry box to finish the costume. Caroline thought with great satisfaction that she looked at least twenty years old.

Mrs. Dainty laid a rose velvet evening cloak lined in white satin over her shoulders, handed her an ivory brise fan, and led the way out of the room. In the carriage Caroline sat up very straight and absolutely still to prevent doing any damage to her toilette. At the theatre her own grandeur made her so shy that she saw little besides the tips of her slippers as she followed Mrs. Dainty's broad back up the stairs to the box Julia had procured for them.

The box was in the center of the left side in the first tier, and as they entered Caroline felt all her senses assaulted at once: the roar of the heaving, restless crowd in the pit, the various scents of perfume and burning candles, and the kaleidoscope of color, all combined, caused her to sink stunned into a chair as she attempted to take in the entire dazzling spectacle at once.

"You must not sit so with your mouth agape like some clodpole just up from the country, Miss Caroline," admonished Mrs. Dainty in a whisper.

"No—no, of course not," Caroline agreed, dropping her eyes,

"but of course, Mrs. Dainty, I *am* just up from the country," she added irrepressibly.

"That's no reason to behave as though you had straw in your hair still," retorted Mrs. Dainty. "Now lay off your cloak and sit back and fan yourself very slowly as though you came to the theatre every night of your life. You'll see everything just as well that way."

Caroline did as she was told, covertly eyeing the chattering, laughing groups, her head moving slowly from box to box, filling her eyes with the beautifully coloured gowns and glittering jewels. When her eyes reached the last box across the theatre, just above the stage, they met the soulful stare of an unusually handsome young man and moved on, only to jerk back in spite of herself. The two gazed at one another for a long moment before Caroline dropped her eyes in confusion. She felt a blush rising up over her bared bosom and quickly laid her fan over it, but the color continued mercilessly up to the very roots of her hair. It was quite five minutes before she dared raise her eyes again, and then she carefully avoided looking in that direction.

There was a sudden rise in the volume of noise and every head in the theatre turned to a box directly across from Caroline. She gasped, as did a number of women in the audience, as she saw the woman who had entered the box, a strikingly lovely lady in a white gown of revealing sheerness which clung to her voluptuous figure lovingly. Her snow-white bosom was exposed almost in its entirety by her low décolletage, and the diamond necklace displayed there flashed blindingly with her every breath. She was surrounded by men who jostled and elbowed one another in an effort to get near her. She threw back her head in a gay laugh and waved a white ostrich-feather fan with sensuous grace.

"Who is that?" Caroline breathed.

"Look away, Miss Caroline. It's indecent, is what it is, and shouldn't be allowed," Mrs. Dainty replied, stiff with outrage, her own head rigidly facing the stage.

"Yes, but who is she?"

"Her name is Harriett Wilson and she's a—she's—never mind, just pretend not to notice her. Disgraceful! She's dampened her skirts!"

Caroline reluctantly dragged her eyes away only to find herself gazing again into the eyes of the outrageously handsome young man. He must be the only man here who isn't staring at that woman, Caroline thought, and was so gratified she allowed herself to reward him with a shy little smile before looking away. Before she had time to think further about this interesting discovery, the lights were lowered and the laughing and shouting died away to a hushed expectancy. The curtains parted and all reality faded for Caroline. She sat rapt and silent to the very end, and was led away by Mrs. Dainty after the final curtain, still speechless, all thoughts of the handsome man gone from her mind.

When Julia arrived home and Caroline joined her for supper, she was almost too shy with adoration to say all the things she felt about Julia's performance. Julia laughed at her and soon put her more at ease by insisting that she have a glass of wine.

"Oh, but my head is spinning so much already!"

"Nonsense, it will do you good," insisted Julia, half filling her glass. She could see the girl was in high alt and thought the wine would calm her and help her to sleep.

Caroline did sleep, almost as soon as her head touched her pillow, and her dreams were as eventful as her day had been, featuring Madame Colette pursuing her with a basin of water crying out that her skirts must be dampened before she could enter the theatre, a roomful of clothes which in the way of dreams she understood she was to try on, and the handsome young man who kept trying to tell her something with his eyes that she could not quite grasp, try as she would.

4

NEVILLE DEVEREAUX STEPPED out of his handsome traveling carriage onto the carefully raked gravel of the sweeping driveway that led up to the large country house and gazed up at the imposing front door, draped now in black crepe. He was too late then, he thought, with an impatient shrug of broad shoulders beneath his many-caped coat. Then, resigning himself and setting his harsh-featured face into a semblance of solicitude, he ascended the steps to the door.

His emotions were not affected in any way by the knowledge that his Great-Uncle Chandos had quit this world for another, since Neville's father had been estranged from his uncle long before Neville's birth. Also since Mr. Devereaux's older brother, Jack, had always been presumed to be Chandos's heir, this estrangement had made no difference at all to Neville's own future. As a matter of fact, Mr. Devereaux had assured his son's future himself by making a fortune in the East India Company, and at the time of his death had been able to leave his son in possession of a fortune many times larger than that of Chandos's.

During his lifetime Mr. Devereaux, a man of strong moral rectitude, had also cut off all relations with his own brother, Jack, in disgust for his degenerate way of life, thus leaving Neville with no contact with his father's people. Now, with the death of his father, Chandos, and Jack, he was the only male left with that name in his family.

Which would account for the urgent letter he had received from a lady he could only assume was the housekeeper, begging him to come to his great-uncle's deathbed. Much as he deplored the necessity for the trip, he could not shrug aside the pleadings of a woman with no one else to turn to for help. At least, no male to turn to, for Neville was aware that Jack had a wife and at least one female child. It was perfectly possible that they too had been summoned and were here by now, which might provoke some uneasy moments if they were inclined to resent the attitude of Neville's father.

Ah, well, one's duty must be done, however distasteful, he thought and thumped the knocker firmly. The door was opened instantly by a tall, cadaverous servant who had obviously been waiting for the sound. He bowed slightly and gazed at Neville expressionlessly. Neville experienced a stab of irritation. Surely the man could be in no doubt of Neville's identity?

"I believe Mrs. Knox-Gore is expecting me," Neville said coldly.

"What name shall I say, sir?"

"Mr. Devereaux!" snapped Neville. Devil take the man, he fumed inwardly.

The servant bowed again and opened the door fully. Neville walked in and removed his hat and coat. The servant took them and laid them on a chair. The interior of the house, as far as Neville could see, was in keeping with the elaborate, well-tended grounds. Great-Uncle Chandos had obviously lived very well.

"If you will follow me, sir," said the manservant, and led the way across the hall. He opened a door, announced, "Mr. Devereaux," and bowed Neville in.

Seated in a large wing chair before a brisk fire was an extremely stout lady of middle years, dressed completely in black except for her elaborately ruffled and beribanded white cap. Each ruffle, however, was daintily edge with black.

Neville, surprised that she did not rise and curtsey as would have been proper in a housekeeper, advanced across the room and bowed. "Mrs. Knox-Gore?"

"Oh, Mr. Devereaux! How kind of you to come so quickly. We are all at sixes and sevens with no member of the immediate family to take charge, and I so overcome with grief for my dear brother I cannot think what is best to do!" She turned her head away and applied a lacy handkerchief to the corners of her eyes.

"Brother?" Neville's tone expressed his bewilderment, for to his knowledge Chandos had had no sister.

"My dear sister, may her soul rest in peace, was the wife of his heart alas for too few years. Ah, poor creature, to be taken so young. But still she is not here to grieve for him today, which must be accounted a blessing. Dear Chandos was inconsolable. He mourned her to the hour of his own death.''

"Ah—er—yes, I see—of course, your brother-in-law. May I offer my condolences, madame.''

"Oh, but it is I who—oh, dear, how remiss of me—such a sad time for all of us—'' The handkerchief was again brought into play.

"The sorrow must be all your own, Mrs. Knox-Gore. I was not acquainted with my great-uncle, as you must be aware.''

"Ah, such a pity, Mr. Devereaux! He was the most admirable man in the world! All kindness and consideration. I could speak forever of his goodness to me and never be finished. Allowing me and my poor fatherless little boy to make our home here. Oh, I shall never forget all he has done for my dear Sidney. He treated him as his own son. Poor, poor boy, to be twice left fatherless.''

"Er—your son is still young, madame?''

"He has attained his majority, sir. The very time when a boy needs a father's guiding hand. And homeless now, too.''

"My dear Mrs. Knox-Gore, I am persuaded you will have been left provided for by my great-uncle,'' Neville said soothingly. "Now, has his solicitor been notified?''

"Immediately, sir. But he has written back to say he will not come as he has had no contact with Chandos since your Uncle Jack died. At that time Chandos wrote explaining how his will was to be changed. The solicitor made the requested changes, returned the will to Chandos, and never heard from him again.''

"Has he a copy of the will?''

"He says not. Sounded somewhat miffed on the subject, for he said Chandos told him two copies were not necessary. He said he knew nothing further in the matter, quite coldly—Chandos never liked that man! At any rate, I would not apply to him further for help. That is when I wrote to you.''

"Then the will must be here in the house. Have you looked for it?''

She looked aghast. "Certainly not, Mr. Devereaux! It was not my place to do so. That surely would properly belong to one of his own blood to do, if not his solicitor.''

"Oh, yes, that reminds me of what I had thought about on my

32

way here. My Uncle Jack left a wife and child, I believe. Have you—"

Mrs. Knox-Gore rose to her feet with a soft shriek, clapping her hand to her large bosom in the general area of her heart, and then swooned forward.

Neville, directly in front of her, caught the heavy body and supported it back into the chair. He then stepped to the fireplace and pulled the cord to summon a servant. In a moment the cadaverous manservant appeared and stood silently surveying the slumped body and lolling head of Mrs. Knox-Gore. He then turned his impassive stare upon Neville.

"Bring brandy—at once!" snapped Neville, again irritated by the man's manner.

Mrs. Knox-Gore sighed and her eyelids fluttered open. "Oh— oh—Moberly—my vinaigrette, please."

Moberly walked to the table beside her, picked up her work bag, and extracted the bottle, which he handed to her.

"I think perhaps a few sips of brandy might be most efficacious as a restorative, madame," offered Neville, though he could see she was not truly in need of it, since she had not lost any color.

"So thoughtful, sir, but I can never abide brandy. Even a few sips muddle my poor brains sadly—even more than—oh, dear, Mr. Devereaux, I have been so remiss. I will never forgive myself, though at the time I was in constant attendance on dear Chandos—indeed, for the last three days that he lingered I never once laid my head on my own pillow—but I should have—oh dear, oh, dear—"

"My dear Mrs. Knox-Gore, you must not upset yourself again. Just tell me quite quietly what the problem is and I'm sure we will find a solution." Neville allowed no trace of his vexation with this feather-headed woman to appear in his tone. It was slowly becoming apparent to him that his business here might not be concluded as expeditiously as he had hoped and he must simply resign himself to the fact. The woman was clearly incapable of coherent thought. He distinctly remembered her letter asking him to come at once as his great-uncle was dying, yet not three minutes before she said she had written to him after contacting the solicitor *after* Chandos's death. Not that it really mattered, he supposed, except that he had little tolerance for the dithering sort of female.

"Well, Mr. Devereaux, I will try to be sensible. So annoying for gentlemen, I know, to be forced to attend fainting women. My own dear husband was just so—oh, the soul of courtesy, of course, but one could always see—''

Neville interrupted the flow of this digression by dismissing Moberly, still an interested if impassive spectator. ''Now, Mrs. Knox-Gore, what is it that has distressed you?''

''Well, it was when you spoke about Jack's wife and daughter. It reminded me quite suddenly—my heart absolutely *leaped* with the shock—such an appalling lapse on my part! There had been a letter, you see, not two days before dear Chandos expired. I had only time to glance at it and then put it—now, where *can* I have put it—?'' She stared into space, seeking the answer.

Neville shifted impatiently. ''Whose letter?''

''Oh—the daughter's. Perhaps you think I had no business to open it, but I knew if Chandos could have spoken he would have asked me to open and read it to him. He often asked me to handle his correspondence, you see, for he disliked writing letters excessively—even reading them. Why sometimes his letters would remain unopened for days. I used to say to him—''

''What did the letter say, Mrs. Knox-Gore?'' Neville asked firmly.

''What? Oh, well, I only glanced at it, as I told you, I was much too distracted with worry and grief to really read it. No one could believe my— However''—she switched back to the subject hastily upon seeing Neville's brows beginning to contract—''the child was writing to notify her great-uncle of her mother's death. Oh, dear, so much death, Mr. Devereaux! But there, in the midst of life, you know, we are—''

''Yes, I know. Now, Mrs. Knox-Gore, if you could find the letter I would like to read it. Just to assure myself that she is all right.'' Neville knew it might take the better part of the morning to get the woman to divulge the entire contents of the letter and a great deal of time might be saved by simply reading it for himself.

''So kind—so thoughtful. Now, I was seated at the bedside, in case dear Chandos should regain consciousness for even a brief moment and require something. I read the letter, just hastily, you know, and laid it aside to—no! There now, I remember! I put it in my apron pocket! I will fetch it at once.''

She hoisted herself to her feet and waddled away. Neville

shrugged and turned to the fireplace, to contemplate the flames moodily. Here was another responsibility devolving on his shoulders, he supposed. Though their fathers had not spoken for years, still the child was his cousin, his only cousin in their very unprolific family, and if he knew anything of the matter, it was most unlikely that Jack had cut up warm when he'd finally stuck his spoon in the wall, for according to rumour he had gambled away every penny he could get his hands on. Though Neville had little taste for assuming the burden of a young female, he knew only too well he would never have an easy moment until he had assured himself of her welfare.

Mrs. Knox-Gore returned, waving the letter triumphantly. "Just as I said, sir, in my apron pocket from that day to this," she wheezed. "But there, I must be forgiven for my carelessness, for it was a time of so much worry I had no mind for anything but to tend poor Chandos and make his last moments easy. Why a morsel of food never passed my lips for four days! Sidney was quite in despair for fear I also would fall ill—"

Neville, to save himself the bother of trying to stem this recital of her trials, simply took the letter and read it, allowing her to ramble on. The letter was brief, dignified, and heart-breakingly young. In it the girl told of her mother's death and the necessity of finding a means of supporting herself, without a trace of self-pity. She asked only for her great-uncle's recommendation if he had among his acquaintance any families with young children who might be in need of a governess. It had been written two weeks before. Well, that settled it, of course. He must take the matter in hand at once.

"As you know, madame, her mother died, and I would say she is quite destitute, for she writes of her need to find employment."

"Oh, dear heaven! What have I done? I blame myself, sir, indeed I do. Had I only read it through I would have seen at once that she must be sent for to make her home here. Oh! But perhaps you think I presume too much in thinking to offer a home not even my own?"

"A charitable impulse could never be adjudged presumptuous, I hope. Besides, who else has more right? This has been your home a great many years, has it not?"

"Oh, quite twenty now, Mr. Devereaux. Twenty blessed years."

"Good heavens! Then your son was but an infant when—"

"Oh, yes, sir. Barely ten years old."

Neville could only utter a blank "Oh" at this surprising revelation, for the son she had described as only now reaching his majority, a term usually inferring the age of twenty-one or thereabouts, was actually thirty years old. Neville immediately envisioned a fat, moping man, overly concerned by his health, continually brooded over by his doting mother.

This image had barely formed clearly in his mind's eye before it was shattered by the entrance of a gentleman in excellently cut riding clothes who, though slender of frame, was the picture of glowing good health. The only truth in Neville's previous image was the part about the doting mother.

With a radiant smile, Mrs. Knox-Gore held out both hands to the young man. "Sidney, darling boy! Did you enjoy your ride? Come and meet your cousin, Mr. Neville Devereaux!"

Sidney strode lithely across to his mother, kissed each of her hands, and then turned with a charming smile to give Neville a hearty handshake. "Welcome, sir. You can't know how happy and relieved my mother and I are to have you here at last. My Uncle Chandos went so suddenly, you see, we had not even the time to receive his final instructions as to how we were to proceed."

Neville blinked at this engaging candour. "Well—ah—I was happy to oblige, of course. I hope, now I *am* here, we all be able to come about quite quickly. There should be no difficulty that I can foresee. The first step, of course, is to locate the will to ascertain just what his wishes were concerning his estate. We will then know exactly where we stand. Or rather, where you do, for there can be no question of my being in any way involved in my uncle's estate. My only role here is as a representative of the Devereaux family. Now, if you would accompany me to my great-uncle's study, I will begin my search for the will."

"So decisive! I do admire that in men. Your dear father, Sidney, was just so. I'm sure I—" But here she caught Neville's eye, and something she saw there caused her to drop the subject of the departed Mr. Knox-Gore, and turn busily to the door. "If you will just follow me, Mr. Devereaux. You'll find everything just as Chandos left it. I could not bear to enter the room. It was there, you know, that he was struck down—just after dinner, it was. I made sure it was nothing more than the pickled crabs. He had a great partiality for pickled crabs and would have them, though they never agreed with him, and many's the time I've had to scold him for indulging himself overmuch. Ah, poor man, poor man." She dabbed her eyes before throwing open the library doors. Neville and Sidney followed her in.

"This was his private retreat, as he always called it, and even Sidney was rarely allowed in. Of course, I never was, nor did I dream of wanting to be. It is very important, I believe, for a man to have occasional privacy from the cares of a family. So he always took his brandy alone here after dinner. It was Moberly who found him, you see, when he brought in the brandy. Then he summoned me. Oh, dear, oh, dear—such a dreadful time! I could not revive him and Mr. Quires, the doctor, was hours getting here—"

While this monologue went on, Neville trod across to the massive fruitwood desk and sat down behind it. The desk was cluttered with newspapers and books. He pulled out the drawers one after another. They all seemed to contain discouraging quantities of letters, bills, and printed tracts, besides the miscellaneous bits that people seem to accumulate in desk drawers. It was clear that a woman's tidying hand had not been permitted here. In fact, the entire room, while elegantly appointed, showed a degree of carelessness that indicated a lack of feminine attention. Books were heaped about on every surface, even on some of the chairs, and the air retained the staleness of pipe tobacco. This was obviously a true retreat. Neville felt he could certainly sympathize with his great-uncle's need for such a place to escape from his sister-in-law's bird-witted conversation.

"Mrs. Knox-Gore," Neville interrupted ruthlessly, "there is a great deal here to be gone through. Perhaps you and Mr. Knox-Gore would be so good as to help—"

"Oh, never, sir!" She raised shocked eyebrows. "It would be a desecration! Sidney and I would not dream of *touching* any of poor Chandos's things. *That* is why we wrote to you."

"Very well," Neville replied, nearly grinding his teeth at the woman's silliness. However, if they would not help, at least he could be rid of her. "Then I had best start at once, if you will excuse me."

"Of course, dear Mr. Devereaux. Such a delicate and morbid

task needs solitude. I confess I would not be equal to it. So many treasured memories stirred up—oh! the pain would be unendurable! If one is cursed with such frail sensibilities as I—''

"Mama, do come away now," urged Sidney, casting a sympathetic smile at Neville. Still talking, she allowed herself to be led away.

Neville set to work at once, but after an hour and three quarters he sat back wearily and ran a none-too-clean hand through his thick black hair in frustration. Every drawer had been turned out, every paper scanned, but nothing resembling a will had come to light. He rose to ring for Moberly.

"Yes, sir," said Moberly, appearing at the door.

"I would like to speak to Mr. Devereaux's valet."

"I am he, sir."

"Oh! Well then—did Mr. Devereaux have a place besides this desk where he kept papers?"

Moberly stared at Neville for a long moment before admitting, "There is a box in the bottom of the wardrobe, sir."

"Bring it to me at once, please."

Moberly bowed and withdrew, to return some moments later bearing a japanned box which he placed silently on the desk before Neville. However, on inspection the box proved to be locked.

"Where is the key?"

"Mr. Devereaux always kept it on a chain around his neck, sir."

"Was it buried with him?" snapped Neville.

"No, sir."

"Then fetch it, man! Why bring the box without the key?" Damn the man, Neville fumed, was he half-witted or being deliberately insolent?

After a pause the man reached into his waistcoat pocket and withdrew the key. "I took the liberty of removing it from the wardrobe drawer, where I had placed it with his watch and fobs when the doctor removed them and handed them to me the night Mr. Devereaux was stricken."

Neville heard this spate of information in amazement. Surely it was the longest speech the man had made, but delivered in the monotonous tones of one reading from a paper. How had his great-uncle been able to bear such a person about him all the time?

The key turned easily, the lid raised with no trouble, but the box did not contain a will. There was only a jeweler's box inside, wrapped in a paper bearing the words: "My mother's pearls. To be given to my niece, Caroline Devereaux." Signed: Chandos Devereaux.

Neville felt a sudden surge of relief, as though a great weight had lifted from his shoulders. This meant the old man had not forgotten the girl, did not hold her father's behaviour against her. In all likelihood he would leave her the entire estate, after suitable acknowledgement of his wife's relatives, which would relieve Neville of the responsibility of her welfare.

Two days later, after every possible corner had been searched, Neville announced his departure.

"Oh, no, Mr. Devereaux! Why, nothing is settled!"

"My dear Mrs. Knox-Gore, it is imperative that I return to London at once and consult with my great-uncle's solicitor. It is possible he did keep a copy of the will, in spite of what he says, or at least still has my great-uncle's letter of instruction. If so, and the signed will does not turn up, we shall have to see what the law says may legally be done."

"The—law?" faltered Mrs. Knox-Gore.

"Don't worry your head about it, madame. It will all be done with the least worry for yourself, I assure you. I will also see Chandos's man of business, and arrange for housekeeping money to be sent on a regular basis until the estate is settled. And of course, even more importantly, I must go to my cousin and make arrangements to send her here to you at once. She cannot be left alone there any longer."

"Oh, indeed, Mr. Devereaux, she must not be. Only send the poor darling to me and I shall be a mother to her. Ah, how I have longed for a daughter. I pray each night that Sidney will bless me in this matter by marrying, but he has been most disobliging. Now I shall have my heart's desire. I will take good care of her, sir, never fear."

Neville went away to pack, leaving Mrs. Knox-Gore still babbling away. Ten minutes later there was a tap at the door and Moberly entered.

"May I pack for you sir?"

Completely taken aback, Neville murmured "Thank you," and stood aside. Whatever other faults Moberly might possess, there was no denying he was neat-handed. In no time at all the boxes were packed, strapped, and being carried to the door. There Moberly turned.

"Mr. Devereaux, sir, I don't know as it's my place, but I think in justice I must not remain silent."

Nevertheless he did so for a very long, pregnant pause. "Well, go *on* then," prompted Neville in a goaded voice.

"Mr. Chandos Devereaux confided to me many times that he planned to make his nephew, Mr. Sidney, his heir—sir," the man replied flatly.

Neville was too astonished to speak for a moment, but then when he had absorbed the idea, he saw that it was not so surprising after all. Sidney had lived here most of his life, he had, according to his mother, been treated as a son of the house, and had a pleasant, engaging manner, besides brains enough to ingratiate himself to a relative who had been very good to him. Of course, he is not a blood relative, mused Neville, thinking of his cousin Caroline, but in a moment he realized the foolishness of such thinking. The man hadn't even known Caroline, any more than he had known Neville, and he was free to leave his money where he liked.

Neville finally shook himself out of his introspection enough to say, "Well, it will certainly simplify matters if a will can be found to that effect," before preceding Moberly down the stairs.

Mrs. Knox-Gore, Sidney smiling pleasantly beside her, continued to wave her lacy handkerchief, continued to call out instructions and admonitions pertaining to travel until Neville's carriage was out of sight around a bend of the drive. Behind her, in the shadow of the doorway, hovered Moberly, his usually inexpressive face marked now by a very definite frown.

— 5 —

NEVILLE STROLLED DOWN Pall Mall, idly glancing into the fashionable shops without really seeing the extravagant wares displayed. He had just enjoyed an outrageously expensive dinner at his hotel, the Clarendon. The manager, M. Jacquir, former chef to Louis XVIII, had bowed and scraped obsequiously, and the best suite had been made ready. In spite of all these amenities, however, Neville's mood was not agreeable.

His visit to his Uncle Jack's estate had been fruitless, the house shuttered and desolate-looking, in a sad state of disrepair. Inquiries in the nearest village had produced the information that the young miss had been taken in Farmer Hatch's cart to Norwich and left at the coach house to await the Norwich-to-London Mail. In London Neville went directly to the London terminal, Black House, but there the trail stopped. There was no remembrance there of a particular young woman arriving from Norwich. From the attitude of the staff he gained the impression that a steady stream of young ladies arrived there daily and it would be an impossibility to distinguish one out of so many, especially as the gentleman was unable to furnish them with a description.

Neville cursed himself as an irresponsible fool for not having asked Farmer Hatch or one of the villagers for a description of the girl, but he had not thought to do so and must now live with the dispiriting knowledge that he had been less than clever. He wondered what the odds were against his locating a girl somewhere in London with nothing more to go on than her name. He would be forced to put a notice in the *Gazette*, he supposed.

He arrived on the pavement outside Watier's, one of his London clubs, and pondered on whether he felt like company tonight. His mood was one of irritable distraction, which might indicate that he return to his hotel and try to read himself to sleep. However, his disinclination for that prudent course was so strong he could not force himself to turn and walk away. The problem was solved for him by the emergence of his friend, Mr. Bartle à Court, from Watier's doors.

"Ah, Dev, didn't know you were in Town! Why do you stand there dithering?"

Neville smiled and held out his hand. "Trying to make up my mind whether I am fit for company or would be better off in my bed."

"In your condition one is not fit to be alone. Come along. I'm off to see Mrs. Daventry at the Regent's Lane. Have you ever seen her? No? Then you are in for a treat. I'll introduce you to her after the play. We're meeting Malby there. He'll be glad to see you. Asked about you only last week."

Without hesitation Neville took the arm held out to him, his mood lightening on the instant, and the two went off arm in arm.

The Duke of Malby, already installed in his box, rose to clasp Neville's hand warmly. "Well, well, old Nevy Devy himself. By the Lord Harry, it's good to see you again! I hope you are planning a long stay."

"You know I'm never happy for long in London, Monty."

"Ah, wait till you see our Divine One! You'll fall at her feet as we all have, and never want to go home again. Eh, Bart?"

Mr. à Court eyed Neville's cynically arched eyebrow and said, "I find it difficult to form the picture in my mind of Dev prostrate before a woman. Have you ever been in such a position, Dev?"

"I'm told I was so before my mother and Nurse, but I've only their word for it as I've no memory of it myself."

His Grace shouted with laughter, drawing many eyes in their direction. Lord Redvers entered with the Honourable Bertie and there were boisterous greetings and much shuffling about of chairs. Lord Redvers immediately began to search the audience anxiously, while Neville sat down with Bertie. Their box was the one directly over the stage and by turning his head Neville was able to see everyone in the theatre. Everywhere his eyes moved they met a pair of feminine eyes waiting to capture his attention. If he had been previously introduced to the lady he nodded politely, but disengaged immediately, especially in the case of the very young females. He had no taste for green buds, and even less for their rapacious mamas, ever on the lookout for suitable *partis* for their marriageable daughters.

"There's my mama signaling me," observed Bertie unenthusiastically. "Got Tessie in tow, so I know what she wants."

"Tessie?" Neville asked.

"Sister," explained Bertie briefly.

"And what does your mama want?"

"Wants me to bring you around to meet Tessie."

"I'm sure I should be charmed to meet your sister," responded Neville courteously, if perhaps less than truthfully.

"You won't then. You won't like it above half, and so I warn you."

"And why is that?"

"Antidote," replied Bertie succinctly.

"How unkind of you, Bertie," Neville said severely, his lips twitching.

"Truth. Not a hint of an offer and out nearly three Seasons."

Neville slid a cautious glance across the theatre to find himself the object of an avid inspection by Lady Buckthorpe and her daughter, a moderately attractive blonde of surely no more than twenty years. She met his eye boldly for a moment before dropping her own in pretended shyness.

"Have no fear, Bertie. She won't be on the shelf much longer."

"Not if my mama knows it, I'll be bound. Wouldn't object to you as a brother-in-law, you understand, but I'd hate to see you leg-shackled to a pert jade like Tessie."

"Thank you for the compliment and the thoughtfulness, Bertie, but fear not. I have no plans for matrimony at all."

"With you there, Dev. Can't think why men do it. Never met a woman *I'd* care to spend more than an evening with."

Neville agreed with him in part. He had had several interesting liaisons with certain little Barques of Frailty which had lasted more than an evening to be sure, but marriage was a very different thing. The female who could interest him in living in the same house with her day in and day out for the rest of his life had not till now entered his life, though when he thought of it at all, he supposed that someday he must marry. He was thirty-five, healthy, and the happy possessor of a large fortune, with no relatives besides this unknown girl cousin to leave it to. A son, he acknowledged, would be nice. However, he would not marry just for that. He was not looking for a brood mare.

"I take that back," continued Bertie after a gloomy pause. "There is one—woman, I mean—but it's no good. She'll never have me. I've asked several times. She only laughs and says I'm too young for her. All bosh, of course, she can't be more than thirty."

"Who is this fortunate lady who has won your approbation, Bertie?" Neville asked indulgently.

"Julia Daventry."

"The actress you are all so mad for?"

"Yes."

"Good Lord, you must have windmills in your head if you think your mama would ever let you marry an actress, Bertie."

"Don't know why not! Craven married Louise Brunton and made her a countess and what was she? Saw her acting myself as Miranda in *The Tempest* and—"

"All right, I give you best." Neville laughed. "Nevertheless, I can't see your mother giving over about Mrs. Daventry without a battle royal. You told me yourself the last time I saw you that she had an heiress all picked out for you."

This reminder apparently did nothing to elevate Bertie's spirits, for he slouched further down in his chair, thrust his hands into his pockets, and stared moodily at his shoes until the curtain rose. He then sat up and leaned forward eagerly, as did the other gentlemen in the box, even Lord Redvers who had evidently not found whoever he had been looking for. Neville found himself eager to see this paragon who had them all dangling at her shoestrings.

When she made her entrance he thought her attractive, but in no way extraordinary until she threw back her head in a delicious trill of laughter. Her flashing dark eyes seemed to look directly into his own, demanding he share her amusement, a joke between only the two of them.

He knew, of course, that she could hardly have distinguished his face and could not have been singling him out in any way; nevertheless he found his heart beating in a disconcertingly irregular way. He lost the thread of the play completely, only her presence, the generous mouth and gleaming white teeth, the thrilling voice reaching him.

At the end of the play, without waiting for the Pantomime, he followed the rest back to the Green Room. While they waited for the actress to join them Neville tried to take himself in hand. He told himself severely that he was not a schoolboy to become infatuated with an actress, that he was not going to make a fool of himself as these friends of his had evidently done, and besides, she undoubtedly had more lovers than she had time for already.

These silent lectures did little to stop his jolting heart, however, when she finally joined them. Her presence was even more vibrant and beautiful up close than from the stage. He stood silently in the background as her admirers surrounded her, making high-flown speeches and begging for the opportunity to spend the evening with her. She was smiling and gracious, but adamant in her refusals to their invitations.

"I thank you all very much, but you know Mrs. Dainty rules me with a rod of iron. Well, Lord Redvers, you are unusually silent this evening," she said, turning to give the young man her hand.

"You were, indeed, wonderful, madame," he said with a startling simplicity. Julia blinked and opened her mouth to reply, but he rushed ahead. "Dear Mrs. Daventry, your—your—young friend—does she not accompany you tonight?"

"Good heavens no! I cannot allow a young girl to be hanging about in a theatre. Most unsuitable."

"I—I—noticed her—last week at the performance of *The Provoked Husband*. I had—hoped to see her here after—"

Julia laughed. "No fear of that. Mrs. Dainty hustled her straight home." She noted the droop of disappointment in his features and took pity. "You may come to my Wednesday, Lord Redvers, and be presented to her there."

His face lit up at once and he stuttered out profuse gratitude. Well, thought Julia, Caroline has an admirer already. I hope she likes poetry. She turned away from him and met the intense, dark blue regard of a man she had never seen before. Their glances held for what seemed a very long moment before Mr. à Court, following her look, recollected his duty and taking Neville's arm pulled him forward.

"Madam, you will allow me to present my very good friend Mr. Neville Devereaux."

She was unaccountably flustered by the steady look he bent

upon her and so did not register his name. She held out her hand and he took it, causing a shock of electricity to race up her arm. He bent to kiss her fingers and she felt her hand begin to tremble at the touch of his lips. She pulled her hand away hastily.

"I—how do you do, sir—so pleased—I must—it is very late— Mrs. Dainty will—" She turned away, feeling as clumsy and doltish as a schoolgirl.

The usual clamour of protest followed her as she went to the door and she turned, her cheeks hot with color. "Please, everyone—I hope—you are all welcome to visit me at home on Wednesday. I will—I mean—good night."

Neville watched with dismay as she vanished. He hadn't said a word, had been as tongue-tied as a sixteen year old! What a figure of fun she must think him, he reflected bitterly, to behave in such a rag-mannered way. Feeling completely out of sorts, he excused himself from accompanying his friends to Cribb's Parlour for a night's carousel, feeling unequal to the task of making the agreeable to a set of Park Saunterers. Thus castigating his friends as well as himself, he tramped glumly back to the Clarendon and got himself to bed. Sleep, however, evaded him for a long, uncomfortable hour while he reenacted his gape-seed performance in the Green Room over and over. At last the words she had spoken as she left finally registered with some relevance to himself. "—you are all welcome to visit me—" Wednesday. That was the day after tomorrow. For some reason he fell asleep immediately.

Julia was so silent on the ride home that Mrs. Dainty asked her sharply if she were sickening for something or simply indulging in a fit of the sulks.

"I am tired and hungry, which I suppose is not so wonderful after an opening," Julia snapped.

"And out of reason cross, missy," retorted Mrs. Dainty, much offended.

"I'm sorry, Dainty," Julia said, instantly contrite. "I've just behaved like a complete widgeon and I'm out of charity with myself."

"What did you do?" Mrs. Dainty asked suspiciously, hoping Julia had not been unforgivably pert to His Grace of Malby. Mrs. Dainty's reverence for titles could not be damped and she nursed a secret ambition to see her former charge a duchess.

"Oh, became all missish upon being introduced to a stranger. I can't remember behaving so since I left Miss Kentish's School."

"A stranger? What do you mean?"

"Only that he was a gentleman I had not met before. Quite—well—different from the usual sort of man who hangs about backstage." She sighed and turned away to stare unseeingly at the dark, silent streets. What she did see was the tall, broad-shouldered figure with the saturnine face and the dark blue eyes that looked so deeply into her own. She shivered at the memory.

Alarm bells were sounding in Mrs. Dainty's brain. A strange gentleman who caused Miss Julia to sigh? A man who caused her to behave missishly? Miss Julia, whom Mrs. Dainty had not seen put out of countenance since she was eight years old? Mrs. Dainty could see she had been too much preoccupied with Miss Caroline and must keep a sharper eye on Miss Julia in future.

"What is this strange gentleman's name?" It was necessary to identify the enemy at once.

"His name? Oh—Devereaux. Neville Devereaux." After only a second's pause she gasped at the same moment Mrs. Dainty turned her head sharply. They stared at one another in astonishment. "Good heavens! What a slow-top I am. Devereaux! What was the first name of Caroline's cousin, Dainty? The one she has never met?"

"I can't exactly call it to mind at the moment."

"Nor can I, but it must be he! Who would credit such a coincidence? I wish I had not been so silly—I could easily have asked him if she was his cousin. I don't even know how to reach him—but there, Mr. à Court or one of the others can give me his direction if it turns out to be her cousin indeed."

"I see no reason for you to make any push to bring them together. She does very well with us and what can he do for her that we cannot?" Not only was Mrs. Dainty jealous of anyone who might snatch Caroline away from her care, she foresaw having this disturbing stranger forever underfoot, a menace to Miss Julia's peace of mind and to her own plans for Miss Julia's future in the ranks of nobility.

"Why, Dainty, he is her only relative! You cannot seriously suggest that we not tell her. As for that, it is perfectly possible they will meet in any case, for I told everyone they could come to my Wednesday afternoon, so perhaps he will come."

And perhaps he won't, she reminded herself, the elation she experienced as she remembered that invitation immediately plummeting into despondency as the doubt entered her mind. For there was no denying she had not behaved in a manner calculated to rouse his interest. He must think her a shatter-brained flea-wit after the performance he had witnessed in the Green Room. No man had had such a paralysing effect on her since Edward, and she had long ago given up the hope of those feelings being roused again, and now—She drooped sadly into the corner of the carriage.

Then her heart gave a painful jump as she thought: But after all, he *may* come! And if he does not I will be forced to write to him on Caroline's behalf.

She smiled and sat up. "Dainty, I vow if my supper is not on the table I shall eat the plates, I'm that sharp-set!"

=== 6 ===

NEVILLE GROPED HIS way up the narrow, dusty stairway to his great-uncle's solicitor's office, trying not to let his broad shoulders brush against the grimy walls. Why the devil, he wondered, did all the gentlemen in this profession insist on inhabiting these centuries-old rabbit warrens? Still, his mood was not blighted by his surroundings, despite the task waiting him. He was grateful to have something to fill this day which intervened before his next meeting with Julia Daventry. For he had quite decided that he would avail himself of her invitation to attend her "Wednesday," and try to recoup his reputation as a cool, mature gentleman quite accustomed to meeting beautiful ladies. He writhed in shame every time he remembered his doltish behaviour the previous evening, and had only succeeded in quelling his discomfort by the projection of a scene in which he confronted her with an air of courteous detachment that while acknowledging her beauty made clear that he was not thrown into nonplus by it.

Mr. Thistlewaite's clerk bowed him into the presence of his master and Neville found himself the object of a silent inspection as Mr. Thistlewaite peered at him suspiciously over the tops of his spectacles. Apparently satisfied that his visitor could safely be invited to sit down, Mr. Thistlewaite indicated a chair.

Neville sat down, his spirits somewhat damped by this chilly reception. Mr. Thistlewaite was as lightweight as his name indicated, a mere scrap of a man, his face pale as parchment, a condition that extended, as far as Neville could see, well past the crown of his head, bald except for the tuft of white hair over each ear.

"Mr. Thistlewaite," Neville began, leaning forward, "it is kind of you to see me. This really is the devil of a tangle, you see, and I am hoping you will be able to straighten the whole affair out for us."

"To whom do you refer, sir, when you allude to 'us'?" Mr. Thistlewaite's voice was as thin and scratchy as his appearance and name gave every indication it might be.

"Well, the Knox-Gores and myself to begin with."

"You have expectations, sir?"

"Good Lord, no! I never met the man."

"I see. Then it is the Knox-Gores who have expectations."

"Well, it seems to me they might be entitled to some! The woman worked as unpaid housekeeper for him for twenty years and he raised and educated the boy."

"You are the oldest remaining Devereaux, I believe?"

"I am. Nevertheless, I assure you my great-uncle would never have felt any obligation toward me because of it."

"Then what is your interest in the matter, sir?"

"Well, good Lord, man, there is this will that can't be found, as you will have gathered from Mrs. Knox-Gore's letter, and the two of them left up in the air as to what is to become of them and this daughter of Uncle Jack's gone missing and somehow the whole mess has been dumped in my lap to sort out. And I'm damned if I know what *to* do!"

Mr. Thistlewaite subjected Neville to another prolonged inspection after this rather plaintive outburst. Suddenly the faded blue eyes twinkled and Neville found himself smiling ruefully in response.

"It is the devil of a mess, sir, isn't it?" asked Mr. Thistlewaite sympathetically.

"Yes, it is, and I'm hoping you will be able to resolve it for us."

"In what way, sir?"

"Well, I had hoped you had kept a copy of my great-uncle's will."

"As I told that silly woman in my letter, I did not do so at his specific instructions. However, even if I had it would not be valid since it would not have been signed."

"The devil! I'm at a loss to understand why he should have insisted on such a crack-brained plan and then hidden the only copy so that it couldn't be found. Was he quite right in his head, do you think?"

"No fear, Mr. Devereaux, your great-uncle was in full command of all his faculties. He was, however, a very difficult man to deal with."

Neville stared at him, eyebrows raised, inviting elucidation, but none was forthcoming. Mr. Thistlewaite contented himself with realigning an already pristinely straight stack of documents on his desk.

"Look here, sir," Neville said forcefully, "let us stop fencing. I've shouldered the deuce of a problem here and I would be grateful for any light you could shed on the thing."

Mr. Thistlewaite sighed and sat back in his chair. "Mr. Devereaux, you understand it would not be ethical on my part to divulge things I deem as confidential between myself and my client, even though that client is dead. However, tell me everything you know and I will help you if it is in my power."

Neville took a deep breath and plunged into his story, beginning with the letter he had received from Mrs. Knox-Gore imploring him to come to Chandos's deathbed and everything that had transpired from that moment. Mr. Thistlewaite listened without comment until the end, and even then allowed quite five minutes to pass before leaning forward, folding his frail white hands together on the desk and contemplating them for another moment of silence.

"Mr. Devereaux," he said finally, "I do not have a copy of the will."

"Do you still have his letter of instructions?"

"No, sir, I do not," but then perhaps in sympathy with Neville's exasperated sigh, he relented enough to say, "though I do remember the contents. Not that they would be of any value in a court of law," he cautioned seeing Neville's hopeful expression.

"But surely—"

"No, no, sir. Disabuse yourself of that hope. After all, anyone, even I, could be thought to have an interest in promoting one heir over another. No court would admit such a thing."

Neville sighed, his hopes almost visibly flying out the window. "Well, I suppose we must just hope that the will does turn up."

"I have found, sir," said Mr. Thistlewaite dryly, "that in most such cases, it does so when it is to someone's advantage to do so. It seems quite clear to me to whose advantage its disappearance is working in this case."

Neville looked at him for a moment. "Are you suggesting the Knox-Gores—?"

"I suggest only that until the will is found they are in possession of a large country estate, with the means, at your instruction, of maintaining it indefinitely. Being quite penniless themselves, this is not an altogether unhappy position for them to be in.''

"But see here, surely they deserve it, and they have no place else to go apparently. Devil take it, Chandos should have made some provisions for them. The boy looked upon him as a father and even the butler confided that on several occasions Chandos told him he meant to make the boy his heir.''

"Is that so, Mr. Devereaux?" said Mr. Thistlewaite noncommittally.

"Not that I claim he should have it all. There is, after all, a much nearer relative, and she's just as needy, by what I can understand. I mean Caroline Devereaux, of course.''

"There is one even nearer, Mr. Devereaux.''

"If you mean myself, sir, I assure you my great-uncle would never have considered me, nor do I want his money. I simply would like to be shut of the whole problem.''

This rather vehement statement caused Mr. Thistlewaite to purse his lips disapprovingly for a long moment. Finally he cleared his throat decisively.

"Very well, Mr. Devereaux, I will tell you what you want to know, though I cannot say I approve of your attitude. As the oldest living relative of a man who seems to have died intestate your own best interest would be best served by"—he was halted by an impatient gesture from Neville—"yes—well, for what good it may be to you, your great-uncle's last will left, to the best of recollection, the interest on a modest sum to Mrs. Knox-Gore for her lifetime, and the rest of his estate to Miss Caroline Devereaux.''

"By Jupiter!''

"But without the signed will," Mr. Thistlewaite said warningly, "such information is useless. If the will is not found, the estate will, in time, come to you.''

Neville looked puzzled. "I find it strange that you have not mentioned Sidney. Surely my great-uncle cannot have meant to leave him out, why he—''

"Sidney Knox-Gore," Mr. Thistlewaite interrupted, rolling the name over his tongue distastefully, "was not in great favour with the old man.''

"Not? But I was under the impression—''

"Mr. Devereaux seemed to have come to the conclusion very early on that the lad was not—not—quite straight. Oh, he would have liked very much, I think, to have taken him on as a son, but there were disagreeable episodes, you see. Something unpleasant involving animals at a very early age, and then he was sent down from two schools for some mischief or other which your great-uncle would never discuss. He was not the easiest man to get along with, your great-uncle, but there were no flies on him. He could see that Sidney was not the answer to his dreams for a son.''

"Good Lord,'' said Neville. "I must say I found nothing to dislike in the boy. He seemed intelligent and charming, and certainly fond of his mother to put up with her flea-brained conversation so patiently.''

"Yes, he has charm. Even I saw it. However, the upshot was, when Jack died your great-uncle wrote to me instructing me to remake his will in favour of Jack's daughter, which I did, and that's the extent of my knowledge of the whole affair.''

After a moment spent digesting this information Neville said, "Which brings me to my next problem. The girl, as I told you, has disappeared. I went to fetch her with the idea of putting her in the care of Mrs. Knox-Gore. As far as I could discover she is somewhere here in London. Can you advise me of the best way to set about finding her?''

"Hmm. Well, I could put a man onto checking the smaller hotels. If her circumstances are as straightened as you think I doubt she will be staying any place very grand.''

"You do that, sir. Here is—'' He reached for his pocket.

"No, no, Mr. Devereaux, I will present you with a bill when our search is concluded. Perhaps you wouldn't mind calling around again, let us say in three days' time at the same hour, and we'll discuss what my man has discovered. As for the will, I would advise that we be patient and see what happens. Something will, you may be sure. An estate of six hundred thousand pounds will not be left cooling for long.''

Neville took his leave, and though nothing was settled in any way, he still felt relieved of some part of the burden of responsibility, and the next day at three in the afternoon was able to present himself at the home of Julia Daventry without any thoughts but the approaching delight of seeing her again. Bartle à Court had informed him that her afternoons usually began at two o'clock, but Neville had forced himself to wait until three.

He was admitted by a dignified butler, who took his hat and gloves and invited him to step into the drawing room, from which a babble of conversation made it clear a considerable company were already assembled.

He halted in the doorway, surveying the crowded room and attempting to restrain his eyes from darting eagerly in search of Mrs. Daventry. Then he heard her delightful gurgle of laughter, a group of male backs shifted, and there she was, in blue-and-silver-striped gauze, her head back and the generous, rosy mouth parted in laughter to reveal a sparkle of white teeth. She saw him at once and after only the slightest hesitation, came forward, hand outstretched to greet him in a calmly friendly manner.

"Mr. Devereaux, how charming of you to remember my day."

"Surely such an invitation from so beautiful a woman could not be forgotten," he riposted smoothly, taking her hand and brushing her fingers lightly with his lips, then releasing it before he succumbed to the impulse to cover it with kisses.

"I'm sure it was only one such amongst a great many," she countered.

"Such a one amongst however many would always stand forth."

They smiled at one another, each silently congratulatory on having conducted this bit of polished flirtation in the accepted style of London drawing rooms which kept avenues open, gave nothing away, and flattered both. Having explored, however, all the conversational possibilities of her invitation and his acceptance, neither seemed disposed to move on to another topic. Fortunately, this impasse was resolved for them by His Grace of Malby who called out, "Here, Dev, can't have you monopolizing our Fair One."

They both turned to him, not unwilling to be rescued before they revealed the eager interest each felt behind the composed facade. They both felt they had surely erased whatever previous impression the other had retained of their first meeting.

"We were just observing, Mrs. Daventry, that young Redvers is a fickle creature, indeed," said Mr. à Court, raising a sardonic eyebrow at the window seat where Caroline sat, staring bewilderedly at Lord Wrexham who was reading aloud from a paper and staring ardently at her between the lines. The afternoon sun struck glints of gold from her dark auburn hair and caused her white skin to seem even more translucent. "Though one cannot fault his taste," continued Mr. à Court judiciously, "your protégée is quite, quite beautiful, Mrs. Daventry."

"Yes, isn't she?" answered Julia, so much unenvious satisfaction evident in her voice that Neville lost to her what little heart remained untouched. "Mr. Devereaux, I believe I have a pleasant surprise for you. Come along."

Julia took Neville's arm and led him away across the room to the window seat. "Caroline, darling, allow me to present Mr. Neville Devereaux to you. Sir, *Miss* Devereaux!"

Caroline, her dark green eyes wide and staring, and her mouth half open in the polite smile she had turned on Julia at her first words, rose slowly to her feet.

"Good God," exclaimed Neville, "of all the unlikely places—"

"You—are you my cousin, Neville, sir?"

"If Jack Devereaux was your father I am. And you've had me in the devil of a pucker, let me tell you!"

"How so, sir?"

"Well, when you disappeared from your home without leaving word of your whereabouts with anyone—"

"There was no one to leave it with," she replied with a shattering simplicity that caused him to open and close his mouth helplessly several times without, however, producing a suitable reply. "My great-uncle did not reply to my letter, you see, so I could only suppose he had no interest, and I didn't know your direction to write, even had it occurred to me you might want to know."

"He never received your letter, and I found you gone when I went to find you."

"Why?"

"Why what?"

"Why did you go to find me?"

"Because—" He suddenly became aware that they were the object of the unabashed curiosity of the entire room, where all conversation had stopped. "Perhaps we should go into all of that at a more suitable moment."

Julia, being thus reminded of her duties, glanced around before saying softly, "You will have dinner with us tonight, Mr. Devereaux, and become better acquainted with your cousin," and walking away. Neville watched her go, vexed at this unexpected interruption to his plans for the afternoon when he had hoped to consolidate his position with this beautiful woman, perhaps paving the way to something more fulfilling than hanging about in the Green Room after a performance hoping for a few words from her. He knew he was being irrational for he should be glad to have found this cousin and thus have one of his problems solved. However, he remembered, he would be coming to dinner, which meant he would be with Julia all evening, and the possibilities of intimacy were surely more easily realized with only his little cousin in attendance than in a room filled with men, all as eager to attach her interest as he.

He turned back to find Caroline regarding him with some anxiety, while Wrexham, still beside her, devoured her profile with his eyes. Really, Neville thought with amusement at Wrexham's open adoration, one could not blame the boy, for the chit was uncommonly beautiful. Her thick auburn curls were held back with dark orange ribands to reveal the breathtaking purity of her features, and her simply cut round gown of orange-blossom muslin displayed her slim, neat figure to perfection. Neville smiled warmly down into the green eyes which cleared instantly and sparkled as she smiled enchantingly back at him.

"Well met, coz," Neville said easily.

"Oh—thank you. I was afraid for a moment I had displeased you past mending. I truly would have notified you of my plans if I had known where to find you. I would have been very happy to be able to do so. There is—no one else you see."

He heard the catch in her voice and impulsively reached for her hand. "I'm a great clod! It was only the shock of coming upon you so unexpectedly. What I should have said was how sorry I was to hear of your loss and how glad I am at my gain. For I have no one else either. We are the last of the Devereauxs, Cousin, and must be doubly close."

Her eyes were shiny with tears at this kind speech, but she blinked them away. She may have lived her life till now in a falling-down mansion with only her mother for company, but she had been well brought up, and knew it was not *comme il faux* for one to cry in company. She turned to Lord Redvers. "Oh, how remiss of me. Are you acquainted with Lord Redvers, Mr.—er—Cousin Neville?''

''Since he was in short coats at least.''

''Yes, you see your cousin is a maggoty creature indeed, Miss Devereaux,'' observed Lord Redvers laughing.

''Oh no,'' she replied forthrightly, ''he is just as he ought to be.''

Neville laughed and sauntered off, and she watched as he rejoined the group around Julia and deftly maneuvered her out of it and into a tête-à-tête with himself. Caroline could hardly take her eyes off this darkly handsome new-found relative. To claim kinship with a man of so much cool self-assurance, with such an air of authority, was vastly reassuring. One needn't feel so entirely alone and unprotected with such a man who acknowledged one cousin.

7

Neville had returned to his hotel to dress for dinner in cream-coloured kerseymere evening breeches, a dark blue coat of Bath superfine and white stockings. Caroline, waiting anxiously in the drawing room for his return, thought he was the most splendid-looking gentleman she had ever seen. She rose and crossed to him.

"Oh, Cousin Neville, how fine you look!" she exclaimed artlessly.

"Thank you," he replied with a laugh, "but I believe a *jeune fille bien élevée* should allow the gentleman to compliment her first."

"Oh, have I said the wrong thing? I'm not used to being much in company you know."

"Don't refine too much upon it. I was only teasing you, in any case. Though I shouldn't care to have you saying such things to other gentlemen in a general sort of way."

"Oh, I would not! *They* would not be my cousin."

Nothing she could have said could have revealed to him more clearly the importance of his appearance in her life. In her tone was proprietorship and complacency, and her unhesitating acceptance of their kinship spoke volumes of her need for family. He must do something for this child—Lord knows, he could afford to. First he would send her to Mrs. Knox-Gore until a decent interval of mourning had been observed, then perhaps he could open the long-shuttered Devereaux House on Green Street and bring both of them back to London for a Season to launch the girl into Society. After all, if the will could be discovered she would be an heiress, and even without the money she might do very well with family and beauty to recommend her. It was clear Wrexham was already dangling at her shoestrings and he was a most eligible *parti*, being rich enough to buy an abbey if he cared to and eldest son to an Earl. And I could always stump up a dowry, he decided suddenly. No relative of mine need be considered a misalliance by the Wrexhams. In fact, with her looks *and* a dowry she could whistle Wrexham down the wind if she chose to and aim for a Duke!

"You are right," he answered her, eyeing the gown of almondgreen gauze over white satin, "and so I may claim the same privilege and tell you you look fine as five-pence yourself."

"Well, that is a paltry compliment, sir!" exclaimed Julia from the doorway with her rippling laugh.

He swung around and for an instant felt that same schoolboyish paralysis he had felt at their first meeting. She was so indescribably lovely. Not perhaps, by the usual standards, but in a deeply stirring, subtly disturbing way that speaks of real femininity to a man. She obviously spoke to most men in the same way, judging from the throngs in the Green Room, who no doubt sensed, as he did, the generous, womanly givingness she seemed to promise.

She looked now, framed by the dark wood of the doorway, like a painting in her gown of dark rose silk, cut low to set off the perfection of her creamy shoulders and bosom. With pulses pounding he managed to keep his head enough to come forward and take the hand she had extended, and kiss it, more lingeringly than he had allowed himself to do before. He straightened up to find her cheeks flushed and her dark eyes wide and soft as she looked up at him. This tiny indication of disturbance in her composure reassured and elated him and he was able to speak to her without betraying her effect on him.

"Ah, I shall leave all the pretty speeches to the younger sprigs. Caroline and I may dispense with those things between us. However, since you and I are not related, I must tell you how extraordinarily privileged I feel to see a Mrs. Daventry more beautiful than the wildest dreams of her most ardent admirers."

"Well, Caroline, your cousin is an accomplished flatterer, as you can see," Julia said with a laugh, turning to the girl, unable to look at Neville or to reply to him directly. She could only pray she would not blush, though she would not have believed it possible she could be so missish after years of the most extravagant compliments. "Ah, here is Belding to tell me dinner is ready, so let us go in."

She led the way to the dining room, where one end of the long table had been set intimately for three, and seated herself at the head of the table with her guests on either side of her.

Belding served them a first course of a pair of dressed partridges with several side dishes, followed by a second course of scalloped oysters, which was removed by a Savoy cake. The conversation, with the servant moving in and out of the room, was confined to talk of the theatre and of the various sights Caroline had seen so far. When Belding had served the Savoy cake and withdrawn Caroline turned eagerly to her cousin.

"Cousin Neville, you were going to tell me why you had gone to find me."

"Ah, yes. Well, you see, your Great-Uncle Chandos died. Your letter arrived during the last days of his illness and Mrs. Knox-Gore was too distracted by nursing him to send you word, which explains why you received no response. Then, when I arrived and asked about you and your mother, she remembered and was most dreadfully upset. We agreed that I would go to fetch you to her. When I learned you had taken the coach to London I came on here to try to find you. You can't think what a relief it has been to my mind to have accomplished my task so easily. Which brings up a question that I have been pondering. How came you to be *here*, Caroline?"

"My mother and Mrs. Daventry were in school together and she spoke of her to me very often. When I didn't hear from Great-Uncle Chandos I couldn't think of what to do until I remembered her and just came along to London to ask her to help me find employment as a governess."

"A governess! Nonsense, you are much too young!" exclaimed Neville.

"Of course she is," agreed Julia warmly.

"Yes," answered Caroline composedly. "I have been thinking about what you've said on the subject and I can see that it might be difficult to be taken seriously at my age, so I have thought of a much more suitable plan. If you—"

"But I have told you, dear child, there is no necessity for you to concern yourself about employment just yet. You will oblige me by not mentioning it again." Julia smiled, reaching over to pat Caroline's hand.

"Before I left my hotel this evening I sent a note to Mrs. Knox-Gore, Caroline, telling her that I had found you. I know how relieved she will be, and what a comfort you will be to her."

"I'm sorry to hear of Great-Uncle's death, though of course I never knew him at all. Who—er—is Mrs. Knox-Gore?"

"Chandos's sister-in-law. She came to housekeep for him when her sister died. She is rather feather-brained, but very kind-hearted and I'm sure you will like her. My plan is to take you to her, I hope in a day or so."

Two pairs of astonished eyes were turned on him as both women spoke at once.

"But I don't want—"

"But she doesn't need to go away from here," Julia overrode Caroline. "Besides, I doubt very seriously that Dainty would allow it."

"Dainty?" Neville inquired.

"My old nurse, then my dresser at the theatre, and now she sees herself, I fear, as Caroline's nurse."

"I see. Well, of course it is very kind of you and Mrs.—er—Dainty to have taken such good care of my cousin, but I think it will be best if I take her to the country to stay with Mrs. Knox-Gore."

"I'm sure I am very grateful to you for thinking of me, Cousin Neville, but I would prefer to stay here," replied Caroline politely.

"But you cannot remain here, my dear. It is not at all suitable."

"Not suitable?" inquired Julia evenly, but with a definite edge of ice in her voice. "Do you imply that I am not suitable to be in charge of a young girl, sir?"

"I imply nothing of the sort, as you must know!" he replied indignantly. "I meant merely that it was unsuitable that she continue to burden you with the responsibility for her care when she has relatives perfectly capable and more than willing to take that responsibility."

"Oh, but I have no intention of being a responsibility to Mrs. Daventry, Cousin Neville," Caroline said eagerly, "I have thought of a way—"

"I assure you, sir," interrupted Julia, not even seeming to be aware that Caroline was speaking, so intent was she upon the contention between herself and Neville, "I do not consider the daughter of my dearest friend in any way a burden. We go on very well together and I am very happy to have her in my home as my guest for as long as I can persuade her to stay."

"That is very good of you, and my cousin and I will be forever in your debt, but I think I must be allowed to know what is best for my own kinswoman."

"I don't know why you must be allowed to do so," flared Julia. "You've never even met the girl before today and then to march in and announce in this high-handed way that *you* have decided what she will do, without even consulting her own wishes in the matter!"

They had become so overheated during this exchange that their voices were raised beyond what is normally considered polite over the dinner table and they glared in a most unfriendly way that could not be considered good conduct in either a guest or a host. Caroline's eyes went from one to the other, dismayed to think she was the cause of disagreement between them, but not knowing quite what to do about it. She wished very much they would let her tell them of her plan, which she felt sure would solve everything.

"I most certainly beg your pardon if I have appeared to you to be behaving in a high-handed way," conceded Neville frostily, "but I must stand firm in my belief that it would be better for Caroline to go to Mrs. Knox-Gore in the country."

"Better than what?" Julia demanded dangerously, her dark eyes glinting. "Perhaps you do not care to have a relative of yours living in the house of an actress. If that is your opinion, I assure you that I receive cards every day to the most respectable drawing rooms in London!"

"I have no doubt. Nevertheless—"

"Nevertheless, you must be allowed to know what is best," she interrupted scathingly. "Well, I do not think it is for the best to take a child who has lived all her life virtually isolated from the rest of the world and force her to return to the country to live with a lady who is a total stranger to her and where she will have nothing to take her mind off her recent loss."

"I believe it is customary to observe a decent period of mourning, which I believe—"

"Fustian!" Julia cut in ruthlessly. "And I cannot agree with a Gothic custom that demands one to practically *entomb* oneself with the dead. It is cruel to drape a young girl in black and force her to dwell on her unhappiness!''

"I shan't *force* her to do anything!'' Stung by her words he could barely keep himself from shouting. He turned abruptly to Caroline. "Cousin, if you are agreeable I will call for you in two days and drive you down to your great-uncle's house.''

"Thank you very much, Cousin Neville, but I don't care to go at all,'' Caroline replied definitely.

He blinked at her, brought to a complete stand. Her refusal was all the more forceful for the calm, collected manner in which it was stated. Neville felt exactly as though he had come up against a solid wall.

Julia would not allow herself to show her triumph by so much as a flicker of an eyelid, and a small moment of silence ensued. Neville finally rose, feeling that further intercourse was absolutely impossible, and bowed to each of them in turn. "Madame, I thank you for the excellent dinner. Caroline, I will bid you good night. Perhaps you will allow me to take you for a drive in the Park tomorrow? Shall we say eleven o'clock?''

"Oh, I shall like that above all things, Cousin Neville,'' Caroline agreed enthusiastically.

He bowed again and trod across to the door and out without another word.

"Odious man!''

"Oh, Mrs. Daventry, I'm sure he did not mean to be so. He really is very kind and I think he truly thought it was for the best. He wouldn't realize how dreary it would be for me and how impossible it would be for me to find employment there.''

"Oh, child, please don't begin that again,'' pleaded Julia, feeling suddenly dismal and very tired as the exhilaration of battle faded.

"Well, of course I don't want to tease, but when you've heard my plan I think you will see yourself that it will answer very well. I can't think why it never occurred to me before. May I tell you of it, please?''

Julia nodded wearily, sinking resignedly into her chair.

"Thank you, dear Mrs. Daventry. The plan, you see, is this. If you would be willing to speak to Mr. Quinn at the theatre, I could probably do very well on the stage.''

"*What!*'' Julia sat up in shock.

"On the stage—as an actress," Caroline explained patiently. "Only in small parts, naturally. I would not expect anything more to begin with."

"Well, I'm sure that is—very condescending of you," Julia replied with a little laugh, amused in spite of herself.

"Then you do think—?"

"Now you listen to me, my girl. You must be all about in your head if you think for one moment I would allow you to do anything so idiotic."

"But, I'm sure I could do it—"

"No! Under no circumstances. It would be most unsuitable for you."

"But *you*—"

"I am twice your age and a widow. I have no interest in Society, or in making a brilliant marriage. It would quite ruin your chances to allow you to do anything so shatter-brained. And if you will take my advice, you won't breathe a word of this scheme to your cousin. If he even dreamed you were contemplating such an idea nothing either of us could do or say could keep him from whisking you off to the country so quickly it will make your head swim."

"Well, I won't then, but I must say it is very frustrating to be told one is too young to be a governess and then that one is shatter-brained for coming up with another scheme that one is *not* too young for. I must find a way to support myself and I really don't have any interest in making a brilliant marriage—or any marriage at all, come to that."

Julia smiled wanly. "Not now, darling, but you will, and even a less than brilliant marriage would be difficult if you were to become an actress. But don't fret, darling, there is no need to tease yourself about it for some time yet. Now, I hope you will forgive me, but I think I will go to my bed, I seem to have the headache."

Caroline was at once contrite and insisted on escorting her to her room where she tenderly kissed her good night and turned her over to Mrs. Dainty.

Mrs. Dainty saw the tiny crease between the delicately arched eyebrows and knew she would receive only short answers, but her curiosity could not be restrained.

"Is he a nice gentleman?"

"He's an officious, meddling, obstinate, m-m-make-mischief!"

Julia was nearly spluttering, her anger flaring up again to combat the hollow feeling she was experiencing.

Mrs. Dainty looked at her in astonishment at this outburst, for her Miss Julia might be headstrong and volatile, but she was slow to anger. Now what could have happened to put her in such a taking? "What did he do, Miss Julia?"

"He thinks Caroline should be sent to some female relative in the country."

"Female relative? I thought—"

"Oh, not a real relative, only the sister of this Chandos Devereaux's dead wife. And of course, Caroline doesn't want to go."

"I should think not, indeed! He can't make her go, can he?"

"I don't see how he could. He can hardly carry her off against her will."

"Then there's nothing to become so overset about," replied Mrs. Dainty comfortably. "I'm surprised at you, Miss Julia, allowing yourself to fly into the boughs over it. After all, the man was only behaving proper to interest himself in the girl, as she's destitute and has no other relative. Would you expect him to wash his hands of her?"

"Oh, of course not, Dainty!" replied Julia crossly, less than pleased to have her own illogic pointed out to her. "It was only—only—the *way* he pronounced his decision as though—as though—" She faltered, not sure herself exactly how he had fired her up so.

"Just you put the matter out of your mind now, missy. A good sleep is what you need," said Mrs. Dainty soothingly, lowering the lawn night dress over Julia's head and tying the lilac ribands at the beruffled neckline.

When she was alone, Julia lay watching the light from the fireplace flickering across the ceiling, her thoughts leaping and jerking about in rhythm with the movement, from sharp words to cold looks and then in spite of herself to the warmth she had seen in his eyes as he had greeted her before dinner, and the touch of his lips on her fingers that had caused that delicious melting feeling in her bones.

She gasped and sat up as she became aware of the direction in which her thoughts were straying. *That* is over, she thought firmly, and a very good thing too, for tonight's brangle has revealed the man's true character. He obviously considers all women as chattels to be disposed of as he sees fit—like—like some Turk! Well, more fool I if after working so hard for my independence I allow myself to be so cow-spirited as to become starry-eyed over such a man just because he's handsome. I, for one, have no intention of allowing him to be in a position to order *me* about! She punched her pillow angrily, threw herself back onto it and closed her eyes determinedly.

Into the silence that ensued a voice within her spoke quite clearly: Not that he would even want to now.

8

MRS. KNOX-GORE, TRODDING across the hall on her way to breakfast, paused to admire with a proprietary air the way the morning sun, striking through the fanlight over the front door, lit up to perfection the large epergne of flowers which stood on a pedestal in the very center of the black-and-white-marbled squares of the floor. She moved forward, changed the position of a yellow rose infinitesimally, and stood back judiciously. Then with a satisfied nod she moved on to the breakfast parlour where she found her son about to attack a very large beefsteak which Moberly had just set before him.

"Good morning, my love. Did you sleep well?" she asked cheerily.

He merely grunted and proceeded with his breakfast. Mrs. Knox-Gore did not seem in any way put out by this lack of response, only requesting Moberly, as she seated herself, to bring her buttered eggs and toast. Moberly turned away to the door.

"Moberly! My chocolate first, if you please," requested Mrs. Knox-Gore gently.

The man halted, turned back to stare from the pot which stood directly before her to Mrs. Knox-Gore in a significant manner which left her in no doubt of his meaning. She very busily took up her napkin and began arranging its folds carefully across her lap. Moberly shrugged, moved forward to pour the chocolate, and left the room.

"That man is getting above himself," observed Mrs. Knox-Gore. "Have you been for a nice ride, darling?" She looked inquiringly at Sidney who neither answered nor looked up. "Sidney! I asked if you have been riding?"

"What else is there to do in this godforsaken hole?" he muttered, continuing to stuff his mouth with beefsteak.

"Why, I'm sure I can't think why you speak so, Sidney. We have our share of entertainments. The Assembly in Tilton is held to be quite as elegant and well attended as any in the county."

"If you think I find any entertainment in being obliged to stand up with that gaggle of whey-faced, cow-footed geese, you have much mistaken the matter, I assure you!" he snarled.

Mrs. Knox-Gore seemed familiar with these sentiments for she didn't attempt to protest, contenting herself with a soothing, "Yes, I know, my love, they are not worthy of you, but it won't be too much longer, I'm sure."

"That is what you always say. In fact, you've been saying it for the past fifteen years."

"Well, but how could I have known he would live so long, dear boy? He was forever complaining about his heart and his liver and I don't know what all! I fully expected him to be carried off any time these past ten years. Ah, well, it is over at last."

"I don't see what is changed. We're in no better case than we were before the old squeeze-crab turned up his toes. And here's Moberly's friend gone off the Lord knows where—"

"Now, you must not fret. I've been doing a great deal of thinking since Neville Devereaux's letter came, and I'm sure I've hit upon a plan much better than Moberly's. I'm sorry now I ever took him into my confidence—"

"Took *him* into *your* confidence?" Sidney broke in jeeringly. "That's coming it too strong even for you, Mama. It was more the other way around and well you know it."

"Only because he sneaked around amongst poor Chandos's private papers and found the will before—"

"Before you did!"

Mrs. Knox-Gore sat up straighter and surveyed her son coldly. "I'm not at all pleased with your tone of voice, Sidney. It is not only disrespectful, but ungrateful. Let me remind you that it is hardly *my* fault that I have been forced to such measures in your behalf. It was not *I* who put your Uncle's back up by my reprehensible behaviour. Nor was it *I* who—"

"Oh, very *well*! Give over, do, Mama!" Sidney's lower lip came out sulkily.

Mrs. Knox-Gore looked as though she would have liked to say a great deal more on the subject while she was at it, but eyeing his handsome face bent over his plate, she relented. Poor boy, she thought, her heart softening. A lad with such looks and such address should not be forced to kick his heels in this backwater, when with the money which should rightfully be his, he could take his place in the first rank of Society. Why, even the daughter of an earl should not be above his touch.

The thought of marriage reminded her of the marvelous plan that had occurred to her during the night.

"Sidney," she said urgently. "I think I see the way out of all our difficulties—and certainly a much safer scheme than allowing some criminal friend of Moberly's to forge a document that might land us all in Newgate. I never really approved of being forced to associate with Moberly."

"You mean you didn't like to share any of the money with him. You were hot enough for the project when he first broached it to you."

"Only because he managed to get his hands on the will," she retorted resentfully. She remembered vividly the night Chandos was struck down. She had ordered Moberly to send someone for the doctor and as soon as the door closed on his back had tremblingly removed the key from around the unconscious man's neck. She knew very well what the key was for, having already made a fruitless search of his desk some months before. She had taken the first opportunity that came her way to continue her search in his room and had found the japanned box in his wardrobe. She had pulled the box out and applied the key and raised the lid, faint with excitement. She had stared down into the open box uncomprehendingly for a long moment. There had been the jewelry case containing the pearls and nothing else whatsoever! She had nearly jumped out of her skin when the door opened to reveal Moberly, who regarded her expressionlessly for a moment. Then, without speaking, he had removed the will from his pocket and held it before her eyes. She had felt the very blood turn to ice in her veins with the cold rage that seized her. If a weapon had been at hand she would undoubtedly have attacked him then and there. He had noted her anger dispassionately and ignored it, telling her she had best sit down and listen to his proposition.

"I should like to be told what business you think you have to remove my brother-in-law's will? I shall send for the Authorities," she had threatened, rallying.

"Do so," he had invited her coolly. "There's a small pittance for you in the will. I suppose you and your son might be able to eke out an existence on it."

"You mean he left Sidney *nothing?*"

"His name is not mentioned."

"The monster! The despicable monster! Well, we shall see about that! I'll burn the thing, I'll—"

"If no will is found, the estate will automatically go to Mr. Devereaux's eldest male relative. Mr. Neville Devereaux, I believe. Now, suppose you save your breath to cool your porridge and listen to me."

Then, in the long wait for the doctor, he had laid before her his plan to have a friend of his make a new will in Sidney's favour, on condition she would give him an undertaking in writing that one-third of the money would become his. Mrs. Knox-Gore, sick with disappointment to find Chandos had left his entire property to some chit of a girl he'd never even seen, and not so much as a farthing to Sidney, had been forced to agree, feeling part of a loaf was better than no bread at all.

She had reluctantly given him her promise in writing in exchange for his handing over the will into her keeping, with the admonition that it must not be destroyed until the forger had made his copy. She had a better reason than that for holding on to it, however. It occurred to her that if for some obscure reason these plans did not work out, she would be left with nothing at all, whereas if worst came to worst she could always produce the will and be assured of Chandos's bequest to her.

They had both agreed that leaving the pearls in the box lent a nice touch of verisimilitude to the entire plan, for surely anyone illegally tampering with the box would not have hesitated to take the pearls and sell them with no fear of discovery since their very existence was unknown.

She realized now that she had been far too hasty. Not only had Moberly's friend disappeared from the neighbourhood ("Taken up by the Authorities long since, no doubt," sniffed Mrs. Knox-Gore, already doubting the wisdom of putting herself in Moberly's power), thus making it impossible for them to replace the original will with the forgery before Neville Devereaux had had to be sent for for appearance's sake, but now this absolutely brilliant solution had occurred to her that would obviate the necessity of using Moberly's friend at all, much less having to share so much as a penny with Moberly himself. Of course, there was the disagreeable matter of the note she had given him, but she was confident she could contrive to get it back from him—by force, if necessary, she thought grimly.

"Now listen to me, Sidney. I have thought of a much better plan. Mr. Devereaux's letter said he had found the wench in London living with that actress and would be bringing her down to me within a few days."

"What's that to say to anything?" he retorted rudely.

"Think, Sidney, think!" urged his mother eagerly. "A young girl, quite destitute and motherless, in my care here with only the company of a handsome young man to cheer her up."

"Be damned to that for a crack-brained idea. I have better things to do with my time than bear-lead a half-grown girl—"

Mrs. Knox-Gore eyed him coldly. "I sometimes quite despair of you, Sidney. I'm sure without me you'd not be able to go on at all. Can't you really grasp the idea? You will court the girl, you will marry her, and the money will be yours without any danger at all. We'll wait, perhaps even a year, before we allow the authentic will to turn up, just to throw off suspicion—"

"A year!"

"Well, say six months, perhaps less," soothed Mrs. Knox-Gore.

Sidney stared broodingly at her for a moment. "Well, I don't like it! Caught in parson's mouse trap before I've even had a chance to live!"

"For once in your life *try* for some sense, Sidney. What more will it cost you than a few months' effort? Once safely married you may leave your wife to me. I shall be very happy for the companionship and you may go your way and have all your amusements as and where you please. With the added advantage of not having to share anything with—"

She broke off as Moberly soundlessly entered the room bearing her breakfast and a letter which he placed on the table beside her plate. She eyed him suspiciously, wondering how much he had overheard. Drat the man, creeping about the house in that revolting way!

"Thank you, Moberly. How lovely that looks, and I'm positively famished this morning," she exclaimed in a falsely gay voice, which evoked no response whatsoever from Moberly, who moved over to the sideboard and began rearranging the silver.

"That will do, Moberly," she said sharply. "Please go tell the housekeeper to air the bed in the Blue Chamber. We are expecting my young niece for a visit."

He turned to stare coldly at her. "Do you refer to Miss Caroline Devereaux?"

"That is true."

"Why is she coming here?"

"That is nothing to do with you, Moberly," began Mrs. Knox-Gore hotly, but seeing a sudden look come into his eyes that quite frightened her, she backed down. "Really, what can I do if Mr. Devereaux insists on bringing her? I can hardly refuse to receive her, can I? Be sensible now and go along," she ended conciliatingly.

After another long stare he turned and left the room. Mrs. Knox-Gore rose and tiptoed to the door. She peeked cautiously out, saw his back retreating down the hall, and softly closed the door.

"That man positively makes my skin crawl. I really must put my mind to some way of ridding ourselves of him. Now, here is another letter from Mr. Devereaux, no doubt to inform me of their arrival."

She broke open the seal and spread the paper open. After only a moment she clicked her tongue in annoyance and tossed the letter petulantly away from her.

"Really, men are such fribble-frabble creatures, always making a tangle of everything!"

"Now what's to do?" Sidney asked indifferently, his mind still probing the idea of marriage.

"The chit won't come, he says. I should like to know what she has to say to anything. She's not of age and I'm sure had he handled it properly—" She broke off in annoyance, poking at the buttered eggs before her with her fork.

Sidney, who had just begun to realize the possibilities of his mother's idea, was jolted by the news that the prize was about to be snatched from his hands; so much so that his usual quiescent acceptance of whatever his mother decided was for the best was now provoked into thought. After a moment an idea came to him, causing his eyes to widen in surprise, so unused to such an event was he.

"Here—I think I may have the answer." His mother looked almost shocked at this unusual announcement. "What's to say I can't go *there?* I'll lay myself out to be nice to the girl and persuade her to come back to visit you. May even get her in the way of developing a *tendre* for me before we get here."

Mrs. Knox-Gore exclaimed admiringly. "Well, you are coming on, Sidney! It's the very thing! Indeed, with your looks and charm there can be no doubt of it! Oh, dear boy, I do believe it is all going to work out! I'll have Moberly pack your valise at once and—oh!—I have it! You'll take her the pearls. Say I wanted her to have them at once, no need to mention Chandos, and it will seem as though it were a gift from me."

Sidney finished his breakfast, his imagination throwing up pictures of himself sauntering into the drawing rooms of London, causing a stir of admiring interest wherever he went.

In the hallway outside the closed dining-room door stood Moberly, one ear pressed to the panel, a grim expression on his saturnine face.

Caroline, on Neville's arm, Julia's maid some paces behind, strolled slowly along through the mild winter sunshine, feeling very sophisticated in her becoming amber wool pelisse, her free hand inside a large swansdown muff. She had been taken up by Neville in his carriage several mornings in a row for visits to some of London's more interesting sights, including the Tower of London, the *Aegyptiana* in the Scenic Theatre of the Lyceum's upper rooms, and Mr. Burford's Panaroma. She had extracted from Neville the promise of a visit to see the famous marbles Lord Elgin had brought back from Greece, and a visit to the Exeter 'Change to see the wild animals, but had amiably agreed this day was much too fine not to be taken advantage of by a walk in the Park.

She had, with a candour Neville had rarely encountered, told him of her life until now, a life whose wretchedness filled him with horror and pity, and a firm resolve to make it up to her if it lay within his power. He was careful, however, not to express his feelings on the subject, for she spoke of it all without a trace of self-pity. On the contrary, what came through most strongly was the happiness and contentment she had experienced, especially in the later years, with her mother, who must truly have been a most remarkabale woman, Neville thought.

"I cannot help regretting that I never had the chance to know your mother. You must miss her dreadfully," he said sincerely.

"Oh, yes, for I know how much she would have enjoyed all this, and of course she adored Mrs. Daventry. My mother was an orphan, you see, and lived with this invalidish aunt, so was not much in company with young people until she went to school. Mrs. Daventry was her first friend. Mama was several years older, but very shy, so Mrs. Daventry, who was a romp and up to all sorts of games, brought Mama out in a way—helped her to be gay and more lighthearted. Oh, Mrs. Daventry is such fun to be with and so kind!"

"Yes, I'm sure she is," he said, somewhat stiffly, "though it must be difficult for you now just the same."

She looked puzzled. "Why, I don't think that it is. Why do you think it must be?"

"Well—I mean to say"—he was more than a little flustered by this forthright question—"just now, I mean, when you are still—grieving."

"Oh, I am not grieving," she reassured him kindly.

"Not—!"

"No. You see, Mama always said that grieving was wasteful—of life, you know. She said life was a gift of God, as far as she could understand, and if one accepted that, one must accept that death was just another, different, gift, which must be accepted as such when He chose to bestow it. I think now she must have been pre-paring me all along. Her parents were both sickly, you see. She always said I had the Devereaux constitution, which I must have, for I am never ill. So you see, she would not like me to turn my back on life and mourn. She would expect me to use every mo-ment of the gift, and to try to make myself happy and inde-pendent. Mrs. Daventry feels the same way, only she won't discuss my future at all. I must earn my living, you see, and I had a wonderful idea—'' She stopped abruptly, flushing and catching her lip between her teeth in vexation with herself at letting her tongue run on unbridled and nearly telling him her idea of going on the stage, which Mrs. Daventry had warned her would be most unwise.

"Well, go on, what was this wonderful idea?'' he asked, smiling indulgently, for of course, there could be no question of his allowing her to earn her own living, even if the prospects were not very good that she would shortly find herself heiress to a considerable fortune.

"Oh—nothing, really. I haven't—worked it out completely and I'd rather not speak of it yet.''

Her flushed face and evasive eyes told him clearly that this was a patent untruth, and also that she was very bad at telling lies. Of course, that was already evident in her forthright conversational style. What an odd child she was, to be sure, he mused. As fragile-looking as a Meissen doll, but of robust good health, and after the secluded life she had led able to find her way quite alone to London, determined to support herself without a single helping hand. Well, except for Julia Daventry, of course, who obviously was bent on keeping the girl by her and supporting her in style, if the gowns the child had been wearing the past few days were any indication. He knew little of feminine fashion, but enough to realize his cousin was being dressed in the first style of elegance, and that could not be done cheaply. Well, there at least he could do something immediately.

"Cousin, there is a matter I have been meaning to speak to you of. Mrs. Daventry has been more than kind—''

"Oh, hasn't she?'' she interrupted eagerly. "I knew you must see it as I did. I do so much want you to be friends, for I love you both so much. I'm sorry I have been the cause of a disagreement between you. Do you not think you could make it up so that we can all be easy together? She was only defending me, you know.''

"Well, I must say, I can't see why you should need to be defended from me,'' he protested.

"Of course I do not, it was only that she didn't want me to be forced to do what I did not want to do.''

"It was never in my mind to force you.''

"I know that, and so does she now, and I'm sure she would like to be friends again. Shall I persuade her to apologise? Will you forgive her then?''

He looked at her narrowly for a moment, then laughed. "You are a complete hand, Cousin Caroline. I can't think where you've learned such tricks.''

"I'm sure I don't know what you mean,'' she said demurely.

"Coming it too strong, my girl. What a figure I should cut if I allowed you to do any such thing. I see your game. Well, I'll do the apologising, since that is what you're angling for.''

"Oh, I knew you would. Thank you!'' She pressed his arm, looking up at him with a blinding smile.

"Now then, where was I? Oh, yes, we were discussing Mrs. Daventry's kindness. I have decided that you must let me make you an allowance—''

"Oh, no! No, I could not!'' she protested vehemently. "There is not the least need.''

"There is a great need. Will you have it thought of me that I cannot take care of my own relatives, but am such a pinch-purse I allow Mrs. Daventry to do so?''

"But I fully intend—''

"Yes, yes, I know, but not just yet,'' he interrupted hastily, not wanting to get into another discussion of her finding employment. "In the meantime, I think I have as much claim as Mrs. Daventry to take care of you.''

"But I really do not need money,'' she said, much troubled.

"Then give it to Mrs. Daventry to repay her for what she has spent on you.''

"Well, I could try—'' she began doubtfully.

He laughed. "Yes, and get a peal rung over your head for your pains, no doubt. Now listen to me, infant. There is every possibility that something will be coming to you from Great-Uncle Chandos if the will can be found, at which time you can repay me if you like.''

"A loan?'' she said, brightening.

"Yes, a loan. Besides that, if you do not take it willingly, I shall be forced to try to give it to Mrs. Daventry and we shall doubtless come to dagger-drawing again.''

This threat convinced her and she agreed. They turned their steps toward Mrs. Daventry's, each with the agreeable sensation of having accomplished what he had set out to do.

9

NEVILLE DEVEREAUX WAS a man whose intelligence could be rated somewhat above those men of his same background and upbringing, but he was very like his peers in his attitudes and beliefs concerning women. To wit: they were delicate, giddy creatures whose reasoning powers were of a definitely inferior quality, and who must therefore be handled carefully and treated with the utmost courtesy, while at the same time being led firmly away from their general totty-headedness onto the paths of intelligent male reasonableness.

He was not, however, so far lost to all sense of justice as not to be able to admit by this time that he had behaved reprehensibly at Mrs. Daventry's dinner table and that he welcomed being cozzened by Caroline into making an apology. But, in truth, he was only dimly aware of the reasons for his unusual lack of control on that memorable evening.

He could admit to the fact that he was unused to having his judgement questioned and had therefore reacted with wrongheaded defensiveness in response. Beneath this surface excuse there seethed only partially understood emotions toward women in general and this woman in particular. Had anyone accused him of putting women into categories of good or bad he would have indignantly denied it. But there was no denying he had instantly placed Mrs. Daventry into the latter category based on the sole fact that she was an actress. That she was, according to his companions, a heretofore impregnable fortress of virtue he smilingly discounted. Naturally, *they* had not succeeded, he thought smugly. But that the walls had been breached he had little doubt, and that he could succeed where his friends had failed he also felt certain of, based on his past successes. His intentions were definitely not honourable, and he had entertained pleasurable fantasies of setting her up as his mistress to the disgruntlement of Malby, à Court, Redvers, and all the rest. Once face to face with her, however, the dream had unaccountably crumbled, though he could not have said why this should be so. She just didn't look like the sort of woman to whom one could offer a *carte blanche*, he concluded lamely.

Below this, and unacknowledgeable, was his fury with anyone who could reduce him to schoolboyish stupidity; a woman who affected his senses so devastatingly he was swept beyond his ability to command his own feelings. Even these past few days, at their few encounters when he had come to take Caroline out for excursions and had behaved with a stiff-rumped cold courtesy, he was aware that he was helpless to really give her up and wipe her from his life. This knowledge outraged a very deep-seated need he had to control the events of his life, which certainly included the bestowal of his heart and affections, neither of which had ever been engaged in his amours until now.

It had only just begun to occur to him that to think of Julia Daventry in this way and still allow his cousin to remain her guest was illogical, which must mean that sometime between their first meeting and their second his assumptions about her had subtly changed.

However hazy these things might be in his mind, there was no doubt of his pounding pulses as he handed Caroline out of his carriage and approached Mrs. Daventry's front door, forming in his mind a graceful apology which he hoped would instantly disarm her into forgiveness.

The information, given to them by Belding as they were admitted, that Mrs. Daventry could be found in the drawing room where she was entertaining a guest, effectively threw cold water on Neville's plan. He could not stage such a reconciliation under the curious eyes of a guest, he felt. He therefore asked Caroline to tell Mrs. Daventry that he would call in the morning with the hope that he would be received, and took his leave, not entirely displeased with the turn of events. More time spent in polishing his speech, and the opportunity to present her at the same time with flowers, would work more surely in his favour.

Caroline made her way to the drawing room alone to find Julia seated before the fire with a very handsome young man who rose with an eager smile at Caroline's entrance.

"Well, my dear, here is yet another gentleman come to claim you for cousin," said Julia in response to Caroline's questioning look. "May I present to you Mr. Sidney Knox-Gore?"

Sidney strode across the floor and taking her by the shoulders kissed her on each cheek in a hearty no-nonsense manner to which she could not possibly take offense.

Nor did she, only laughing up at him. "Well, Mr. Knox-Gore, I am very happy to make your acquaintance, though I'm not sure we can precisely claim cousinship."

"Pooh! I do not care for that finicky counting on one's fingers of relationships. We are near enough to being cousins and since I have no other you will surely not be so cruel as to deny me the privilege," he replied, smiling coaxingly down into her eyes.

"I hope I will never be accounted cruel, Mr. Knox-Gore."

"Then you will call me Sidney?"

"I will call you—Cousin Sidney, if that will please you," she agreed, her eyes twinkling.

"Very well, indeed!" he replied enthusiastically, as he led her over to the fire and watched with admiring eyes as she removed her pelisse and bonnet.

Julia watched them with amusement, congratulating herself anew on the choice of this costume for Caroline, for the high-waisted amber muslin gown became Caroline mightily, setting off the dark green eyes and auburn curls to perfection. Julia was also pleased by the entrance of this attractive young man into Caroline's life, for gratifying as the child might find Lord Redvers's attentions, Julia herself was not entirely sure, having heard of Redvers's lineage-proud mama, that it was wise to allow their association to develop any further. Not that Caroline had given any indication of having allowed her affections to become engaged as yet. Nevertheless it was not a bad thing for her to become aware of her attractions for other young men, and Sidney's admiration was certainly apparent from the moment he set eyes on her, as even Caroline could not possibly be unaware, though she behaved, Julia noted with amazement, without the least loss of composure. Why, she might be a seasoned debutante! What an unusual young girl she was, to be sure.

Sidney seated himself beside Caroline on the sofa. "My mother's health is not strong enough at this time to face the

79

journey to London, so she sent me as her envoy to tell you that nothing else could have kept her from coming to you instantly. I'm to convey her love to you and her hope that you will consider making her a visit when it is convenient for you to do so."

"Oh, how kind! Of course I shall visit her, you must assure her of that. I hope her illness is not serious?"

"Only exhaustion, I think. My Uncle Chandos required a great deal of nursing, you see, and she could not be persuaded that it could safely be left in the hands of anyone but herself."

"Poor soul!" exclaimed Caroline.

"She will make a good recovery, I'm sure, though of course it is very lonely for her now."

"Oh, dear, how dreadfully selfish she must think me for not going to her at once," said Caroline in dismay.

"Now, Caroline, my dear, you are not to allow yourself to feel guilty. I'm sure, Mr. Knox-Gore, your mother must understand that Caroline herself has been through an ordeal recently and needs this chance to recover from it," Julia interposed.

"Nothing could be more certain, madame. She bid me to do what I could to entertain my cousin and make London pleasant for her. I'm to take her to the opera and the theatre and—oh, yes"— he pulled a long, flat-tooled leather box from his pocket—"she sent this."

Caroline looked at Julia, who smiled approval, before hesitatingly taking the box into her own hands. She opened it and gasped, "But—oh, no, I couldn't take them—"

"Are these your mother's pearls, Mr. Knox-Gore?" Julia asked.

"They were her sister's," replied Sidney, with no hesitation, "and she felt sure her sister would have wanted Caroline to have them." This explanation was nicely calculated to convey the impression that the pearls had come to Mrs. Knox-Gore on her sister's death.

"I'm—I'm honoured she should have wanted me to have them, Cousin Sidney, and it is very kind of her, but I'm not sure it would be right for me to accept them." Caroline turned to Julia for enlightenment.

"Why, my dear, as to that, I see no reason why you should not. I must say, it is very handsome thing for her to do."

"Indeed it is," agreed Caroline. "I cannot imagine how she could bear to part with them."

Sidney laughed easily. "She says she has no occasion to wear them, and she is sure you can put them to very good use. So be easy on that score, Cousin."

Julia rose to order refreshments and over wine and cakes Sidney requested the pleasure of escorting the ladies to the opera that very evening. Julia, with no performance of her own, was not averse to seeing others labour, and agreed. Presently Sidney went away to engage a box for a presentation of the great Catalini at Covent Gardens.

The ladies repaired upstairs for an inspection of their wardrobes. Between a discussion of the rival merits of the shell-pink gauze worn before to see Julia perform and a sea-foam-green net trimmed with embroidered leaves and acorns in dark green and silver, Caroline spoke of the felicity of having yet another relative, which reminded her of the message she had been charged with.

"Dearest Mrs. Daventry, my cousin Neville is much distressed by what has happened between you and has begged me to request that you will receive him tomorrow morning when he means to apologise. Please say that you will see him," she entreated.

Julia, whose own anger had dissipated days before, to be replaced by real regret that she had allowed such an uncomfortable situation to continue, was only too happy to agree, and promptly went off to her own room, ostensibly to choose her gown for the opera, but really to choose one for Mr. Devereaux's visit.

When Belding tapped at her door the following morning Julia was still in the throes of indecision. A yellow striped muslin and a pea-green sarsenet had been discarded and she was just in the process of removing a deep blue jaconet with long white muslin sleeves gathered in every three inches with velvet riband of the same blue.

Nurse returned from the door to inform her that Mr. Devereaux had arrived.

"Oh, Lord! This one will have to do. Quick, Dainty, button it back up!"

"I'm going as fast as I can, missy, and I'd like to know what you're so up in the boughs about? I thought you was mad as fire with him, calling him a make-mischief and I don't know what all."

"Well, he's come to apologise, so I must be friendly again and make it up for Caroline's sake, mustn't I?"

"Don't go lettin' him cozzen you into taking her away," warned Dainty, pushing Julia into the chair before her dressing table and attacking the dark curls tousled by the trying on of dresses. "Take deep breaths, for goodness sake, missy. Will you meet him all gasping like that?"

Julia tried to concentrate on slowing her breathing, taking anxious little peeps into the glass at the same time. There was no disguising the flushed cheeks and the extra sparkle excitement lent to the deep brown eyes. She concentrated even harder for calm. When she felt she had herself well enough in hand she rose and walked with a stately tread out of the room and downstairs.

Neville turned sharply at her entrance, feeling his breath catch in his throat, as always, at her beauty. They advanced hesitantly toward each other.

"Mrs. Daventry, I hope this poor offering and my most abject apologies will induce you to forgive my boorish conduct the other night," he said, holding out an exquisite posy of violets in a dainty ivory holder. She took it, bending her face over it to hide her pleasure, and to savour the sweet leaping of her pulses at the sight of him. It is not, she thought, that he is an Adonis like Lord Redvers, it is the sense of strength he conveys, and the promise of tenderness. But I *must* not give way to such thoughts *now*, of all times.

She raised her eyes, striving for the right tone. "I fear we were both hasty, sir."

"Then shall we start over?"

"Yes, let us try." She smiled warmly in spite of her resolve to maintain a cool friendliness. "Will you take a glass of wine or a cup of tea?"

She motioned him to a chair and rang for Belding before seating herself on the sofa. He took a chair facing her. "I have not thanked you for the flowers," she continued. "They are lovely, though where you can have found them this early in the season I cannot imagine."

"They are lovely now in their proper setting," he replied meaningfully. In spite of all she could do her eyes dropped from his steady gaze. She forced herself to raise them. "Why do you always look like a painting?" he mused wonderingly.

Fortunately, Belding entered at this moment with wine. By the time they had been served and he had withdrawn, she had herself, she hoped, well enough in hand to take charge of the conversation.

"Mr. Devereaux, you may perhaps be wondering at your cousin's absence."

"Only to be grateful," he murmured.

She continued hurriedly, "She has been taken for a drive by another cousin."

"Another cousin? She has no other cousin."

"Well, perhaps not strictly so, but he said he considered her in that light, and she did not object."

"Very amiable of him, I'm sure. What is the gentleman's name?"

"Mr. Knox-Gore."

"Sidney? Good heavens! I had no idea he was in London."

"He came at his mother's behest, he told us, to help entertain Caroline and beg her to visit when she feels able to do so. She is not in the best of health, he told us, or she would have come herself."

"She seemed very well to me. But then she is quite—er—stout, so perhaps travel is not comfortable for her, though why she should want to come—well, never mind, it was kind of her. Still, why Sidney should—" He stopped, not wishing to say anything unkind about the fellow who had seemed quite pleasant even though Mr. Thistlewaite had hinted at some unpleasant qualities.

"Yes?" she said encouragingly.

"Oh, nothing. Only that he needn't have put himself out."

"He seemed quite eager. In fact, he has already begun, for he took us to see Catalini last evening and we enjoyed it prodigiously."

"Oh, I see."

"And your cousin was ravishing. Mr. Knox-Gore had brought his mother's pearls as a gift from her to Caroline, and they were perfect with her sea-foam green—"

"His mother's pearls?"

"They had been left her by her sister, as I understood him."

"Ah! Those pearls. They were not Mrs. Knox-Gore's. They were her sister's, however. But Great-Uncle Chandos had put them away for Caroline."

"Why, I made sure from what he said they were a gift from Mrs. Knox-Gore," said Julia in some puzzlement.

"A small misunderstanding, no doubt. I found them myself in a locked box my great-uncle kept in his bedroom. However, it was thoughtful of her to send them—should have brought them to Caroline myself."

Julia opened her mouth to protest further, but decided it was too hazy a remembrance of the conversation with Sidney to risk any contention that might disturb their newly acquired amity. She offered him more wine instead.

"Now, Mrs. Daventry, lest I get too far behind Sidney, I hope you and Caroline will do me the honour of allowing me to escort you to Lady Heather Knowlton's ball day after tomorrow. She's by way of being a distant relative of my mother's and when she heard I was acquainted with you she would not let me leave her house until I had promised to try to secure you for her ball. She is also eager to meet Caroline, of course."

"You are—sure, Mr. Devereaux?" she pressed doubtfully.

"Very. She seems to think it will be some sort of feather in her cap to capture you, since none of the other hostesses have managed to do so. I hope you have not a deep-seated aversion to balls, Mrs. Daventry?"

"Oh, no. It is only that I have not accepted such invitations before. But of course, this will be Caroline's first ball. I do not like to deprive her of it."

"Then you will come?"

"Yes—yes I—we will come," she said with a breathless little laugh.

"Then I will put in my request now for the first set of dances and at least two others, one to be the waltz."

"You are very specific in your requests, Mr. Devereaux."

"I know exactly what I want," he said in a voice thickened with feeling that brought the colour flooding into her cheeks again, "and if I dared I would ask for every dance. I will content myself, however, with the pitiful few I have mentioned. I know full well that if I do not have your promise before we arrive, I will not even be able to get near you after." He rose and bent to take her hands, pulling her to her feet to face him, so close that only their clasped hands separated them. "You have not answered my requests yet," he reminded her softly.

"Oh—yes—I shall be happy—" she gasped.

He bent his head to press his lips against each of the hands he still held. "Thank you. I will take my leave now while I still retain enough sense of what is fitting to stop me from asking for much, much more. I'm very greedy, it seems, where you are concerned."

He kissed the hands once more before relinquishing them, then stepped back, bowed, and left the room quickly.

She stood where he had left her until the door had closed behind him, then sank limply onto the sofa, her hands pressed to her fiery cheeks. Why—why he made *love* to me, she thought, and, what is more—I *let* him!

10

LADY KNOWLTON WAS much gratified on the day before her ball to receive a positive deluge of notes from young gentlemen, all of whom had previously sent their regrets to her card of invitation, but who now found themselves happily able to be present after all. From despair she was raised to the happy felicity of looking forward to a dreadful "squeeze," the aim of every hostess, and though puzzled she wasted no time trying to plumb the mystery. She sent orders to her cook to triple the number of lobster patties and to her staff that the third drawing room must be cleared for dancing after all.

The explanation lay in the fact that Redvers, calling during the afternoon of the day Neville had tendered his invitation, was met by a bubbling Caroline who was filled with all the excitement proper to a young girl going to her first ball.

Lord Redvers promptly requested the first dance, asked Julia for the second, and rushed away to pen a note to Lady Knowlton that his previous engagement having been cancelled he looked forward with pleasure to attending the ball. That evening he was unwise enough in his own interests to speak of it to Bartle à Court and His Grace of Malby, and so word gradually spread that the Divine One would accompany her protégée to Lady Knowlton's ball.

Sidney heard of it that same evening and presented himself very early the next morning at the Clarendon where he was fortunate enough to find Neville still at breakfast, and after some rather transparent angling was able to secure Neville's assurance that his relative would send Sidney a card. He then sped around to Mrs. Daventry's where he begged the pleasure of at least two dances with his new-found cousin.

On the eve of the ball Lord Knowlton, generally a complaisant, good-natured gentleman, stood fretfully beside his lady greeting guests. He had a decided distaste for evening parties not dedicated to the whist table. He was awaiting the arrival of his special cronies, which would signal his disappearance into the library where the whist tables had been set up for those disinclined to dancing.

Ordinarily not the most observant of fellows, even he was astonished by the very early arrival of a large number of young men whose habit of making a more fashionably late entrance was the despair of every hostess.

"Demmed odd, if you ask me," he muttered, eyeing the group of gentlemen clustering around the door of the ballroom.

"What is, my dear?" asked his distracted wife.

"All those dandified Park Saunterers over there. You may depend on it, there's something havey-cavey going on when that lot condescends to come early."

"Nonsense, Fortesque," she replied, turning away to greet new arrivals.

Caroline and Julia, on either side of Neville, were inching their way slowly up the crowded stairway. Neville and Julia found the crush boring, but Caroline was enjoying herself hugely. She had never seen so many elegantly dressed people in all her life and was happy to be able to look about as much as she pleased. Apart from this was the fluttering of nerves in the area of her diaphragm at this first essay into the world of Society which made the delay of their entrance into the ballroom rather welcome than otherwise. She found many eyes turned in their direction, but assumed the looks of admiration were for Julia, magnificent tonight in a gown of white silvered lamé on gauze, with a Turkish turban of bright blue fringed in gold, and Caroline saw nothing she felt could possibly compare with it.

Her own gown, while not so sophisticated, gave her courage, for she knew she had never looked better. It was of the palest orange India mull over white satin, with short puffed sleeves in the French fashion, the low-cut bosom shaded modestly with delicate lace, the high waist defined with deeper orange velvet riband embroidered with gold clover leaves. The same riband edged the deep scalloped flounce at the hem of the long, straight falling skirt. Her auburn curls had been piled high and threaded with a narrow gold riband. Her only ornament was the pearl necklace, unless one counted the sparkling emerald of her eyes or the perfect cameo of her face.

Their reception by Lady Knowlton when at last they reached the top of the stairs could not have been more flattering. She positively gushed her pleasure in welcoming the famous Mrs. Daventry to her house, and declared Neville's little cousin destined to break more than one heart before the evening was over.

When Lord Knowlton noticed the stir of excitement at the ballroom door he exclaimed, "Ah ha! So that's it then!" before beating a hasty retreat as the pack of eager young men bore down upon the party, each one anxious to claim a dance with the glorious Mrs. Daventry before the other male guests could discover her presence. Julia had promised every dance before they had even entered the ballroom, and Caroline had received her share of attention also. Their entrance caused a high-pitched buzz of inquiry over the entire length of the room. Women of all ages looked them over critically and for the most part despairingly, for there could be no doubt that between them, Julia and Caroline threw every other female in the room into the shade.

One who didn't feel at all intimidated by two such dazzling beauties was a large, imposing lady in puce satin, whose proud bosom held, as on a shelf, an astonishing display of jewels. She was engaged in conversation with Lord Redvers, bent attentively before her, but when the new arrivals entered she waved him aside and raised her *face-à-main* for a thorough, businesslike inspection of them. Redvers whirled around, muttered something to her, and made his way with all speed to Caroline, where he drew her apart from the crowding gentlemen, grandly ignoring all protests. Had he been capable of looking away from her he would have seen the large lady beckoning him indignantly. She beckoned in vain, however. When the sets were formed for the first dance Lady Wrexham, for it was indeed Redvers's mother, watched with undisguised affront as her son led out a girl totally unknown to her, a state of affairs she found highly unsatisfactory. With her fan she rudely poked a gentleman standing with his back to her and demanded to be told who the girl was.

"Madame, I do not know," he replied coldly.

"Fetch Lady Knowlton to me," she ordered imperiously.

He stiffened for a moment, but under her challenging eye swallowed his outrage, bowed, and went away to do her bidding. Lady Knowlton, however, was much too busy to attend her, so Lady Wrexham could only watch in fuming impatience as her son moved about the floor with an unknown young woman upon whom he gazed with much too evident adoration.

Lady Wrexham was not the only person there who watched. Sidney, just arrived, eyed them narrowly, but felt secure in the knowledge that the next dance was his. A few couples away on the floor Julia, dancing with Neville, also noticed.

"Lord Redvers must learn to dissemble a bit, I believe. He is creating gossip," she commented.

"Ah, well, poor wretch, I suppose he cannot help himself," responded Neville feelingly.

"I think he should make an effort for his own sake. Caroline is much too level-headed to be impressed by a languishing air."

"As are you, Mrs. Daventry. I wonder what would impress you?"

"Why, I think most women—"

"You are as unlike most women as a rose to a dandelion," he broke in with a smile.

"I think Lady Knowlton must be having one of the more successful balls of the season," she said, hurriedly changing the subject.

"And all because of you."

"I? What have I to do with it?"

"Well, I know for a fact Malby and à Court had declined, as well as most of the rest of that set, including Wrexham. Lady Knowlton was quite in despair, I assure you. Then they learned that you were to come and changed their minds."

"Good heavens!" exclaimed Julia, between amusement and dismay.

"I'm thankful I had the forethought to engage you beforehand. You have not forgotten that you have promised me two more dances, have you?"

She smiled at him and his heart turned over. "No, sir, I have not forgotten."

He held her eyes for a timeless period and they were both helplessly caught by the strength of their growing feelings for one another. Julia knew that without words he was making love to her here before all these people, and not only did she allow it, but her heart leapt with joy and the blood sang hot through her veins in response. She experienced a fierce longing to feel his arms about her, to—

They were separated at this point by the figure of the dance and for a brief moment Julia was entirely confused by the abrupt withdrawal of his eyes and hands. She became aware of eyes watching her curiously everywhere she looked. Dear Lord, she thought, I have created more gossip than poor Redvers! She realized in her agitation that she was panting for breath as though she had been running and that her breast was visibly heaving. She forced herself to take slow breaths, and when they came together again refused to look into his eyes for fear she would lose control once more. Instead she occupied her mind with taking herself to task for her unseemly behaviour, her thoughts shot through with lightning forks of longing to succumb to this harsh-faced man, to give herself without thought of the price. These flashes were followed almost instantly by a fear of disturbing her long hibernating emotions lest, once roused, they might brush caution aside and sweep her into an affair over which she would have no control. Between these two extremes sanity reasserted itself to remind her that she was still the Vicar's daughter, and would never be able to face him again if she heeded her present longings. She had been in the theatre long enough to know that with only a few, rare exceptions, marriage was the last thing a gentleman had on his mind when he began a flirtation with an actress. She forced herself now to look straightly at the near certainty that Neville Devereaux's intentions did not include anything beyond a *carte blanche*.

She was in a very subdued mood as they left the floor, her mind grappling with this unacceptable truth.

"A pound for them," he said with a quizzical smile.

"I beg your—oh!''—she laughed an artificial little laugh that caused a small crease of worry between his brows—"they are not worth so much, sir, I assure you." Before he could continue in this probing strain she looked about, caught sight of Lady Wrexham. "Who *is* that lady?" she asked, awed.

"Wrexham's mama. A formidable woman who keeps Wrexham on a very tight rein."

"I hope she will not be unkind to Caroline," she said worriedly.

"I have no doubt she will make herself as unpleasant as possible. She's deep in negotiation with the Countess of Charn for her eldest daughter for Wrexham. Hortense, poor girl, is a dish-faced tomboy devoted to her horses and dogs, who's been on the shelf since her come-out four years ago, but she is connected to at least half the best families in England and has a very large dowry. They are taking bets at White's they will make a match of it before the month is out."

"Revolting! Surely his own mama should realize how unsuitable a match it would be for Lord Redvers. Oh,dear! He is leading Caroline to her—perhaps I should—"

"Don't concern yourself, my dear Mrs. Daventry. I would stake my cousin against an army of Lady Wrexhams!"

Indeed, Neville had every reason to be confident, for Caroline, presented reverentially to his mama by Redvers, had met that lady's glacial regard with a deep curtsey and a blinding smile.

"Devereaux? Then since you arrived with him, I take it you are related to Neville Devereaux?"

"My cousin, Lady Wrexham."

"Where are you from, if you please?" the old woman asked in an offensive tone of voice that clearly implied Caroline could not possibly be from anywhere recognizable by polite Society.

"From Worcestershire, madame," answered Caroline imperturbably.

"Ah! Jack Devereaux's girl then?"

"Yes, Lady Wrexham."

"Scoundrel!" pronounced Lady Wrexham emphatically.

Caroline's lips twitched, but she replied gravely, "Was he so, Lady Wrexham?"

"Handsome devil though," Lady Wrexham said, unexpectedly, her face softening momentarily. "Broke many a heart, I can tell you. Threw himself away on some nobody, I heard."

Caroline's chin came up. "My mother," she reminded the old lady softly, but with a note of steel in her voice.

Lady Wrexham opened her mouth for a retort, but possibly for the first time in her life restrained herself.

A small silence followed while both ladies plied their fans: Caroline composedly, Lady Wrexham exhibiting some agitation. She was not accustomed to being faced down by a chit barely out of the schoolroom, and besides was experiencing a rare feeling of guilt for her inexcusable behaviour.

Caroline's thoughts were not concerned so much with the mother as with the son. Throughout the encounter Lord Redvers had stood by silently, flushing uncomfortably at his mother's insulting tone, but seemingly unwilling to protect Caroline from it. Was he so paltry a creature that he dared not draw his mother's ire down upon his own head by protesting? Much as she had come to like him for his gentleness, and of course for his open adoration of her—for it is nearly impossible for one to dislike a person who shows one so much flattering admiration—she hoped he would not prove to be spineless, for his own sake.

She glanced up at him and he smiled uncomfortably at her. She decided she must come to her own rescue. "Sir, would you please take me back to Mrs. Daventry? I believe the set is forming for the next dance and I have engaged to dance it with Mr. Knox-Gore."

"*Mrs. Daventry?*" gasped Lady Wrexham in scandalized accents, "Is that who—?"

Finally Lord Redvers acted. Grasping Caroline's arm he turned her away from his mother, saying, "Of course, Miss Devereaux, how thoughtless of me."

Caroline turned back, dropped a respectful curtsey to Lady Wrexham, and smiled prettily before allowing herself to be led away, leaving Lady Wrexham with her mouth still acock.

Lady Wrexham closed her mouth, sniffed, ordered a hapless gentleman just passing to fetch her a glass of champagne, and sat back to fan herself into a semblance of calm while she considered the situation. That her son was smitten by the wench was only too plain for all to see, and Lady Wrexham thanked God that Hortense was not in London to also be witness, for the Charns were not the sort to suffer any insult, real or imagined.

Lady Wrexham conceded grudgingly that Caroline was a pretty-behaved girl, and there was no denying she was a real little beauty, enough to turn any man's head. But if Redvers thought he would be allowed to whistle Hortense and her impeccable blood lines and immense fortune down the wind for some girl whose mother was a nonentity and whose fortune was in her face he would have to be shown the error of his ways in no uncertain terms, thought Lady Wrexham grimly.

Neville, who had relinquished Julia to Redvers, happened at this moment to have the misfortune to look in Lady Wrexham's direction and could not pretend to misinterpret her imperious signal for him to join her at once. Putting as good a face on it as possible he made his way to her side.

"Well, Devereaux, you are full of surprises. Did you bring that young woman up from the country with you?"

Neville bowed. "My dear Lady Wrexham, how very good to see you again. I needn't ask how you do, for I can see perfectly clearly that you do very well indeed."

Lady Wrexham was not interested in an exchange of niceties. "I hope you ain't got Wrexham in your eye for her, for if you have I tell you to your face it won't do."

"Why, as to that, I must confess I had not thought to look for a husband for her. She is very young, you see. And I fear that when the time comes, I will have very little to say to the matter."

"I hope you are not serious, Devereaux. Since Chandos's death you are certainly responsible for her."

"What is your opinion of the girl, Lady Wrexham? I know your taste to be impeccable."

She eyed him suspiciously. "Don't come the pretty to me, Devereaux. I've known you since you were in leading strings, and I've no remembrance of your consulting my taste before."

He laughed. "Caught fairly! However, I would like to hear what you think of her."

"She is too pretty for her own good, but she has conduct and— backbone," she ended, surprising Neville considerably.

"She has indeed," agreed Neville, giving the old lady a warmly approving smile that immediately charmed her into a more forthcoming humour.

"I'll tell you what, dear boy, you ought to be able to bring off a respectable match for her if you don't aim too high. If you'll take my advice, you'll find one of those Cits whose papa is rich as Golden Ball, looking to marry up. They'd take her for her entrée into Society. After all, the Devereaux name ain't to be sneezed at, even if the mother was a nobody. But don't think you can get a title for her with no dowry."

"But why should you think she has no dowry?" inquired Neville, stung by her inference that one of his blood could do no better for herself than to marry into trade.

"Jack Devereaux can't have left a penny—not the way he lived—so don't get all niffy-naffy with me, my boy."

"No, he didn't. But my father settled ten thousand on her before he died." The answer popped out without any thought on his part, surprising even himself a little.

She looked at him speculatively. She was as aware as anyone could be that her son did not need to marry for money, but she was a very greedy old lady; besides she would have felt she was doing less than her duty if she did not arrange the best possible match for him.

"Is this some Banbury tale you've giving me, Devereaux? I know for a fact that your father never spoke to Jack for over twenty years."

"Nevertheless, it is true. However, that is a mere pittance, for I believe she will be my great-uncle's heiress, in which case—"

"Chandos cut up warm, did he?" she barked.

"Very," he replied succinctly.

"That puts a different complexion on the matter, of course," she conceded, then remembered something else. "What is the gel doing in company with that actress?"

Neville stiffened immediately at her tone. "She is living with her, at the moment," he replied coldly. "Mrs. Daventry was Caroline's mother's bosom bow."

"Ah! No doubt. Her mother was a Crofton, whoever they may be," she said contemptuously, clearly indicating her view that such people would naturally be on speaking terms with actresses.

"Perfectly respectable family, as I remember. And Mrs. Daventry's father is a vicar, I'm told—"

"Vicar or not, the girl should not be appearing in public with such a person, much less be living with her."

"Mrs. Daventry has entrée to any drawing room in London. I don't believe you can possibly have heard anything to her discredit," retorted Neville with some heat.

"Never mind all that roundaboutation," snapped Lady Wrexham, "where is the chit's mother? Why is she not here protecting the child's good name?"

"She died, Lady Wrexham."

"Recently?"

"Quite recently, yes," admitted Neville, uncomfortably sure of what was coming next.

"What! And you take her into company?" gasped Lady Wrexham disbelievingly.

"Yes, I do! I do not hold with the barbaric custom of—of draping so young a child in black. She should be helped to forget her loss." The irony of defending himself with Julia's words to him on the subject fleetingly occurred to him, but he had no time to dwell on it.

"Rubbish! The gel should be in mourning. I can't think where you've come by such an odd notion, Devereaux. You quite shock me. I don't know what your dear mother would have thought if she were alive to hear you express such impious sentiments."

"My mother was a very kind and sensible lady, so no doubt she would have agreed with me. I'll bring you another glass of champagne, Lady Wrexham." He bowed, seized the empty glass from her hand, and departed without giving her a chance to say anything further.

On the floor, Julia had watched this encounter, having little doubt of the content of at least part of the conversation judging from the disapproving glare she had encountered from Lady Wrexham at one point. Redvers, on the other hand, had missed it entirely, being much more preoccupied with the vision of Caroline in animated conversation with Mr. Knox-Gore. The two of them seemed to be enjoying themselves hugely, if his easy laugh and her sparkling smile were anything to go by.

"I wonder who came off best?" mused Julia aloud as she watched Neville hurry away from Lady Wrexham.

"I beg your pardon, Mrs. Daventry?"

"Your mama and Mr. Devereaux. I was just wondering about their encounter."

"Oh—I didn't notice. Mama no doubt," he said with glum conviction.

Julia noticed the direction of his glance and said sympathetically, "Do not refine too much upon it, Lord Redvers. They are by way of being cousins, so no doubt she feels at ease in his company."

"They are perfect strangers, and not really related at all," he returned, refusing comfort.

She studied his unhappy face for a moment. "Then perhaps it is that she feels more at ease with someone who does not make her feel so self-conscious."

"Do you say that I do so? I'm sure I can think of nothing I've done to make her so."

"You never take your eyes from her face when she is in the same room with you, Lord Redvers. It is very difficult to behave naturally when you feel your every movement is being observed."

"But she is so beautiful I cannot help myself," he said plaintively.

"Also, I think she finds it difficult to take seriously anyone who writes verses to her eyebrows," continued Julia determined to tell him everything now that she had started. "First, because she is not in the least aware of how very beautiful they are. Second, she has had to struggle all her life just to survive, which has made her into a very practical young lady. She cannot be expected, therefore, to respect, or even to understand, someone who has nothing else to do in the world but languish at her feet in rapt contemplation of those eyebrows, however perfect."

He mulled this over while they were separated by the dance. When they came together again, he said, "She thinks I'm a fool then?"

"Oh, no, Lord Redvers, I'm sure she would never think such a thing of anyone unless he proved, beyond doubt, that he was so," Julia assured him, smiling encouragingly at him, praying he would take her meaning, for she quite liked the boy and was sure his silly affectation of Byronic histrionics was all part of youthful uncertainty. He impressed her, despite the pose, as an intelligent lad who would finally realize the ridiculousness of a very bad imitation of one who was himself a poseur.

She had the pleasure, as the evening progressed, of seeing that some of her meaning had sunk in, for Redvers ceased following Caroline about with his eyes, and though he looked somewhat abstracted, led out a number of delighted young ladies onto the floor.

It was the only pleasure she was experiencing, however, for as the evening progressed and she passed from one pair of arms to another doing a fine job of acting as a woman having a happy time, her spirits were sinking lower and lower. Her imagination finally presented her with a series of pictures of herself receiving a slip on the shoulder from Neville Devereaux. By the last one she had felt her first stir of anger that he should dare to make such a suggestion to her.

When he came to claim his second dance, the waltz, she had some difficulty in keeping up her determinedly pleasant front. She had decided she could not give way to her feelings here, not only for her own reputation, but for Caroline's. She therefore forced herself to turn a smiling face up to Neville, but even he could see that it was an empty smile, that it did not reach her eyes.

"Now, my dear, I can see that something has displeased you. You will tell me who has offended you and I shall call him out at once."

"I cannot think what you mean, Mr. Devereaux. I assure you the entire evening has been charming. I have not danced for many years, and I find I like it very much."

"You have not had enough gaiety in your life. I hope you will allow yourself more of it now."

"Oh, I expect I shall be seen everywhere now, routs, masquerades, *fêtes champêtres*, for Caroline will be sure to be flooded with invitations."

The music swept them around the floor seductively, and it took all her resources not to allow it to sweep away her anger with it. She had learned the steps of the waltz even though she had not expected to be actually dancing it, but she had never realized the power of the actual fact of moving about the floor in a man's arms to such romantic music. Especially when that man was looking down into her eyes, his own speaking to her of love, his hand warm at her waist, his very presence drawing her to him powerfully. She bit her lip hard and looked away from him, beginning to chatter meaninglessly about the other guests. When he attempted to speak of something concerning only the two of them, she laughed gaily and pretended to misunderstand him. When he led her off the floor at last he was distinctly puzzled, though he made no reference to her behaviour, only handing her over to her next partner with another warm smile before walking away.

Caroline, meanwhile, had truly enjoyed her conversation with Sidney as they danced. He had skillfully led her on to happy reminiscing about her mother, expressed his admiration for his own mother who had been in a like position of having to fend alone for her child, and told Caroline how much courage she herself had shown in coming to London alone. He made no effort at this stage to make love to her, sensing it would hamper his cause rather than forward it. Sidney was not truly very intelligent, being used to having his thinking done for him by his mama, but in the area of engaging the affections of women he had developed the process to an art, it being the one area where his mama could not follow him.

He had seen at once that though grass green, Caroline was of a rare independence of mind and in the habit of taking a long, assessing look at everything before she made any judgements. She therefore could not be swept off her feet by romantic tarradiddle.

His plan was to get her to trust him, to feel safe in his company, to turn to him with confidences. Once on a footing of familiarity with him, and completely at ease, he would gradually let her become aware of his own very warm regard for her. Not blatantly, of course, but with the subtle inference that he was aware he stood little chance with her and would therefore not embarrass her with his deeper feelings. This he felt sure would disarm her and cause her own feelings toward him to be stirred. He congratulated himself that so far he had not put a foot wrong.

When Neville came to request Julia to go down to supper with him she said carelessly that she believed she had already promised that honour to His Grace of Malby and turned back to her conversation with a young lieutenant of the Light Bobs who was fanning her face as they spoke.

Affronted, Neville bowed coldly and left her, fuming inwardly that she had not the courtesy to save supper for him since he had escorted her here. What the devil had come over her to change her in the space of a moment from the warm, giving creature she had been at the beginning of their first dance to this coolly disinterested beauty?

By the time of their third dance she had worked herself into a rage she could no longer conceal from him. His own quick temper, primed by the supper incident, leapt into flame, and by the end of the dance, their conversation had settled into a desultory exchange of cold, inconsequential nothings, every word glinting with ice.

On the carriage ride home Caroline and Julia sat side by side with Neville facing them, his back to the coachman. Caroline at first chattered happily about the evening, but gradually her enthusiasm ebbed as she became aware that the other two were each staring out the windows in opposite directions, not only not speaking to each other, but carefully not looking at each other either. The silence became more and more glacial, and Caroline began to fear they would never reach home. They have quarreled again, she thought with despair, and realized that her good work as peacemaker was all to do over.

= 11 =

IN THE WEEK that followed Caroline found it impossible to implement her good intentions toward the two most dear to her in all the world. Neville, once bitten, was more than twice shy and informed Caroline when she approached him on the matter that while he hoped no one could accuse him of rudeness, and of course he harboured no unfriendly feelings against Mrs. Daventry, he still could not bring himself to make the first move toward reconciliation, especially since he had done nothing to reanimate Mrs. Daventry's anger toward himself.

"She is perhaps a victim of her own—er—volatile temperament. I have heard that truly great performers must have this quality," he told Caroline when she continued to press him, "and though I am a great admirer of her abilities on the stage, I find that same temperament, when applied to real-life friendships, too wearing. I simply cannot keep up with the vagaries of her emotional ups and downs."

Caroline's protests that Mrs. Daventry was the most even-tempered, good-natured soul alive were met by Neville's disbelievingly raised eyebrow, and a change of subject.

She had even less success with Julia, who of course could not confess the shameful reason for the withdrawal of her favour from Neville to this innocent young girl. Instead she met all Caroline's attempts to reconcile the two of them with a bland denial that anything was wrong.

"But my dear child, I'm sure I don't know what you can mean. There is no quarrel between your cousin and myself."

Caroline puzzled fruitlessly over the problem and finally consulted Mrs. Dainty.

"Mean to say they two have kicked up another row?"

"They say not, Mrs. Dainty, but they are so—so—*polite* toward each other. It causes an absolute chill in the air when they are in the same room."

"Hmmm. She's not been up to snuff on stage either these past two three nights. I'd best look into it."

She marched determinedly into Julia's room and began her attack at once. "Now then, missy, what's bothering you? And don't tell me naught because I know you much too well for that."

"What's on my mind at the moment is whether this bonnet is becoming to me or not," replied Julia, who was seated before her glass, contemplating from different angles a confection of satin straw with a deep poke lined in pleated yellow silk, and matching yellow silk roses about the high crown.

"You know that shade of yellow makes you look sallow, so take it off, do!" Julia removed the offending bonnet and rose to replace it in the striped hat box bearing the name of one of London's leading modistes. "And you know that is not what I was speaking of."

"Well, what *are* you speaking of?" demanded Julia crossly.

"You're off your feed for one thing. Haven't eaten a proper meal in days. P'raps that is what's affecting your performances."

"Affecting my—! What do you mean? What is wrong with my performances?"

"Well—I don't know eggzac'ly. Sort of—dull—they are, if you was to ask me," replied Mrs. Dainty judiciously.

"Dull? *Dull?* I suppose those five curtain calls last night were the result of my dullness?" retorted Julia indignantly.

"Pooh! They'd do that if you was only to stand there and grin at 'em. Take it from me, missy, you're off," said Mrs. Dainty firmly, for she considered herself, after five years of observation, as fine a judge of Julia's acting abilities as the critic Mr. Leigh Hunt.

A crease appeared between Julia's brows, for even she had to concede that Dainty was generally right in these matters, and since she knew well that her mind was still doing battle with her heart over the matter of Neville Devereaux, it meant she was allowing her personal life to intrude into her professional one, which would never do.

Mrs. Dainty noted the frown. "Now what is bothering my darlin' girl? Tell old Dainty." She put a gentle hand to Julia's cheek. Julia felt the tears start at the sympathy in her old nurse's voice and turned away from the comforting hand abruptly.

"Nothing. Truly, Dainty. Perhaps I'm only tired."

"Now then, you were never good at fibs, Miss Julia. Miss Caroline says there's bad feelings between you and Mr. Devereaux. Is that it? Has he said something to turn you up like this?"

"Oh, no, he's *said* nothing," replied Julia with just enough bitter emphasis on the verb to unconsciously give herself away.

Mrs. Dainty held her peace. She could see Julia was on the verge of tears and it was never wise to upset her before a performance. But she had much to mull upon.

So it was nothing he'd said, she mused. Something not said then? Something Miss Julia had hoped he'd say? For Mrs. Dainty was not so blind she had missed that joyousness with which Julia had dressed for the ball last week. Mrs. Dainty had not seen her girl like that since Mr. Edward had been taken from her. Mrs. Dainty had immediately relinquished her dream of ducal splendor, for if Mr. Devereaux could make her darling that happy then she must have him. While they were away dancing that night, Mrs. Dainty had spent the evening dreaming of setting up a proper household with a man at the head of it as it should be, and with nurseries upstairs in her charge again. Her arms fairly ached already with the need to hold a babe of Julia's.

Julia's cold silence on her return from the ball had somewhat dimmed Mrs. Dainty's dream, however, and now it seemed in danger of disappearing altogether, for none knew better than Mrs. Dainty how carefully Julia guarded her heart. Feeling quite sure she understood the problem, the old nurse returned to her attack again that night as she helped Julia make ready for bed.

When she had tucked Julia in and tied the ribands of her nightcap in a fetching bow beneath her chin, Mrs. Dainty sat down on the side of the bed and took Julia's hand in her own.

"Dearest girl, old Dainty knows what's troubling you. Now I can see that you like Mr. Devereaux more than somewhat and—"

"Oh, Dainty, *please!*"—begged Julia, pulling her hand away.

"Let me finish, darling, do. I say you're too eager. You was always wanting everything to happen *at once*, since you was ever so small. What I say is, you've only known Mr. Devereaux for a pair of weeks and I vow he's for sure smitten with you. But gentlemen take their time about these things. He'll speak, but you must be more patient.''

"If you mean you think he'll come up to scratch, Dainty, you're far out," retorted Julia.

"That's a vulgar expression that I never thought I'd hear coming from your lips, Miss Julia," reproved Dainty loftily.

"Not nearly so vulgar as what he really intends!"

"Not—why, what do you mean, missy?"

"If you want the word with no bark on it, he only means to offer me a *carte blanche!*"

"*What!*" Mrs. Dainty nearly shouted in her shock. "He has never said such a thing to you, surely not, Miss Julia?"

"Not yet. But that is what he intends, you may be sure. That is all any of them would offer, including Malby, if I gave them the opportunity. The only offer of marriage I've had was from Bertie Buckthorpe."

"Did he truly offer, Miss Julia? And you never told me! What did you say to him?"

"Dainty, the boy is half my age. What would you have me say to him?"

"Well, of course, he ain't really what I would want for you. Not too bright in his upper works, and he'll only inherit a baronetcy," replied Mrs. Dainty. "Still it shows—"

"It shows he's not too bright, as you said," responded Julia bitterly. "Oh, please, Dainty, please don't go on. I'm so tired and— oh, I cannot discuss it anymore!"

Mrs. Dainty saw the futility of pursuing the subject further at the moment, for when Julia got her back up in this way, it was best to let the matter rest until she showed a more reasonable frame of mind. Kissing her forehead and wishing her to sleep well, Mrs. Dainty blew out the candle and tiptoed away. She was resolved, however, to take the first opportunity to have a few words with Mr. Neville Devereaux. She found it difficult to credit Julia's version of that gentleman's intentions, for she had found him, in their few encounters, consistently pleasant, courteous, and respectful.

She found no opportunity to approach him at once, however, for his visits were brief and he did not come every day as before.

Caroline herself saw little of Neville during this time for she had indeed been deluged with invitations: for carriage rides in the Park, afternoon calls, musicales, dinner parties, and dancing parties. She found herself dividing her time for the most part between Sidney Knox-Gore and Lord Redvers, the most persistent of her admirers, who vied for her constant attention.

Lord Redvers had surprised her by calling the day after the ball, his hair cut stylishly, his usual loose, carelessly worn jacket replaced by a beautifully fitting coat from Stutz, and the loosely knotted scarf he was want to affect replaced by a precisely tied neckcloth holding up starched shirt points. His buff-colored pantaloons did nothing to conceal his well-muscled thighs, and his Hessians had been polished to a mirrorlike finish. Nor did he arrive carrying his usual role of parchment.

When Caroline first saw him she was dazzled by this transformation. She said nothing about it, however, though consumed with curiosity as to the reasons. She asked him to be seated and sat, hands folded in her lap, patiently waiting for his daily rhapsodic ode to her perfections. Instead, she found him gazing pensively into the fire.

After a moment she said, her eyes twinkling, "Well, sir, has the Muse deserted you?"

"What?" He turned startled eyes upon her. "Oh—oh—I see. Yes, I suppose so, or at least, I have deserted her. I don't believe, you know, that she had ever been with me at all." He smiled ruefully.

"Oh, I'm sorry. I shouldn't have made a joke of it."

"I expect you had every reason to be amused. It was all fustian, I see that now. I'd no real talent for verse. I must apologize for all I made you listen to."

"Well, it was not so disagreeable to hear oneself praised," she admitted fairly, "even though I could not truly believe it. I'm glad to learn that it was all fustian."   !

"Oh, no! Those things I said in the poems were all truly how I felt, only I had not the ability to say them in that way. I was always too shy, you see, for compliments and flirtations, and it was a way to express admiration—almost as someone else—outside myself, if you see what I mean."

"Why, of course, it's perfectly simple when you explain it so," exclaimed Caroline warmly, "and now you don't feel so shy and can just be yourself. Really, it was quite clever of you, when one thinks about it, to have worked out a way."

He grinned. "And at the same time, I am shamed to admit, cause considerable annoyance to my mama, which afforded me a great deal of wicked gratification. She has always been rather overpowering."

Caroline giggled. "Yes, so I noticed. Does she browbeat you?"

"She used to, but no more," he replied simply, but with total conviction.

"Good!"

"I told her outright this morning I'd no intention of making an offer of marriage just to oblige her, fully expecting the devil of a row, but she took it without a blink. I should have stood up to her years ago."

"Never mind, you've done so now," replied Caroline approvingly. "What would you really like to do?"

"Do?"

"Yes. You know, now that you're no longer going to be a poet."

"Oh. Well, I guess I hadn't really got that far in my thinking, though I suppose what I should really like best of all would be to return to High Mallows and look after my estates. That is all I've ever really wanted to do, but Mama was determined I should cut a swath in Society and capture a great prize in the Marriage Mart. She said I—" He flushed suddenly and stopped.

Caroline looked at him sympathetically, able to guess by the way he coloured up and by his confusion that his mother had said something he was too modest to repeat. No doubt it was something about his extraordinary good looks and high birth. There was every reason for her to have great expectations for there was no denying he was the handsomest man Caroline had ever seen. Any mother might be forgiven for having ambitions for such a son.

"Well, now you're your own man. You can go to High Mallows and live your life the way you want, even pick out your own wife."

"Oh, I've already done so—though she probably thinks me a great looby and will not have me," he replied, giving her a very direct and meaningful look.

Caroline met his glance squarely, not pretending to misunderstand him, for she despised missishness. "Perhaps she will not, but you must first let her become acquainted with the new Lord Redvers. I'm sure she will like him better than the old one."

He understood and was content to allow the subject to drop. In the week that followed, though more determined than ever to have her, he allowed it to appear that he was less so, by granting her more freedom from his ever-hovering presence. She was able to observe him now from more of a distance.

He continued to call every day, however, and there was rarely an evening they did not attend the same party. He did not always find her at home, of course, for there were a number of young blades dangling after her now, and there was also Sidney, who managed to get himself invited everywhere, for hostesses were always happy to welcome a personable, well-behaved young man, and he was, after all, related to the Devereauxs, as he made sure to tell everyone. He knew very well how to make himself agreeable, and when he was not dancing with Caroline, was always available and amenable to stand up with a young lady whose hostess felt was being neglected, however much an antidote.

Caroline had come quite to look forward to seeing him, for he always knew who everyone was, and had a fund of amusing stories. He also encouraged her to tell him of her conquests, though she laughingly denied any such, but she unknowingly told him a great deal more of her feelings than she realized. He noticed at once the alteration of her regard for Wrexham, though she said nothing.

Caroline herself was barely aware of it. She only knew that she no longer thought of him with a sort of amused tolerance and was very much aware of him when they were in the same room together. One evening after a dinner party, their hostess decided there were enough young people present for an impromptu dance, and sat down to the piano to play for her guests. Sidney led Caroline out onto the floor. She stood up with him willingly enough, for he was an excellent dancer, but she was aware of a small stab of disappointment that Lord Redvers had not been by her side to solicit her hand first. She looked around and saw an unusually beautiful girl enter the room, her pale blond hair and dazzling white complexion seeming to light up the doorway. Caroline saw Redvers detach himself from the group of gentlemen with whom he was standing and rush across the room to greet the girl enthusiastically. The girl's bright blue eyes lighted up with happiness and she held both her hands out to him. They stood talking excitedly together until the boulanger was finished. The hostess immediately swung into a lilting waltz and Redvers led the ravishing blonde ont the floor.

Caroline, who had been instructed that young women who had not been given permission by one of the patronesses of Almack's, must not dance the waltz in public, had very properly taken a seat beside Lady Knowlton, who had brought her to this party tonight, since Julia was performing. There were few couples dancing, but no one in the room, including Caroline, had eyes for anyone other than Lord Redvers and his partner as they swung in perfect unison around the floor, their steps so well matched it was obvious they had danced together often. They gazed into each other's eyes, both smiling, seemingly oblivious of the audience they had attracted, not only for the beauty of their dancing, but for their compelling handsomeness as a couple.

Caroline finally could bear to watch no longer, and sat staring at her white-gloved hands in her lap until the music came to an end and there was enthusiastic applause. She looked up then to see the girl laughing up at Redvers from a deep curtsey while he bowed profoundly before raising her and leading her off the floor.

"What—what a beautiful girl," Caroline said with as much casualness as she could command. "I don't believe I've ever seen her before. I know she was not at dinner. What is her name?"

"Why, that is Georgianna Brough. Isn't she lovely? I believe I heard that she had to attend a dinner her aunt was giving and came on here after. She is Wrexham's cousin, you know."

"Oh, is she," was all that Caroline could think of to say in reply. After another few moments she turned impulsively and told Lady Knowlton that she would like very much to be taken home as she had a most fearsome headache. Lady Knowlton was immediately all sympathy, saying it was no doubt the result of too many late evenings, and hurried her away.

In her own room at last which she had longed for all the way home she did not find in privacy the solace she had hoped for. Her mind was filled with the vision of Redvers laughing down into the eyes of the shimmering blonde, and moment by moment their obvious adoration for each other grew in Caroline's mind, matched by a growing pain deep inside her that she could not at first identify. It took quite some little time for her to finally come to the realization that what she was experiencing was a shameful jealousy. Never having had such feelings before she had no knowledge of how to deal with them. She tried to lecture herself on the fact that she had no claim on Lord Redvers, but this proved to be of little help. The pain grew, and she found sleep, when finally in the early hours of the morning it came to her, less than the escape she longed for.

She could not remember her dreams when she came down for breakfast the next morning, but they could not have been happy, so oppressed was her spirit. She sipped her chocolate with disinterest while crumbling a piece of toast. Julia commented that she had shadows beneath her eyes and that she had obviously been going at too headlong a pace, suggesting that she cancel her engagements for the entire day and spend it in bed resting. Caroline agreed listlessly and wandered away to Julia's desk in the small drawing room to pen a note of excuse to this evening's hostess.

Belding, not having been informed to deny her, came to announce Mr. Knox-Gore before she could finish her note and escape upstairs to her room. She greeted Sidney wanly.

"Why, what is this, Cousin? Are you not well?" he said, taking her hand and studying her face carefully.

"Oh, only tired, I think."

"I was sorry to find you gone so suddenly last night. I was so worried I claimed the privilege of cousinship to call this early. I needed to reassure myself that you were not ill."

"It was no more than a silly headache," she said with an apologetic little smile.

"Surely it came on very suddenly?"

"Why—yes, it did. While I was sitting with Lady Knowlton, so she brought me home at once."

"Ah. That was during the waltz, I recollect," he said musingly.

She felt hot colour staining her cheeks and turned away, but he did not miss her reaction. He took his leave shortly, and walked away down the street, a thoughtful frown between his brows. So, he thought, she develops the headache while watching Wrexham waltzing with the gorgeous Miss Brough? Time, I believe, to get the chit away from here before matters can develop further. Drat the girl! Just when I'm beginning to find my way about London!

== 12 ==

THAT EVENING SIDNEY, having decided he would not attend a musicale both he and Caroline had been invited to since she would not be there, and he had no interest at all in dancing attendance on any of the other females who would be, wandered down Pall Mall feeling jaunty with freedom and trying to decide how best to spend it.

He encountered Lord Redvers, who had called at Mrs. Daventry's, learned that Caroline was not receiving and would not be going out that evening, and who had decided, like Sidney, to seek diversion some other way.

Sidney hailed him enthusiastically, and after an exchange of pleasantries, Sidney insisted that Redvers join him for dinner. Redvers had never really cared for Sidney very much, but felt he could not be impolite to Caroline's cousin, so was at last persuaded and they set off to Daffy's together where they enjoyed an excellent dinner in a private dining room. When Sidney ordered the third bottle of wine, Redvers began to make his excuses for departure, feeling that the courtesies had been observed, and that Sidney was already feeling his wine. Sidney was so adamant, however, in his insistence that Redvers not leave that he was finally persuaded to sit down again. He sipped very infrequently, however, from the wine Sidney insisted on pouring for him, for he had no interest in spending a drunken night in company with Sidney.

Sidney, already befuddled by having had the lion's share of the first two bottles, didn't notice Redvers's abstemiousness, but pulled his chair around to the fire, and slouching low on his spine, stretched his long legs toward the flames and tongue loosened by drink began telling all the latest crim. con. stories he had picked up on his rounds of London drawing rooms. He laughed uproariously at his own wit and did not seem to notice Redvers's lack of response. Having finished the bottle he sent for the waiter and ordered a bowl of Daffy's special punch, a brew notorious for causing very sore heads the morning after indulging too freely in it. After a few cups of it, he turned from jollity to moroseness, staring moodily into the flames for a long period of silence.

Redvers, having accepted a cup but not bothering to taste it at all, began to think of slipping away.

"Tell you what, Wrexham," said Sidney suddenly, "'tis women cause the trouble in the world. We'd be far better off without the stupid bitches!"

"Oh, now really, I don't think—" protested Redvers.

"S'truth! Pulling our shtrings to see us dance. M'mother the worst of the lot, damn her to hell. Always telling me what I must do. I hate 'em, d'ya hear? *I hate 'em all!*" He banged his hand down forcefully on the arm of the chair for emphasis, then sank into another brooding silence.

Redvers, profoundly shocked by this speech, surreptitiously began feeling in his pocket for coins to pay their shot, determined to take his leave before things became any worse. Before he realized what was happening, he found Sidney's hand clamped about his free wrist, and looked up startled to find Sidney leaning close to stare intently into his eyes.

"Like you, Wrexham, like you very much. You're a very handsome boy. Could grow very fond of a pretty fellow like you."

Horrified, Redvers jerked his hand away, scrambling backward so quickly his chair overturned as he rose. He stood there for an instant, shocked speechless.

Sidney sneered. "Petticoat lover, eh? Beautiful but dumb. Like having your strings pulled by some dirty female. Well, don't make any plans based on Caroline. I've plans for that bitch myself."

Redvers's hand came around of its own volition and slapped Sidney's leering, wine-red face with a sharp crack that knocked him sprawling onto the floor. He then spun on his heel and left the room.

His first impulse was to go immediately around to see Caroline and tell her that she must never see Sidney again, and he set off on foot at a furious pace. Then, the emptiness of the streets reminding him of the lateness of the hour, he began to slow his steps, finally turning them toward his own home. As he walked along he began to realize that he had been very foolish to think he could tell this unsavoury tale to an innocent young girl, and she would be bound to ask why she should refuse to see Sidney anymore.

He reached home and went to bed, hoping a good night's sleep would be of benefit to his thinking on the matter. But once in his bed he found sleep elusive, for suddenly it occurred to him that Sidney might call him out, and morning might bring only Sidney's friends to make the arrangements. There could be no question of not accepting the challenge if it came, much as he disliked the idea of shooting at someone, not to speak of being shot at. He was not a coward, of course, and had practiced shooting at wafers at Manton's, but he knew he was not accounted as even particularly skillful with a weapon, much less as a crack shot.

This worry, together with the recurring vision of Sidney leaning forward to make his unspeakable insinuation, combined to keep sleep at bay until dawn was breaking. As a consequence he rose past midday the next morning.

Sidney, on the other hand, woke very early. His head ached abominably and his eyes were bloodshot, but he grimly went about his business without heeding his discomfort. He penned a short note to his mother, then made his way to an agency where he hired a respectable-looking lady's maid, placed her in his carriage, or rather in Chandos Devereaux's carriage, and drove around to Mrs. Daventry's. He had made up his mind that he would take Caroline away this very day—within the hour if possible, before Redvers could come around with any tales.

Belding allowed his displeasure to show on his face at this early caller, but Sidney persuaded him that it was a matter of greatest urgency that he speak with Miss Devereaux at once.

Presently a somewhat breathless Caroline hurried into the drawing room, dressed, but with her hair loose down her back.

"Cousin! I came as quickly as I could. What is it?"

He took her hands, his face a compound of worry and admiration. "How—how beautiful you are! I wish I could just stand looking at you. I dislike distressing you, but I have had some troublesome news and must leave for home at once. I simply could not go away without seeing you to explain. My mother has written asking me to return since she fears she is more ill than she had thought. I believe she is frightened, all alone there with only the servants to care for her.''

"Oh! How dreadful! Is there no female relative who could be sent for to nurse her?''

"No. Unfortunately, we are all alone, she and I, and must take care of one another. She will have to make do with my poor services, I fear.''

"But—surely—a woman must attend her—'' Caroline faltered, then with decision said, "I will go to her.''

"My dear Cousin, how very noble of you to make such a sacrifice.''

"Please do not be silly. Of course it is not noble when it is only my duty. I have meant to go visit her, and what better time than when she needs me? I'll just pack a valise.'' She turned away to the door, but then turned back, frowning slightly. "Oh—I had not thought—Mrs. Daventry will undoubtedly insist that I take a maid for the journey—''

He smiled his most engaging smile. "Caroline, my dear, in the sure knowledge that you would offer what I could not bring myself to ask for, I've hired an abigail to travel with us. It is only a matter of two hours or so, but I agree with Mrs. Daventry that it would not be proper for you to be unattended.''

"Why—how thoughtful of you, Cousin Sidney,'' Caroline replied slowly, somewhat taken aback. "Very well then. I'll not be too long. I must speak to Mrs. Daventry, of course.''

She hurried off to Julia's room, where she found her still abed, but sitting up, taking her morning chocolate. Mrs. Dainty sat by the window, mending a torn ruffle on one of Caroline's gowns.

Caroline bent down to kiss Julia's cheek. "Forgive me for bursting in this way, but something has happened. I've decided I will leave at once to visit Mrs. Knox-Gore and—''

"What is this?'' demanded Mrs. Dainty, dropping the gown and rising to her feet.

"She is ill, you see, Mrs. Dainty,'' Caroline went on hurriedly, "and there is no one to care for her. Cousin Sidney just came to tell me and of course I said I would go.''

"The woman must have servants to tend her. I don't see any call for you to go tearing off in this madcap way—'' began Mrs. Dainty indignantly.

"I think it is my duty to go—'' protested Caroline.

"Now, now. Both of you hush and let us discuss it calmly," interposed Julia. "Caroline, my dear, has Mr. Knox-Gore come to ask you to go with him to nurse his mother?"

"He didn't ask me. I offered."

"But my dear child, I can hardly allow you to go off alone with him, even though he does claim to be a relative, and I don't see how I can go with you. I suppose I could send Dainty—"

"But that won't be necessary. You see, he hired a maid to make the journey with us so all would be proper. She is waiting in the carriage now."

Julia's eyebrows rose in astonishment. "How very—ah—sure he must have been that you would offer."

"If you ask me, 'tis strange doin's and I don't like it above half," declared Dainty with a dark look at both of them.

"Please don't worry. It is only two hours away and I shall only stay until she has recovered. I can't really do less"—Caroline looked at them pleadingly—"after she sent Sidney here to see that I enjoyed myself and her pearls and everything. You must see that I had to offer to go."

Julia opened her mouth to tell her what Neville had revealed about the pearls, but then decided it would not be nice to repeat it at this point, since it was probably only a misunderstanding and didn't affect the real issue of whether Caroline was right to go nurse Mrs. Knox-Gore. "Well, my dear, just as I would not allow you to be forced to go there before, now I cannot force you to stay here. Dainty and I will help you pack a valise." She set down her cup of chocolate, threw back her covers, and felt with her toes for her slippers. She went off arm-in-arm with Caroline to decide which gowns would be suitable and Dainty followed, grumbling dire predictions.

Less than an hour later Caroline was handed up into the carriage, while Julia and Dainty waved from the doorway.

"Promise me you will write to me as soon as possible," Julia called.

"Oh, I will—this very evening, I promise you, and you must answer me at once." She threw kisses to them both as Sidney gave his horses the office to start and they drove away.

When Redvers woke at noon, he could not know Caroline and

Sidney had left London nearly three hours earlier. His sleep had been sporadic and disturbed and he was feeling out of sorts. However, the news that no one had called cheered him somewhat. Possibly Sidney had been too foxed to be able to remember what had transpired last night. The problem however, remained for Redvers. It was a full hour before his muddled brain cleared and it came to him that the obvious person to consult was Neville, of course. He dressed as quickly as possible and set forth to the Clarendon Hotel. However, he was greeted there with the news that Mr. Devereaux had returned to his country estates and was not expected back in London for several days. In frustration, Redvers turned his steps toward Mrs. Daventry's.

Julia was reading a terse little note she had just received from Neville, informing her and Caroline that he had been called to the country for a few days and would call upon his return, when Belding came to announce Lord Wrexham. She sighed in resignation and bade him show the gentleman up. Her hard-and-fast rules against receiving visitors other than on Wednesdays had been completely shattered by the introduction of Caroline into the household.

"Mrs. Daventry, I hope I do not disturb you? Is Caroline at home?"

"No, she is not, Lord Redvers. Won't you sit down?"

"Oh, thank you—we had no engagement, you understand. I suppose I will see her this evening at the Elliot's."

"I fear not, sir. Caroline has gone away for a visit to the Knox-Gores."

"The—the—good God!"

"Why, Lord Redvers, whatever is wrong?"

"She shouldn't—he is not—I—" He floundered to a halt, utterly unable to think of how to complete the sentence. It was unthinkable that he should reveal Sidney's true character to her, any more than he could have to Caroline, or any other female for that matter. "I *wish* Neville had not gone away at just this time!" he said, finally, with great vexation.

"Yes. I have just had his note advising us that he is called away. But it is only for a few days. I expect he will be back by the end of the week."

"I really cannot like Miss Caroline going there. I—I—don't much care for Knox-Gore."

Julia's lips twitched at this. "Do you not, sir? Well, that is understandable, I think."

"No, no, it is not—that! It is only—that I don't think he has a very nice character."

"You must not worry, Lord Redvers. Caroline will not be there long. It is only that Mrs. Knox-Gore is unwell and Caroline felt she owed it to her to offer her help. Mrs. Knox-Gore has no other female relatives, it seems. I expect Caroline will have little time to be in Sidney's company."

He stared gloomily into space, unable to take comfort from her statement, and presently took his leave.

Julia wandered about aimlessly, too restless to settle to anything. The house seemed strangely empty. She realized that she already missed the excitement and change Caroline had brought into her life. She finally forced herself to settle down before the fire in the drawing room with the manuscript of a new play with an enchanting part for herself. She looked up eagerly, however, when Belding appeared.

"Lady Wrexham, madam."

"Good Lord! What on earth—? Well, show her up, Belding, and bring refreshments," she added, welcoming any diversion, even one so unexpected as this.

Lady Wrexham, tall, stout, and overpowering in a purple pelisse and a fearsomely unbecoming mauve bonnet featuring plumes, grapes, lace, and large purple silk flowers, plowed inexorably across the drawing room.

Julia rose and dropped a respectful curtsey, determinedly turning her fascinated eyes away from the bonnet.

"Mrs. Daventry, I've called to see Miss Devereaux," announced Lady Wrexham, coming straight to the point and ignoring the amenities as usual.

"How do you do, Lady Wrexham? Will you be seated?"

Lady Wrexham look about, chose a large wing chair which looked capable of containing her bulk, and lowered herself majestically into it. "Please summon Miss Devereaux," she commanded.

"I fear I cannot oblige you, Lady Wrexham. Miss Devereaux is not at home."

"Not at home?" repeated Lady Wrexham astounded, clearly unused to finding people away when she condescended to call. "When does she return?"

"Not for a week or so. She has gone to attend a female relative who is ill."

"A female relative? It was my understanding the girl *had* no relatives other than Neville Devereaux."

Belding entered here with a tray containing wine and a plate of Queen's cakes. He poured and served each of them a glass of wine, and put the cakes conveniently near Lady Wrexham's hand before withdrawing.

"She actually has none, of course. Mrs. Knox-Gore is only related to her by marriage, but I think when one is so bereft of relatives one tends to treasure even such tenuous connexions, don't you?"

Lady Wrexham looked at her with an expression that clearly said such a state of affairs was somehow reprehensible and the fault of the orphan, before reaching for her third cake.

"She will be devastated to have been absent when you called. I shall write and tell her and perhaps she may be allowed to return the call when she is once again in London?"

"I do not approve of young females gallivanting about the countryside," pronounced Lady Wrexham between bites.

"Well, it is a very short trip and she was accompanied by a maid and escorted by Mrs. Knox-Gore's son, Sidney."

"I don't like that young man. Don't like him at all. One can see he is hanging out for a rich wife."

Now Julia had all this while been trying to work out the reason for this call. Lady Wrexham was notoriously high in the instep and rarely went out of her way to make calls at all. That she should take the trouble to come here—and Julia was aware that her own position as an actress made it even more wildly improbable that the old woman should do so—just to visit a young girl with no prospects at all, to Julia's knowledge, was unfathomable. She could only imagine the dreadful woman had noted Redvers's infatuation and had come to warn Caroline off. This thought made Julia sit up straighter, prepared to do battle with Lady Wrexham if necessary.

"As far as I know, Lady Wrexham, the Knox-Gores are perfectly respectable people. Mrs. Knox-Gore was Chandos Devereaux's wife's sister. Caroline felt she had to go attend her when she learned the woman was ill and alone.''

"Very commendable, though I must say I have never met so many people with such a lack of relatives in so short a space of time.'' She reached for another cake and sat consuming it thoughtfully, finally pronouncing, ''Actually, now that I think about it more, it might be much the best thing, seeing Miss Devereaux has no closer female relative to care for her.''

Julia stiffened. "Caroline is in my care, Lady Wrexham.''

Lady Wrexham popped the last of a cake into her mouth and stared at Julia as she chewed. "You are an actress, Mrs. Daventry?''

"I am.''

"You seem a very intelligent young woman, with a sense of what is right. So you must admit that it cannot be to Miss Devereaux's advantage to be your protégée.''

"I do not think it has been to her disadvantage, madame. My credit is good enough to insure her entrée to the best drawing rooms in London. Now, I do not like to be rude, but I have a manuscript to study and am not in the habit of receiving callers. It interferes with my work. I'm sorry that Caroline was not here to receive you. I will tell her of your call.'' She rose, chin up and waited, her breath coming rather fast and her cheeks flushed by the end of her speech.

Lady Wrexham took the last cake, and devoured it in two bites before carefully wiping her fingers on the napkin Belding had given her. She took a deliberate sip of wine, and setting the glass aside, rose with great deliberation.

"I congratulate you on your cook, Mrs. Daventry. Please advise me when Miss Devereaux returns.'' She bowed her head briefly and trod across to the door. There she turned and said, ''You will do, Mrs. Daventry—good backbone there,'' and left.

Julia, quite faint with the shock of her own rudeness and this unexpected accolade, felt her knees give way and sank back down onto the sofa wordlessly.

13

AFTER AN UNEVENTFUL journey, Caroline had her first glimpse of her great-uncle's estate. The house was large and solidly built, sweetly situated on a slight elevation in the landscape, and the park surrounding it looked well tended.

She was not so impressed with the butler who admitted them, however. He looked at her darkly and barely acknowledged Caroline's presence. When Sidney instructed him to show Miss Devereaux's abigail to a room, the man turned away without a word. Sidney motioned Margaret, the maid, to follow and after a nervous glance at Caroline the woman picked up her case and scuttled after the butler.

Sidney frowned, then shrugged. "Now, Cousin, I know how eagerly Mama must be waiting for you, so if you are agreeable I will take you to her straightaway. Unless, of course, you would prefer to go to your room. Perhaps you are tired?"

"Pooh! I hope I am not so delicate that I should require rest after a two-hour drive. Let us by all means go to your mother."

They proceeded together up the wide, imposing staircase. Sidney knocked softly on a door just at the top of the stairs. They entered to find that apparently Mrs. Knox-Gore was not so eager as her son had thought, for she was sound asleep against her propped pillows, snoring softly through her gaping mouth, her nightcap slightly askew.

Sidney stepped quickly across to the bed and shook his mother's shoulder brusquely. "Mama, for heaven's sake!" His voice was distinctly annoyed.

Caroline had all she could do to suppress the giggles irresistibly rising in her throat.

Mrs. Knox-Gore jerked awake and sat up wildly. "Wha—?" she muttered bewilderedly.

"Mama, Cousin Caroline is here to take care of you," he said slowly, giving her a significant look.

She sank back against her pillows, one hand to her heart, "Oh, my dear, how you startled me." She pulled her cap straight. "Where is the darling child? Why didn't you bring her to me at once?"

"I have brought her." He turned and held out his hand. "Cousin Caroline, here is my dear mama."

Caroline came forward, her eyes still brimming with laughter, dropped a curtsey, and took Mrs. Knox-Gore's outstretched hand. She was abruptly pulled forward into a stifling embrace against Mrs. Knox-Gore's capacious bosom. Caroline heard a tiny crack and felt quite sure the smart little white plume on her bonnet was broken. She was finally released and sat up.

"Oh, the pretty thing!" exclaimed Mrs. Knox-Gore ecstatically. "Oh, the perfect little *doll!* Dearest child, how good to have you here at last! Sidney, Sidney, is she not a little beauty? You have quite lost your heart to her already, I'm sure!"

"Mama," said Sidney, warningly, "I'm sure you should not be allowing yourself to become so excited."

"Oh—oh, to be sure, my dear. I shall pay for it," she sighed dolorously.

"Mrs. Knox-Gore," said Caroline, "I will just go and change into a more suitable gown and come straight back to try to make you more comfortable."

"Of course, dear child, of course. And Sidney must order you some luncheon."

"That would be very nice. Perhaps it could be brought to me here and we can share the meal."

"A charming idea. Sidney, show Caroline to her room. I've had it all made ready, just next door to my own, and then go down and make the arrangements for luncheon, if you please."

In her room, Caroline found the new abigail hanging her gowns away in the wardrobe. "Oh, miss, your lovely bonnet!" she cried.

Caroline went across to the dressing table and surveyed herself in the glass. The plume had indeed been broken and drooped crazily over the brim of her bonnet, giving her a rather addled appearance. This reminded her of Mrs. Knox-Gore's tilted nightcap and she began to giggle. The abigail cheered up at this sign of lightheartedness and began to smile as she continued her unpacking. "What gown will you have, miss?"

Caroline untied her bonnet ribands and handed it to her. "Oh, the green merino, I think. And then you must go along to the kitchen and have some food, Margaret."

"Thank you, miss, though I hope that Moberly person won't be there. Fair turns me up, he does." She shuddered.

"Has he been unpleasant to you?"

"Not to say in words, but such looks he gives me. Shrivels me up, it does."

"It is just his manner, I think. I doubt he even realizes the effect it has on people. He glowered at me, too. There now, that will do, I think." She patted down the lace collar that primly trimmed the plain merino round gown Julia had chosen as most suitable for attendance in a sickroom. The green was only slightly darker than Caroline's eyes and set them off perfectly. She went next door and rapped lightly before entering. Mrs. Knox-Gore turned to smile wanly.

"How charming you look."

"Thank you. Mrs. Daventry has very good taste and she chose all my gowns."

"How modest of you. Her task was not so difficult when she had such a beauty to dress. However, it was very kind of her to give them to you."

"Yes, it was indeed. However, I have begun to repay her from the allowance my cousin insists on giving me."

"Very proper of him. But he can well afford it. Rich as Golden Ball. Not like some of us who have had to struggle and scrimp to make ends meet, eh, little girl?"

"Er—no, indeed," Caroline replied politely, though it was difficult to believe Mrs. Knox-Gore could ever have struggled very much. Her enormous girth bespoke a large appetite, well catered to, and the lace trimming her nightcap was alone worth enough to keep a normal family in food for several weeks. "Shall I just shake up your pillows, Mrs. Knox-Gore?"

"How kind," murmured the lady as she sat forward. "Oh, my dear, how good to have one of one's own to care for one's comfort.

The maids have done their best, but they have their chores and cannot sit with me. They are always in a hurry. But you are like my very own daughter. I felt it the moment I saw you.''

Caroline calmly continued straightening the bed covers, only smiling in response. Indeed, she could think of nothing to say to these effusions. She had felt no immediate affinity for Mrs. Knox-Gore such as she had experienced with Mrs. Daventry or Cousin Neville, but then it was not her usual way to rush into judgements about people. All she knew of Mrs. Knox-Gore so far was that she was extravagant in her speech and that she overindulged in food.

This last was proved when Moberly, followed by a maid, entered with a table he set up beside the bed. Then he unloaded the dishes from the tray held by the maid, placed a chair for Caroline, and left. Evidently they were to serve themselves. Caroline was surprised that Mrs. Knox-Gore said nothing about her servant's attitude, but held her tongue. She filled a plate with chicken a la tarragon, boiled mushrooms, and French beans, and spreading a napkin across the broad shelf of Mrs. Knox-Gore's bosom, handed her the plate and then sat down to serve herself. It was clear that loss of appetite was not one of Mrs. Knox-Gore's symptoms, for she had second helpings of everything and three apple tarts before lying back with a sigh. Caroline rang for Moberly to remove the remains of the meal. When he was gone she asked if Mrs. Knox-Gore would like to be read to, an offer eagerly accepted.

Presently, as Caroline read from a romantic novel, Mrs. Knox-Gore fell asleep and Caroline tiptoed away to her own room, where she wrote the promised letter to Mrs. Daventry. Then taking her pelisse and bonnet she went downstairs and, leaving her letter on the hall table, went out to walk in the shrubberies. It was a mild winter day and she enjoyed the sweet, clean country air and remembered days like this out-of-doors with her mother.

Presently, she went back up to her room, removed her outer garments, and went back to Mrs. Knox-Gore. She wondered why she had seen nothing of Sidney since her arrival, but did not mention it to Mrs. Knox-Gore, who was sitting up again, gazing out her window contentedly.

"Ah, you're awake! Did you have a nice nap?" said Caroline brightly.

"Lovely, my dear. Oh, I know I shall go on famously, now you are here."

"Have you had the doctor, Mrs. Knox-Gore?"

"Oh—yes."

"What did he think wrong?"

"Only that I had overtaxed my heart nursing dear Chandos, and now must rest."

"I see. Then we must see to it that you do so. Will you like me to read to you again? Or perhaps you would like me to answer your letters for you?"

They passed the remainder of the afternoon pleasantly enough together and presently, when the sun sank below the trees, a maid came to see if Mrs. Knox-Gore was ready to dress for dinner.

"Dress?" Caroline exclaimed in surprise, "but, surely you won't leave your bed?"

"Oh, you see, my dear," Mrs. Knox-Gore began, improvising rapidly, cursing Sidney in another part of her mind for not warning the silly abigail not to come up this evening, "I know Sidney will be looking forward to seeing you at dinner and I feared you would feel you must stay here with me."

"Well, of course I must—"

"No, that is just what I will not have, or you will become too bored with me. You must have some relief. I'll stay here and Jenny shall serve me dinner, if you will go down to keep Sidney company."

"Very well," Caroline agreed, laughing. She was not really sorry to give in, for a change would be welcome. She therefore left Mrs. Knox-Gore in charge of her abigail and went away to dress for dinner.

When she opened her door she found Margaret awaiting her, a fire crackling cheerfully in the fireplace and the curtains drawn tight to shut out the cold night.

"Oh—how comfortable it looks! You've made it so homelike," Caroline exclaimed with pleasure.

"Thank you, miss," Margaret said, much gratified to have her work noticed. She helped Caroline out of the merino gown and into a dressing gown, and when Caroline sat before the glass to let down her hair, Margaret calmly took over, removing the pins and catching her breath admiringly at the thick cascade of auburn curls.

"Ah, miss, yer hair be a treat to look at," she said, brushing the long strands carefully.

"Why, thank you, Margaret. I'm afraid I have never been able to dress it properly—beyond bundling it up any old way."

"Never you fear, miss. I have the art, though I say it as

shouldn't. I was dresser to Lady Sarah Barraclough!"

There was enough pride in this declaration to cause Caroline to say impetuously, "But then how were you free to come here with us?"

Margaret flushed and her mouth tightened. "I was let go," she replied stonily.

"I'm sure it was unfairly done then!" declared Caroline warmly, thoroughly ashamed to have caused Margaret unhappiness by prying so thoughtlessly.

Margaret's eyes filled with tears at this unexpected championing and her story poured out: Lady Sarah, turning around suddenly while Margaret was curling her hair with hot tongs, the explosion of rage at the burn mark on the fair, white neck, and the angry dismissal after four years of devoted service. Caroline exclaimed indignantly and sympathetically and within ten minutes had earned Margaret's unswerving devotion.

She watched proudly as her new young mistress left for dinner in her white muslin gown, and pondered gratefully on the mysterious ways of the Lord, who had seen to it that she had been sitting in the Agency waiting room when Mr. Knox-Gore had come rushing in to hire an abigail.

Caroline made her way downstairs, where she found Sidney waiting for her at the drawing-room door.

"Ah, there you are, Cousin. My mother sent word that she had persuaded you to join me. I hope you are not exhausted with your nursing?"

"Very little nursing, sir, has been required of me. You will not take it amiss, I hope, if I say that I don't think your mother ill so much as tired and perhaps lonely. She is quite lively now, and of good appetite."

He took her hands and held them for a moment. "You are very kind, Caroline. I think being alone here may have caused her to exaggerate her symptoms. I hope you will not think I tried to deceive you just to get you here?"

"Of course I will not. It is very natural to be concerned for the health of one's mother, and if she overstated her illness I'm sure no one can blame her. She wants companionship, of course. When I go back to London I think you should hire someone for her."

"I should like to do so very much, but you see, we could not pay the wages. I know this will seem unlikely, but Mother and I have only the allowance Uncle Chandos made us, which his man of business continues to pay until the estate is settled."

"But—" She looked about the elegantly appointed room in bewilderment.

Sidney took her meaning at once. "Ah! You are wondering at the style in which we live. That too is provided by the estate. When it is settled it is most likely we shall have to move from here."

"But surely your uncle will have made provision for you and your mother," she protested. "Why, you are undoubtedly his heir."

He started to protest, but bethought himself that it might be wiser to let her think so. The supposed heir to a large fortune could not be lightly dismissed as a prospective husband. Even if she secretly sighed for Wrexham's title, she seemed too down-to-earth a creature to entertain any real hopes that his family would allow him to throw himself away on a penniless nobody.

"Well, I suppose myself to be," he replied modestly, "for he was the only father I remember and I loved him dearly, and have every reason to believe he felt the same for me. I admit to some impatience, of course, for I am eager to settle down. I am almost as impatient for my own family as dear Mama is for grandchildren," he said, looking confidingly into her eyes, hoping to see her blush or show some signs of confusion, as most young girls would at such an intimate confession which could hopefully be interpreted as a preliminary to a proposal.

Caroline, however, looked at him composedly and answered, "Naturally you would feel so. I think all children who have no brothers and sisters or who are orphans feel that very strongly. I have always hoped to marry young and have a large brood of children."

"I don't think there can be any doubt that you will do so, judging by the admiration you have already excited. One could barely fight one's way to your side."

She laughed. "Surely you exaggerate, sir. Besides Lord Redvers there were very few—"

"Oh, I discount him," he interrupted to plant his first little dart.

"You—discount him?" She looked startled, he was happy to note.

"Why, yes. According to gossip he has made a match of it with the Charn girl. The announcement is expected daily."

"Charn? Surely you mean Brough?" Caroline felt something leaden and approximately the size of a cannonball settle in her stomach.

"Georgianna Brough? Oh no, she is a cousin and I believe he had hoped to marry her some years ago—terribly in love, they say, but their families would not allow it." He looked up. "Ah, here is Moberly to announce dinner."

"Wonderful," she said summoning pride to her aid, "I admit I am very hungry. It must be the country air." She took his arm, smiling gaily, determined not to allow him to see how much she was disturbed by his revelations. It was only her resolve to keep this objective above all else that enabled her to firmly banish the picture of Redvers waltzing with his beloved Georgianna, or on his knees asking for the hand in marriage of this mysterious Charn girl. She forced herself to eat heartily, though it was as though she were forcing down sawdust, and as soon as she politely could, excused herself, using the country air again as an excuse for excessive sleepiness.

Once in her bed and alone, she could not hold the visions at bay any longer, and felt a lump rising in her throat at the pain they caused her. After a time of determinedly swallowing the lump she was calm enough to look more clearly at the problem. Was it possible, she wondered, that this pain was falling in love? Was she, in fact, in love with Lord Redvers, or was it only her vanity, puffed up by his attentions and now resentful that they should be shared? She saw him clearly in her mind's eye, smiling at her, reading his poems to her, leading her through a dance, and felt her heart warm at the remembrances. Surely his was too open a character to play games with her while in love with one girl and in the process of offering marriage to another? No, she would not believe it of him.

Comforted, she tucked her hand under her cheek and fell resoundingly asleep, not five minutes after climbing into bed. No doubt the country air had had is effect, after all.

Sidney went straight to his mother's room when Caroline's door closed. He was feeling pleased with what he had accomplished this evening, but less than pleased with his parent.

He leaned close and began whispering fiercely at her. "For

God's sake, can you not try to keep in mind that you are supposed to be ill? She has already mentioned going back to London.''

"But dear boy, I stayed quite quietly here all day long.''

"Keep your voice down! She is only next door, remember. I can't hope that you managed to curb your appetite at lunch," he said sarcastically.

"You cannot mean for me to confine myself to broths and jellies and invalidish slops. Why I really should become ill," she protested, really alarmed at such a bleak prospect.

"If you take your lunch in her company that is exactly what I expect. I must keep her here for as long as possible. I daren't cause her to take fright by proposing too abruptly. I must detach her from her London friends carefully, encourage her to feel she has only us to rely upon. She left a letter on the hall table to Mrs. Daventry which I have burnt. If she doesn't get a reply she will feel Mrs. Daventry doesn't care for her as much as she thought. But I need time to execute this plan, and if you bounce around and stuff yourself in front of her she will not feel needed and take herself off back to London.''

"Oh Sidney, I cannot—" she protested weakly.

"Now, you listen to me. This was *your* scheme. If you are interested in bringing it off, I don't think the sacrifice of a few meals is too much to expect, not after the sacrifice you expect *me* to make!" he grated out savagely, the whispering voice lending an even more sinister threat to his tone.

His mother, almost frightened by the rage blazing quite clearly in his eyes, cowered back against her pillows. "Yes—I mean, no— oh, do go away Sidney and stop looking at me so or I shall swoon. I'll do whatever you say!''

He turned on his heel and left her without another word. As he quietly closed the door and walked softly away down the hall his rage was mixed with exhilaration at the tongue-lashing he had just administered to his domineering parent. It was the first time he had let her see his true feelings. Always before he had been too dependent on her support and protection to be other than mulish or pouting. It had only come to him as he was berating her and saw the fear in her eyes that *he* was now in the dominant position. It was a heady thought! Yes, by God, now *he* was in charge. *She* needed *him*!

=== 14 ===

IN THE NEXT four days the routine followed very closely that of the first day of Caroline's stay. She attended Mrs. Knox-Gore until that lady's afternoon nap, then Caroline wrote her letter to Julia, took her walk, and returned to attend Mrs. Knox-Gore until dinner. She then said good night to the old lady, dressed for dinner, and spent the evening with Sidney.

The only change was that Mrs. Knox-Gore's appetite disappeared startlingly. The second day she had refused everything but a clear broth and a chicken wing, and seemed quite cross and restless for the rest of the day until the dinner hour approached, when she brightened up and bid Caroline good night quite cheerfully.

Caroline began to fear the lady was more ill than she had first supposed, and the appetite she had displayed on the first day only the result of her stimulation at Caroline's arrival. She saw the days passing with no apparent improvement and thought she had become quite spoiled and selfish for even thinking this relapse would delay her return to London.

She felt that if only she had had any response to her letters to Mrs. Daventry she could have settled down to doing her duty in a more wholehearted frame of mind. She simply would not have believed Mrs. Daventry could ignore her in this way. Perhaps she felt it was too much trouble to write, or perhaps she felt she had nothing interesting to write about, or—

Oh, what was the use, thought Caroline unhappily, she should write! She must know how much I would want to hear from her and about my friends. Of course, I do not expect Lord Redvers to write, but I would think Cousin Neville might have wanted to know how I go on. What is wrong with all of them? Have they forgotten me so quickly? Her letter to Julia that day was somewhat plaintive.

At dinner she was less attentive than usual, and the food seemed unappealing. Sidney watched her toying with an exceptionally well-cooked fillet of turbot in Italian sauce.

"You do not care for fish prepared in this way, Caroline?" he inquired gently.

"Oh"—she looked down at her plate—"oh no, it is only that I had too large a luncheon, I think. I was not used to eating so heartily twice a day. I shall become quite stout if—if—" she stopped in confusion, not liking to mention returning to London when his mother was so obviously not recovering.

"You miss your friends very much, I fear," he said sadly.

"Please do not concern yourself about that. I doubt they have the leisure to think of me, in any case," she replied, despising herself for the note of self-pity she heard in her voice.

"No one could forget you," he assured her, "but it is wise of you to accept that Londoners live very shallow lives, always looking for someone to divert them, to take up and lionize for a few weeks then drop for a new excitement. We country people stand fast when we offer friendship. For this reason I hope you don't pine too much for London."

"I am perfectly content," she said with a brave show of lightness, "or at least I should be so if I could see some improvement in your mother. My friends do not need me so much as she does."

"Nor as much as I, Caroline," he said with an intense look.

She studied his face calmly, realizing that he had ceased using the prefix "Cousin" a day or so ago. "I think you must be bamming me, Cousin Sidney. You have, it seems to me, a great many interests and affairs to attend to to keep you away from home every day. You are very independent, I think."

"Dare I interpret that to mean you have missed me?" he replied, leaning ardently across the table toward her.

"Cousin Sidney, you must not—"

"No"—he allowed just a touch of bitterness to shade his voice—"I know I must not! I know very well that you are far too beautiful to throw yourself away on a mere *Mr.* Knox-Gore of no definite prospects."

"You insult me, sir," she gasped. "Surely you do not suggest that I am dangling after a title!"

"Forgive me, my dear Caroline!" he cried. "I had no right to impute such a thing to you. I had no right to speak at all. I never meant to, truly. My feelings for you overcame my resolve. Say you will forgive me!"

"Well, of course I will. But I hope you are not allowing yourself to believe your feelings for me go beyond what I am persuaded you cannot truly feel."

"I fear it is far too late for me to hope to control my heart, Caroline, but you have my assurance that I will not annoy you with my feelings again, knowing it is distasteful to you," he said in a crushed voice, managing to convey hurt pride.

"Oh, please do not speak so, Cousin Sidney! I'm sure I didn't mean for you to think it is distasteful to me, only—"

"Then I may hope?" he cried, his eyes lighting up with eagerness. "Please say that you will allow me to speak of it again someday. Your feelings toward me will change, I know they will."

She looked at him in dismay, torn between the need to set the matter straight at once, and her dislike of hurting him. She did not doubt his sincerity, but she found this profession of love from him somehow distasteful and thought back swiftly over their friendship to see if she had ever said anything to encourage him.

"Cousin Sidney," she said finally, "though I don't think my feelings for you will grow beyond the sisterly fondness I feel for you now, I won't forbid you to speak of it again—someday."

In the hallway, Moberly raised his ear from the panel of the dining-room door and stared balefully down the hall. So, he thought, the rogue is already making his move? They are really going through with this scheme to marry him off to the girl and cut me out? Well, I'll see to that!

He went straight to the kitchen where Margaret was having her supper in company with Mrs. Knox-Gore's abigail and told Margaret that Mr. Knox-Gore was sending her back to London at once.

"But Miss will—"

"Miss Devereaux did not hire you. You are in Mr. Knox-Gore's employ and he wants you gone," he rasped, glaring at her ferociously. She cringed away from him. "Get upstairs and pack your box. The carriage will be waiting to take you into the village to catch the stage. Quick now!" he barked.

Margaret jumped up and ran up the back stairs. In less than ten minutes she returned, eyes red with weeping. Moberly took her out to the carriage, wordlessly handed her her wages and the fare back to London, and returned to the house, closing the door firmly.

That is the first step accomplished, he thought with satisfaction. He had no worries about the rest of the staff since, with the exception of Cook, they all came from the village or nearby farms and did not sleep on the premises. He could simply tell them not to return until sent for. As for Cook, her room was at the very back of the house, over the kitchen, and she was a notoriously heavy sleeper.

The first thing that Caroline noticed the next morning was that the room seemed colder than usual. She sat up and saw only gray ashes in her fireplace, where a cheery blaze ordinarily greeted her each morning. Then she realized Margaret had not appeared with her morning chocolate. The evening before when she had not been waiting to help Caroline into bed had puzzled Caroline somewhat, but still being unused to the services of a personal maid, she had not given it serious thought. She had proceeded to put herself to bed as she had done all her life. For Margaret not to appear in the morning, however, seemed odd. Perhaps the woman was ailing, though she could not imagine, if this were true, why someone had not come to inform her of it. But then, at least so far as the servants were concerned, this was a very strangely run household, headed by a butler of unmitigated insolence.

Caroline shrugged, rose, and rang, but no one came, so presently she washed in cold water and dressed herself in her green merino. She searched out her cashmere shawl against the chill and pinned it around her shoulders with a brooch, and hurried out of the room, anxious for some news of Margaret.

As she passed Mrs. Knox-Gore's room she heard voices and stopped. Surely that was Moberly speaking—perhaps he would be able to tell her where the maid was. She scratched at the door and opened it. Moberly turned his head to stare and Mrs. Knox-Gore, a large forkful of York ham halfway to her mouth, which was wide open to receive it, looked up, a picture of comical guilt. On her lap was a loaded tray of food.

Caroline stared at it blankly for a moment. "Why—why—Mrs. Knox-Gore, you have regained your appetite! How wonderful!"

She spoke overenthusiastically to cover Mrs. Knox-Gore's obvious embarrassment.

"Ah—I—Well, yes, I don't know how it came about, but I woke this morning feeling absolutely famished and—my dear husband was used to be just so after an illness, and so cross and difficult once he regained his taste for food. Now I don't feel in the least cro—"

"Will that be all, madame?" inquired Moberly rudely.

"What? Oh! Oh, yes, thank you, Moberly. Do tell Cook how lovely everything is, and do what you can about getting new staff immediately."

He turned away. Caroline said, "Moberly, I came in to inquire about Margaret. Is she ill?"

"She left last night, miss."

"Left? But why?"

"She said she could never abide the country," he replied.

"How odd. She said nothing to me."

"Will that be all, miss?"

"Yes, I suppose so," she said, much puzzled and somewhat hurt by Margaret's defection. Moberly left the room.

"Not to worry, my dear. Servants behave so oddly. Why, Moberly was just telling me none of the servants appeared this morning. I'm sure I don't know what the world is coming to when servants can just leave without notice in this exasperating way, never thinking of the inconvenience."

She paused for breath and Caroline spoke quickly. "Is there anything I can do for you now, Mrs. Knox-Gore?"

"No, no, dear child. I'll just finish my breakfast while you go down for your own."

"I'll come back directly," Caroline assured her, making a hasty exit before the woman could begin talking again. She made her way slowly downstairs, still disturbed by Margaret's abrupt, secretive departure. In the five days of their acquaintance she had grown to like the woman very well and had always found her to be open and honest.

She sat down in the dining room and presently Moberly came with a pot of hot chocolate, which he placed before her. He fetched her a cup and stood waiting. She gave him a long, cool stare, wondering what *made* the man so insolent, and why the Knox-Gores stood for it.

"Please bring me some toast, Moberly."

He turned on his heel and left the room. Outside the door he stood for a moment grinding his teeth in frustration. The little idiot had spoiled everything! His plan depended on her coming down without seeing anyone but himself. Now he had to postpone and hope that tomorrow morning the circumstances would prove more favourable.

Caroline ate her toast when it was brought to her and then returned to Mrs. Knox-Gore, who was seated at her dressing table trying on a new cap, a froth of lace ruffles, though she was still in bed gown and wrapper.

"Oh, there you are, child. Do you think this cap becoming? I ordered it before you arrived. Are you surprised to see me out of my bed? I thought there would be no harm, if I did not exert myself too much. I feel ever so much better. I do believe I'm on the mend. I owe it all to you, darling. Your good care of me has made all the difference."

"I'm glad if that is so, though I can hardly feel that I've had much to do with it," replied Caroline, moving over to make the disordered bed.

"No, no, you must not do such chores, my dear," protested Mrs. Knox-Gore.

"There are no maids yet to do it. Fortunately, I have always made my own bed until I went to Mrs. Daventry's, and I don't in the least mind. Perhaps you would like to spend the morning on the chaise longue?"

"Yes, so I will. And this afternoon I will take a very short walk in the shrubberies with you."

"Oh, I really would not, if I were you, Mrs. Knox-Gore," protested Caroline, still labouring under the notion that she was dealing with a genuine invalid.

"Very well, my dear, if you think it unwise," agreed Mrs. Knox-Gore comfortably, settling her bulk onto the chaise. "Perhaps we could have a nice read through the papers. They've just come from London."

"Of course. There were no—letters for me, I suppose?"

"Why, no, not today," Mrs. Knox-Gore said and handed her the newspapers. "Read the Court news first, child."

They lunched together in Mrs. Knox-Gore's bedroom, the older lady's appetite evidently back to stay, and passed the afternoon quietly.

When Caroline went down to dinner she found Mrs. Knox-Gore in rustling mauve taffeta waiting for her. "Cook came up to help me dress as a surprise for you and darling Sidney."

Her darling Sidney did not look all that overcome with joy by the surprise when he came in, but he said nothing, only offering an arm to each and leading them into the dining room.

Nor did his expression lighten as he watched his mother eat hugely of the two courses served to them mutely by Moberly, who had evidently had little luck recruiting new staff in the village, for he served the meal unassisted.

Sidney was not his usual self this evening and Caroline could only believe he felt inhibited by his mother's presence. Mrs. Knox-Gore, on the other hand, seemed not the least put off by his taciturnity, chattering away in her aimless way until Caroline's nerves began to twitch with irritation. Thankfully, Mrs. Knox-Gore said she would not wait for the tea tray, but would go straight up to her bed. Caroline was happy to use the excuse of helping Mrs. Knox-Gore to bed to escape the smouldering looks she encountered from Sidney each time their eyes met. He seemed to be trying to remind her of his ardent feelings.

In spite of these discomforts, however, Caroline felt a lightening of her spirits and was astute enough to realize the cause: Mrs. Knox-Gore's recovery must surely signal an early escape back to London.

When she passed Mrs. Knox-Gore's door the following morning she heard the clink of china and presumed the woman was having her breakfast and did not require her presence. Humming softly to herself she tripped lightly down the stairs, noting with pleasure the strip of sunlight laid across the black-and-white tiled floor of the hall through the fanlight. It was definitely a more golden colour, not the pale, thin sunlight of winter. It would soon be spring!

She rang for Moberly and took her seat. In a moment he appeared with the steaming pot of chocolate.

"Good morning, Moberly," she said cheerfully, with a dazzling smile.

He checked almost imperceptibly, then grunted and came to

place the pot before her. He moved to the sideboard behind her where the china was laid out. Caroline, waiting for her cup and saucer, was still smiling at her pleasure in the sunny day when she felt something cold and sharp laid across her throat. She gasped and a hand came around to clumsily stuff a napkin into her open mouth, at the same time as Moberly whispered menacingly into her ear.

"Not a sound! This knife is sharp! Now, stand up and put your hands behind you—very slowly." She did as she was bid, her mind tumbling chaotically as she tried to make reason out of this insane event. The knife disappeared while he quickly tied her wrists together. Then with another napkin he bound the gag in place very tightly, and the knife returned to its place, blade prinking lightly against her throat.

"Now we will walk out and down the hall quietly and quickly. Understand?"

She nodded her head, very carefully, and he took her arm with his other hand and led her out of the room and down the hall toward the back of the house. They passed through his pantry and to the door leading to the cellars. Around a slight jut in the wall was the entrance to the kitchen, where Cook could be heard loudly intoning a doleful hymn as she worked.

Moberly opened the cellar door, pushed Caroline down a few steps, and closed the door softly behind them. At the bottom a candle guttered in a bracket, obviously placed there in advance to leave his hands free from the obligation to carry a light. He opened the first door they came to, and she had time to notice its heavy bolts before he pushed her in and told her to sit down. He then pulled more cord from his pocket, bound her ankles tightly, and left without another word, leaving her in total, smothering darkness. She heard the heavy thud of the bolt being shot into place, followed by his footsteps fading back up the stairs—then nothing.

Moberly hurried back to the dining room. She'll do for now, he thought. I'll finish the job later. He checked the dining room, straightening the cloth where she had rucked it slightly, set her chair back into place, picked up the still-steaming chocolate pot, and returned to the kitchen.

"The young one hasn't come down yet," he remarked sourly to Cook.

"Probably above with the Missus."

"I'd best go see if she wants her breakfast up there," grumbled Moberly. "No consideration, these toffs. Run me off my legs and think nothing of it." He made his way to Mrs. Knox-Gore's room. "Miss hasn't come down. Thought she might be up here," he said abruptly.

"Why, I haven't seen the child this morning. Perhaps you should tap on her door. She might like to have her breakfast up here."

Moberly went to do as he was told. He came back in a moment. "She's not there. Bed's made. No sign of her."

"How odd. Well, no doubt she went for an early walk since the weather is so fine."

He said no more, took her breakfast tray, and left. An hour later Mrs. Knox-Gore rang for him again. "Has Miss Devereaux returned from her walk?" she demanded.

"No."

"But this is very strange! Send Cook up to me. I'll dress and come down. And Moberly, you must hire staff today. This situation is intolerable."

Mrs. Knox-Gore made her way downstairs to the drawing room to wait. But the day passed, hour by slow hour, and there was no sign of Caroline. Mrs. Knox-Gore became so upset she could not do real justice to her luncheon. She wished desperately for Sidney to come home. Where on earth did the boy go every day? Why could he not stay at home sometimes, she wondered wildly. By the time he did arrive, in the late afternoon, she was close to hysteria.

"Oh, Sidney, why must you come home so late? The girl has disappeared and I'm near dead with worry. Just like your father, never around when a person needed him."

"What do you mean?"

"He was always off riding around—"

"*No*, you fool! What of the girl?" he shouted in exasperation.

"Don't raise your voice to me in that way, Sidney! I won't stand for it." She pouted. "The girl has not been seen all day. Moberly thinks she went away last night—or at least very early this morning before anyone was awake."

"Went away? Nonsense! Where would she go?"

"Well, of course I don't *know*, Sidney! That is why I'm so

upset. I mean to say, why should she just go off in this way? She seemed perfectly happy. She never even mentioned wanting to leave. Oh, what shall we *do?* Did you—press your suit too warmly—try to embrace her or—"

"Don't be ridiculous!" he snarled.

"Oh, dear, I'm sure my nerves are fretted to threads. I can't think why you didn't propose to her. I'm sure she was only waiting for you to speak. Perhaps that is it! Perhaps you didn't show her your feelings and she—"

"Of course I showed her. I came very near proposing night before last and she all but accepted. At least she said I might speak of it again. I suppose she thinks it is more genteel to wait for the second proposal before giving her answer," he said sneeringly.

"Then why should she run away?"

"Who says she has? Lord, a dozen things could have happened. She may have gone for a walk and twisted her ankle or something."

"Good heavens! I never thought of such a thing! We must search for her, Sidney, at once. Do you take your horse and ride over the Park and I'll order the carriage and drive toward the village. Oh, you are clever to have thought of it! If only you had come home sooner!"

= 15 =

THAT SAME DAY, as Caroline was going down to breakfast, Redvers, in London, called at the Clarendon as usual to learn if Neville had returned, found that he had not, and proceeded, as had become his custom, to Mrs. Daventry's. Five days had passed with no letter from Caroline and he was determined not another day should go by without word of her, or more preferably, to her.

Julia, when she received him, could not hide her own worry about Caroline. She could not imagine how she could have been so careless as to let the child leave without getting the Knox-Gore's direction so that she could write to Caroline and beg her for just a line or two for reassurance. No doubt the poor thing was being run off her legs nursing a sick old woman, but still—

"I don't need to ask—I can see from your face you haven't heard yet," said Redvers grimly.

"No, I haven't, and I vow I shall comb her hair with a joint stool when she does return for causing us all this worry. Really, it is so unlike her."

"Exactly! It is unlike her. There is no word from Devereaux yet and I won't wait another day. I'm going to her at once."

"But *where?* We don't know where the place is. All I know for sure is that he once mentioned the house was near Wychcombe. That would be about two hours from here."

"I'll find it," he promised.

"I'm not sure you should—is it really necessary, after all—" she began doubtfully.

"It is necessary to me."

"Is there something—do you know something unpleasant—or is this only your dislike of Sidney? What is it?"

"I—I can't really tell you," he replied with embarrassment, "but I assure you I know a side of his character that he does not show the world, and I do not like it at all. Even less do I like the idea of his dangling after Caroline."

"Oh, surely he is not dangling! I have only seen cousinly interest—"

"He is not her cousin, and in my opinion he will make a push to engage her affections, he as much as told me so, though he doesn't like women at all—" He stopped and his face flamed.

"Doesn't like women? Why, he behaves charmingly with women. I'm sure you must be wrong."

"No, I'm not! We had dinner together, the night before Caroline left. He drank a great deal and said some really shocking things when he became foxed. I've been wanting to speak to Neville about it, but I won't wait any longer. I will take my chaise in case I can persuade her to come back with me. If I leave now I should arrive by midday."

Julia looked doubtful at this precipitate plan. "You know, Lord Redvers, I fear we may be rushing too headling into panic. After all, Caroline went to nurse Mrs. Knox-Gore. It is possible the woman was more ill than she told Sidney. If she requires constant care it is possible Caroline has no time to write."

"We'll soon know," he replied, not giving way an inch in his determination to go. "I will report to you at once, either by letter or perhaps by bringing Caroline back. You will definitely have word by this evening."

He took his leave and Julia, in spite of her misgivings, was somewhat comforted by his going.

Redvers returned home, called for his chaise and pair to be brought around at once, and set off for Wychcombe at a spanking pace which would do doubt have brought him to his destination at the predicted time had not the off-side horse cast a shoe. He was forced to walk him into the next village and wait for over an hour for it to be reshod. Then, after a few more miles, a trace snapped and there was another fretful delay while repairs were made. It was by now close to two o'clock and he was famished. Spying a likely-looking inn he decided nothing was to be gained by arriving faint with hunger and he pulled up. Forty-five minutes later, in much better spirits for the excellent raised pigeon pie and mushroom fritters he had been served, he set off again and arrived without further mishap at Wychcombe at about three o'clock.

However, he discovered to his dismay that it was not to be made simple for him. He had forgotten that Mr. Devereaux's estate lay somewhere in the vicinity of Wychcombe, not in the village itself. It took an exasperating further hour of inquiry, during which he became convinced the entire place was inhabited solely by village idiots, before he found someone who could send him in the right direction.

As he was approaching a pair of imposing gates, a carriage careened out and passed him carrying a very stout lady who eyed him incuriously. He drove up to the front door, and since no one came to take charge of his carriage, he tied his horses to an ornamental railing and took the steps two at a time to give the knocker a resounding thump.

Inside, Moberly was just rubbing his hands together with satisfaction, feeling rather better disposed toward the world than was usual for him after seeing the discomposure of the Knox-Gores as they set off on their fruitless missions. He felt it served them right to be in a stew, and a wild-goose chase was no more than they deserved for scheming to do him out of his share of the old man's money. When the door knocker sounded he leapt into the air with the shock of it. He finally called himself a fool and went to open the door a cautious inch and peer out suspiciously at the tall gentleman who stood waiting. "Yes?" he asked discouragingly.

"Miss Caroline Devereaux, please."

"She is out."

"Then I will see Mrs. or Mr. Knox-Gore."

"They are all out."

"Then I will wait," replied Redvers firmly and stepped forward, forcing Moberly to stand back.

Swept by complete panic, Moberly lost his head. Fearing that one or the other of the Knox-Gores might reapear at any moment, and without giving thought to why he should care if they arrived and found a gentleman here inquiring for the girl, his hand went out to the heavy ash cane in the hall stand and brought it crashing down on the side of Redvers's head just as he was turning to hand Moberly his hat.

Moberly caught the full weight of the falling body as Redvers crumpled, and though he staggered, managed to keep his feet. He hoisted the heavy body over his shoulder with some difficulty and made his way waveringly toward the cellars. He unbolted the door and bent to allow the body to slide to the floor, stepped back, bolted the door again, and ran back to the front drive with all speed. There he untied Wrexham's horses and, glancing fearfully about for any sign of Sidney, who he knew was exploring the park, hurried off to the back of the house, and followed a path that struck off into a copse of trees behind the stables. Out of sight in the center of the copse he hastily tied the horses to a tree, still harnessed to the chaise, and sped away without a thought for their possible needs in the way of water or feeding, any more than for the unconscious body he had dumped so carelessly into the cellar.

Caroline, after some time of fruitless struggling with the cords at her wrists, had given up when a sticky wetness told her the cords had abraded her delicate skin until it bled. She then attempted to stand up. She got as far as her knees, but with hands and feet bound there was no way to get further. She slumped back to the floor in defeat, tears welling in her eyes.

What on earth am I doing here, she wondered. What could Moberly's purpose be? Unless he had simply gone mad! Yes, that must be it. She thought of Mrs. Knox-Gore and was unable to prevent an image of her lying murdered in her bloodstained bed—! She pushed the picture away, shuddering. And Sidney? His fate was less clear since he had not been in the house at the time Moberly's sanity had given way. She could only pray he might escape his mother's fate and rescue herself before—

She tried not to dwell on her own fate: why had the man brought her here rather than killing her at once? The only answer that occurred to her was too terrible to contemplate. Death itself would be preferable, she thought dramatically.

Her green merino and cashmere shawl were no match for the dank chill of the unheated room and the cold stone of the floor, and it seemed that interminable, uncountable hours must have passed since she heard those bolts shooting home. She shivered uncontrollably from time to time, and occasionally drifted off into a semi-sleep from which the pain in her shoulders woke her and forced her into a sitting position in a vain attempt to ease them. Her hands and feet had long ago lost all feeling, and her jaw ached from the tight binding that held the nauseating gag in her mouth.

When the bolt clanged and the door swung open she was roused from one horror to another. In the dim light of the open doorway was a grotesquely misshapen figure. She screamed in terror though only a muffled sound came through the gag. Before her wildly staring eyes the figure disintegrated, a part sloughed off onto the floor with an ugly thump, and the upright figure remaining was recognizable even in the dim light as Moberly. The door closed immediately, the bolt shot home, and she was again in smothering darkness—but no longer alone!

Her heart leapt with hope as she hitched herself an inch at a time in the direction of the body. Her feet finally made contact and she nudged the body gently, then less gently, but there was no response. The searing ache in her shoulders and the cloth cutting viciously into her cheeks suddenly doubled their pain in her disappointment and her eyes filled with tears. Then she mentally took herself to task for being such a baby and settled herself to wait patiently until Sidney regained consciousness. He must have returned to the house in the late afternoon as usual and been taken unaware as she herself had been. Then another thought occurred to her, one so dreadful she felt as though the very blood froze in her veins in an instant, and she caught her breath sharply.

Suppose—suppose he was not going to regain consciousness? Suppose he was—dead! Rigid with horror she sat for what seemed hours before her need to know one way or the other caused her to hitch closer and bend forward until her cheek touched cloth. After a moment of fearful listening she realized her ear was against—yes, a knee! She moved her ear to one side and came into contact with a boot top, then sitting up again she inched herself in the other direction along the body and bent forward again. And there, faintly but distinctly, beneath her ear she heard the beating of his heart. She sat up and allowed her tears to flow unchecked.

Now she must wait, and because she was exhausted from the effort and suspense she eased herself back down onto the cold floor, carefully not touching the inert body next to her, and after a time fell into a light doze. She was wakened some time later by a moan and sat up hastily, making gurgling sounds of inquiry to alert him to her presence. After more groans the body began to stir and with the rustling sounds of movement her hopes of deliverance from her painful bonds rose and her heart began to pound. There was a more pronounced sound and then a gasp and she deduced Sidney was sitting up. She made her hideous noises again.

"Who is that?" he whispered. She made a grunting response. The hands moved up her shoulder and over her face, feeling the cloth tied over her mouth, and then up over her nose and forehead. "Caroline! My God, Caroline, is it really you?"

She responded in what she hoped he took for an affirmative, while her mind grappled with the strangeness of Sidney's voice. It didn't sound at all like Sidney, it sounded—it sounded like Redvers! Meanwhile the hands were fumbling at the knot behind her head and she obligingly hitched around to make it easier for him. In another second the knot was open and she felt exquisite relief as the cloth was pulled free. She turned aside and spat out the nauseating wad of napkin.

His hands moved down and began to struggle with the knots at her wrists. Presently they also were free and she could not prevent a sob at the pain of release she felt in her shoulders and numbed hands. He gently eased her paralyzed arms into their proper position and began chafing her wrists, murmuring brokenly all the while, "Oh, poor darling, how could he hurt you so—dear little hands—don't cry, my darling—" After a time he took her into his arms, soothing his hand over and over the tumbled curls, while she cried heartily into his neckcloth. He freed one arm to grope in his pocket and handed her a handkerchief which she took gratefully, being in dire need. She blew her nose, wiped her eyes, and pulled back.

"It *is* you! I thought it was Sidney."

"Sidney? Why should you think that?"

She told him of her fears that Moberly had gone mad and murdered Mrs. Knox-Gore in her bed and had been lying in wait for Sidney's return in order to dispatch him also. She related what had happened to herself at breakfast, though not able to tell him what she had all too vividly imagined her own fate to be.

"Do you mean to tell me you've been here like this the entire day?"

"Well, I can't be sure how long I've been here. It has seemed years! What day is this?"

"Saturday."

"Then it has only been since this morning," she said wonderingly. "What time did you arrive?"

"Close on five. How long was I unconscious?"

"Nearly an hour at least." He made a movement of withdrawal. "Where are you going?" she cried, clutching him.

"Just to explore the room, my love," he said with reassuring tenderness. Reluctantly, she released his coat and he rose.

"Damn!" He stood swaying unsteadily.

"What is it?"

"Only a little dizziness." He moved off cautiously in the blackness, reaching, after only a few steps, a damp wall. He followed it around the entire room, a matter of a moment, and returned to her. "A very small room," he commented as he sat down and put his arm around her again. "Only one door, bolted, of course, and no windows. At least none within my reach. A storage room of some sort, I suppose. I think we had best make some sort of plan."

"What sort is possible?" she asked, not finding anything unnatural about nestling confidingly closer into his embrace.

"Well, they can't mean to keep us here forever. Someone must come, if only to give us food and water."

"Well," she said doubtfully, "I have been left for a full day— why, I've had nothing to eat since dinner last night!" she remembered indignantly. "Anyway it doesn't seem to me there is much interest in our comfort."

"Well, then, they will remember that I am not bound and will come back to do so."

"Why—I hadn't thought—now why should I be and not you?"

"I don't know. I think it was a mistake. Perhaps they had not time to spare at the moment for some reason. In any case I think they will remember and come back and we must be prepared for them."

"Why do you say 'them'? It is Moberly who has gone mad."

"I'm not so sure of that. From what I've learned of Knox-Gore's character, I wouldn't put it past him to be part of the scheme."

"Sidney? What do you mean?"

"I can't tell you that," he answered gravely, "it isn't proper for female ears, but you may take my word for it. Why, that is the reason I came!''

''Good heavens! I'm so all about in my head I never thought to even wonder about that. Why *are* you here?''

He gave her an abbreviated version of his evening with Sidney, his frustration at Neville's absence, and his own and Mrs. Daventry's worry at not hearing from her.

''But I wrote her every day,'' she protested.

''Your letters never arrived.''

''So that is why *she* didn't write. I thought you all—she had forgotten me.''

''As though I could forget you, even for a moment. Oh, Caroline—darling!'' He pulled her so close she gasped, though she was not at all inclined to resist him. His presence, after all her frightened hours alone was too comforting to give up, and the cold made his arms about her and the warmth of his large body almost a necessity. Below all these practical considerations lay something more, something sweet and waiting which she didn't attempt to explore in this dark and dreary place. It was something for the sunlight.

''You were saying something of a scheme,'' she reminded him.

''What scheme?''

''Well—actually I don't know, and I can't for the life of me imagine what it could be, but there is something strange going on. That butler gave me a reception on the north side of friendly but he certainly didn't strike me as mad.''

''To have nearly killed you? I call that mad! And I can assure you that Mrs. Knox-Gore cannot be part of any scheme. She is—rather foolish, but she has been very kind to me. As for Sidney, he fancies himself in love with me, but has never behaved in an ungentlemanly way.''

''Thank God!'' he breathed, his arms tightening about her. ''You—you do not return his feelings?''

''You must know I do not,'' she answered simply. He did not ask for an explanation of this statement, nor make any comment. He, also, felt this was not the time or the place to speak seriously of love.

''Now we must make a plan. Since we cannot get out, we must

wait for someone to come. And we must be prepared."

"What can we do?"

"We must move over to one side of the door. When he opens it I will hit him as hard as I can. I'm as tall as he and much heavier and I should have no trouble overpowering him."

He rose and helped her to her feet and they groped about until they found the door, then settled down beside it, their backs to the wall. He removed his coat and wrapped it about her shoulders against her protests that he would now be cold.

"I am never cold," he declared stoutly.

They sat quietly for a time in the thick dark. "Redvers," said Caroline presently, in a matter-of-fact way made possible by all that was obvious but unspoken between them, "who is Georgianna Brough?"

"Georgie? My cousin. Great gun, Georgie, you will like her. Up to every rig and row. Lord, the scrapes she has lead me into!"

"And the Charn girl?"

"Someone my mama had in her eye for me, but I told her it wouldn't wash."

This clearly was an adequate explanation for Caroline since she said no more but nuzzled into his shoulder in a contented sort of way.

"That's right," he said protectively, pressing her head closer, "you must rest—sleep if you can. I'll keep my ears sharp for his footsteps. We must just—wait."

=== 16 ===

AFTER LORD REDVERS had left her, Julia, assured of having some word of Caroline by evening, settled down to study her lines for the role of Isabella in *The Fatal Marriage*, a forthcoming play. During the afternoon she ordered the horses put to and, dressed in a ravishing poppy-red velvet pelisse lined with sable, and a matching red silk bonnet trimmed with a broad striped riband, set off for a ride in the Park. The day, though brisk, was fine with a definite hint that spring would soon come. There were a great many others also taking advantage of the good weather and Julia was forced to have her coachman pull up several times to exchange greetings with friends and acquaintances. One who fell into the latter category was Lady Wrexham, who waved her to a stop imperiously.

"Well, madame, *where* is Miss Devereaux?" she demanded in a tone that seemed to imply Julia was deliberately concealing her.

"She has not returned from the country, Lady Wrexham. Is it not a lovely day?"

"We must hope this restless streak in her will be curbed with maturity," answered Lady Wrexham severely. "Young people should not be encouraged in these directions. Wrexham's gone gallivanting off to the country also without so much as a by-your-leave."

"How remiss of him to do so without your permission," replied Julia blandly.

Lady Wrexham eyed her suspiciously, but Julia met her eyes unflinchingly. "I'll bid you good day, Mrs. Daventry. Please bring your protégée to drink a dish of Bohea with me when she returns." With a stately nod she motioned her coachman to move and was borne away.

Julia smiled impishly as she was carried in the other direction, for not only had she given the old lady as good as she got, she had also been given to understand that Lady Wrexham no longer considered her unacceptable by condescending to invite an actress into her drawing room!

Julia's buoyant spirits lasted through a visit to Madame Colette, where she could not resist a blue sprigged muslin gown for Caroline and a delectable chip straw bonnet for herself to celebrate the coming of spring. As the carriage approached her own home she felt certain she would find a note from Wrexham at least, or Caroline herself at most, awaiting her. Neither of these anticipated pleasures were there, however, and her high spirits were somewhat doused. Upstairs she found Mrs. Dainty mending linen, which she dropped as Julia entered, giving her a hopeful look.

"No word yet, Dainty, but it is early still. You'll never believe it, but I just encountered Lady Wrexham in the Park and she condescended to chat with me. What is more she has even invited me to bring Caroline for a visit when she returns. The only thing I can think of to account for such amiability is that she has decided Caroline will do for Wrexham after all."

"Why should she not?" demanded Dainty, flaring up defensively. "Even she cannot be so lost to common sense as not to see Miss Caroline's worth any dozen eligible girls she may have picked for the boy."

Julia laughed. "Well, we shall see. I think when I have changed I'll curl up with a book in the back drawing room until dinner. And since I've no performance tonight I believe I'll have a sherry."

Several hours and two glasses of sherry later, Julia was telling Belding to put back dinner for the second time. He looked at her with disbelief.

"But, madame, Cook will—" he faltered.

"Cook will have to contrive somehow. I am awaiting the arrival of Miss Caroline, or possibly only Lord Wrexham. If anyone comes show them up straightaway," she ordered, thinking of a possible messenger if not Redvers himself, with or without Caroline.

Belding tottered away reluctantly to bear the bad news to Cook, whose temper was uncertain at the best of times. Julia went downstairs after a further frustrating hour to pace from room to room on the lower floor, standing for long moments to stare out the windows at the disobligingly empty streets. She finally retreated upstairs again to the back drawing-room fire and her discarded book. After only a few moments, however, she tossed it aside and sat staring into the flames, nibbling at her knuckle nervously.

It was past nine o'clock when Belding showed Neville into the room, and Julia sprang up to meet him, all her previous animosity forgotten in her relief at having someone to share her worry with. She came forward swiftly, both hands outstretched. "Neville, thank God you've come," she exclaimed impetuously.

Neville was taken completely aback, not only by the warmth of her greeting when he had expected a chilly reserve, but by her use of his first name. His heart melted as usual at sight of her, her brilliant dark eyes alight with emotion, her warm, generous mouth pronouncing his name so sweetly. He took her hands and pulled her closer so that he held her hands against his chest. "Is something wrong, my dear?" he asked, his eyes devouring the lovely face so close to his own, all his former irritation instantly wiped away.

"It is Caroline! Oh, I may be foolish, but I cannot help worrying. If only you had not gone away just then."

"My agent sent word that I was needed to settle some business on my estate. If I had known you needed me nothing could have kept me from your side." His arms slid about her and pulled her even closer. "Will you forgive me?" he asked, his voice low and husky with emotion.

Her eyes were wide and searching for a moment before she said, "I—yes."

With an inarticulate moan he snatched her close, raining kisses on her brow and eyelids and cheeks, before seeking her mouth, which immediately softened at his touch, her arms creeping around his neck, one small hand caressing the back of his head. They finally drew apart to stare wonderingly at one another. He laughed rather shakily. "What torment you've put me through these past days."

"Did I?" she said softly, almost shyly.

"Minx! You know full well you did. I adored you from the first moment I saw you! You turned me into an idiotish, tongue-tied schoolboy. No woman ever affected me so!''

He tilted her chin up and ran his fingers lovingly over her lips, something he had longed to do since he had first seen her. She stood docilely, face raised, eyes closed, rapt in her enjoyment of his touch at last. He kissed her lightly in a delicious series of little kisses that kindled the blood in her veins almost unbearably. She pulled away with a breathless little laugh.

"Oh, Julia, how beautiful you are! I shall never tire of looking at you. Even when you are cold and angry with me you are enchanting. Though Caroline says—''

She had been dreamily running her fingers over his cheeks, but at his last words she started. "Oh, good God! How *can* I have forgotten. Oh, Neville, you must do something. She has gone away to the Knox-Gores and I've had no word for five days, though she promised faithfully to—''

"Whoa! Slow down, my love. Let me hear the story more slowly. She went to visit the Knox-Gores and has not written. What exactly is worrying you?''

"Well, it was something Lord Redvers said as well as not hearing from her. Evidently Sidney revealed something not very nice to Redvers, which he refused to repeat to me. He has been most anxious to consult with you about it. He was foxed, of course— Sidney, that is—so of course when Sidney took Caroline away so suddenly Redvers was very upset. He kept checking your hotel every day and then coming here to see if I had heard from her.''

"But did you not write to scold her for her forgetfulness?''

"I could not. Sidney took her away so suddenly I didn't think to get his direction.''

"What was all the urgency?''

"His mother was ill and wrote to ask him to return home at once and Caroline felt it was her duty to go along to nurse her. They were gone in less than an hour after he came to tell her of it.''

"You allowed her to go off alone in a carriage with him?'' he asked, a slight edge of disapproval in his voice.

"Of course I did not!'' she cried indignantly. "He had hired an abigail on his way here and had her in the carriage waiting—which is suspicious, when I come to think of it.''

"Well, perhaps he was very certain of Caroline's response, which I think was the only proper one, and wanted to save time. But since all was respectable I cannot understand why you are flying into the boughs. She is perfectly safe with Mrs. Knox-Gore, though she may be bored to death with the woman's silly chatter. As for Sidney, I think he may be spoiled and overprotected by his mama, but not dangerous in any way."

"According to Redvers, Sidney—"

"Oh, I think that we may assume that Redvers speaks from jealousy."

"I don't assume anything of the kind. Whatever he knew of Sidney worried him enough to go there this morning to seek some assurance that all was well. He was to send me word by this evening or bring Caroline back, but I've heard nothing and I'm nearly fretted to death. I think you should go at once to see what is wrong."

"Go at once? My dear Julia, I have just arrived in town after a very long and tiring journey. Only duty brought me here at such an hour or I should have been in my bed hours ago."

"Duty!" she cried incredulously.

"I thought it was my duty to stop in passing to inform my cousin of my return," he replied stiffly.

"If you are so set upon your duty, sir, I should think you could make some push to reassure yourself of her safety!"

"She is perfectly safe."

"You know nothing whatever about it—nor care, it seems."

"Julia, you are being unreasonable. There is no evidence to cause you to start such a hare as this. I cannot account for this hysteria—"

"I am *not* hysterical! But I am very angry and disgusted."

"I think it would be best to take my leave now. You are tired and distraught."

"Good night, sir," she said coldly, turning away from him.

"My dear, ask Mrs. Dainty to give you a sleeping draught. I'm sure a good night's rest will show you this picture in a more reasonable light." She remained stubbornly turned away and did not reply. After a moment he murmured good night and went away.

Julia stormed into her bedroom, muttering darkly, gave Dainty a garbled version of Neville's unreasonable attitude, and went to bed supperless, resolutely refusing to allow herself to dwell on the earlier part of the evening for as long as she could keep her anger fed. Exhaustion finally burned out rage, however, and the memory returned piercingly, filling her with such a physical longing, she began to cry childishly. She wiped her eyes with the edge of the sheet, calling herself a fool for having allowed herself to forget his hard-headed, contumacious character.

She woke feeling chilled and hollow, as though only the cold gray ashes of both rage and love were all that remained. She sat at the table, sipping uninterestedly at her morning chocolate, the mail, when she found no letter there from Caroline, disregarded. Belding came in presently to announce a "person" was calling, asking for a word with her.

"A *person?*"

"Ah—a woman. Margaret Brown is the name she gave."

"Well, then, I'll see her here."

Belding went away and returned with a middle-aged, pleasant-looking woman who bobbed a respectful curtsey and stood twisting her fingers together nervously.

"Mrs. Brown? Can I help you?" asked Julia kindly.

"Well, madame, I hope I'm not forgetting my place, but I thought if the young lady was back I could explain why I went away without no word to her like that."

"I'm afraid I don't quite understand. Do you refer to Miss Devereaux?"

"That's right, missus. The gentleman hired me as her abigail. It was that butler, see. He came and said Mr. Knox-Gore wanted me gone, just when I was having me supper. He had the carriage waitin' and bundled me away so quick I hardly had time to pack me box. I felt bad, I did, 'cause I'd grown that fond of young Miss, even if I only knew her a few days."

"When was this?"

"'Twere two days ago, madame. I would have come at once, but I've been obliged to seek another place."

"Have you done so?"

"Not yet, missus. Places are that hard to come by now, you wouldn't believe."

"Then you will stay here. I'm sure Miss Devereaux will be happy to have you attend her again when she returns."

Julia rang for Belding, told him Margaret was to be Miss Caroline's abigail and to take her to the servants' quarters and attend to her. Margaret released an avalanche of gratitude, interspersed with little bobbing curtsies, before finally being persuaded out of the room by Belding.

Julia leaned her elbows on the table to support her chin and considered what she had heard and what she knew. First, Caroline not communicating for five days, though she had promised. Then Redvers going after her and neither sending word nor returning as promised. And now Margaret Brown, hired by Sidney and dismissed on a moment's notice three days later. A night's sleep did not present the picture in a more reasonable light as promised by Mr. Neville Devereaux. Very well, then, she thought, rising decisively to her feet. *I* will do something. She rang for Belding, ordered the horses put to, and went upstairs to dress.

"You're *what?*" shrieked Mrs. Dainty. "I'll not let you go gallivanting off alone on such an errand!"

"Try not to be so foolish, Dainty. I'm thirty years old and surely have proved I'm able to take care of myself. I shall have Bob Coachman with me if I need any assistance."

"You're not thirty," replied Dainty, hitting on the one indisputable fact.

"Near enough. Now get out my claret merino and put some things into a valise for me, a dinner gown and night things in case I'm forced to stay over. And don't argue. I'm going and that is all about it!"

Neville rose late due to a nearly sleepless night of tossing about, reliving those few precious moments of passion with Julia when they had been open to admitting their feelings; also reliving the dispute which followed and wondering, despairingly, why they seemed always to end up at daggers drawing every time they met. He longed for her with his entire being and yet could cheerfully have shaken her until her head rattled for her stubbornness.

Having resolved to give her the better part of the day to cool down, he strolled around to his club and occupied the morning as best he could with the few friends he found there. He met Malby after luncheon and they rode together in the Park and, at Malby's insistence, dined together. He declined Malby's pressing invitation to make a night of it at Cribb's Parlour and walked around to Julia's close on eight o'clock.

Belding, answering his knock, informed him that Mrs. Daventry had gone away, but might be back in Town tomorrow.

"Gone away? Gone where?" demanded Neville.

"I'm sure I couldn't say, sir," replied Belding mournfully.

"Is Mrs. Dainty here?"

"Yes, sir."

"Step up and tell her I would like a word with her if it is convenient."

Belding showed him into a small waiting room, brought him brandy in spite of Neville's protests, and finally went away to fetch Mrs. Dainty. She came bustling in presently, neat as always, but flustered-looking. "Oh, Mr. Devereaux, how glad I am you've come at last! I'm that upset. Here's Miss Julia gone off after Miss Caroline and not come back, though she left before ten this morning."

"Gone after Caroline? But why on earth—" Neville felt completely at nonplus by this development.

"Well, sir, she has been that fretful for days, not hearing and all, and then Lord Wrexham here at all hours stirring her up. Then this morning comes this woman Mr. Knox-Gore hired as abigail to Miss Caroline telling of being turned off at moment's notice after only a few days. Miss Julia made up her mind there was something havey-cavey in the business, and she's that headstrong, Mr. Devereaux, there is no stopping her once her mind's made up, so off she went this morning and no word from her since."

She finished her recital by folding her hands over her waist and fixing him with an expectant look, clearly waiting for him to offer a solution, or at least some comfort.

Neville uttered a sharp *"Damn and blast!"* before turning away to pace about the room rapidly. He stopped to stare blankly into the middle distance for a long moment, then sighed, ran a distracted hand through his hair, and then banged his fist on the mantle.

"Of all the crack-brained starts! Well, I shall go after her, of course, though I shall have to rouse the whole household no doubt, for I cannot arrive before midnight."

"Oh, Mr. Devereaux, I'd be that grateful if you'd go, for I'm worried, I'll admit to you."

And so Neville found himself riding out of London at an hour when, unless engaged for the evening, a gentleman would ordinarily be sitting by his fire with a brandy thinking pleasantly of bed.

= 17 =

JULIA, MEANWHILE, HAD found her way with far less difficulty than Redvers to the Devereaux estate, arriving well before midday and announcing to a surly Moberly that she would like to see Miss Devereaux.

"She is not here," he replied shortly.

Julia gave him a cold stare, raising her eyebrows to indicate her displeasure at his manner. "Then I will see Mrs. Knox-Gore," she replied with all the hauteur at her command, feeling very much like Lady Wrexham.

After a brief battle of wills, he submitted with a marked sullenness and stepped back to admit her. "Wait here," he said, indicating a hall chair, and went away.

Much affronted, Julia drew herself up, preparing to do battle if he returned with a negative answer. However, in a moment he came back and indicated that she was to follow, and led her across the hall, opened a door, and stood back to allow her to pass into the room.

She found a stout lady in a much beruffled cap seated before the fire, looking up at her fearfully. "Mrs. Knox-Gore? I'm happy to see that you are somewhat recovered. I am Julia Daventry. I've come to fetch Caroline home."

"Oh—oh—Mrs. Daventry—Caroline has spoken of you so often I quite feel we are old friends. How I look forward to seeing you on the stage! I love the theatre and have read about your splendid talent, of course. Mr. Knox-Gore was used to take me to the theatre upon occasion when we were first married, but after he was taken from me, I had to forgo such pleasures."

She paused for breath and Julia said hastily, "Could you send for Caroline, Mrs. Knox-Gore?"

"Caroline—yes—ah, you see, she has gone out to visit some friends in the neighbourhood and has not returned, the naughty child."

"I see. Well, of course it is gratifying to know she has made friends so quickly here, though I must admit I am disappointed. I have missed her sadly. Was she at home yesterday to receive Lord Wrexham?"

"Lord Wrexham? No one called to see her yesterday." Mrs. Knox-Gore looked genuinely puzzled.

"How odd. He said he was coming. Perhaps he lost his way."

The door opened abruptly and Sidney hurried in. He halted in shock at sight of Julia and before he could prevent it a slight frown drew his brows together. He recovered himself quickly, however, and came forward, all affability.

"My *dear* Mrs. Daventry, this is a pleasant surprise!"

"She came to fetch Caroline," Mrs. Knox-Gore interposed swiftly before Julia could respond. "I told her that Caroline is visiting friends today."

"Visiting—ah yes, of course, the Debenhams. A daughter just Caroline's age. They were fast friends at once."

"Delightful. You won't mind if I wait for her?"

"Mind? My dear Mrs. Daventry, I shall insist. How often can we be so honored? I'll have Moberly show you to a room at once. You will want to refresh yourself after your journey."

"If you could also have someone bring up my valise and attend to my coachman and the horses, I will be grateful."

"Of course, of course."

Moberly was rung for, sent to fetch the case and direct the driver to the stables, then when he returned to lead Julia upstairs. He opened the door for her, set her valise down, and left. After a moment of indecision Julia softly opened the door again, and hearing voices, tiptoed to the railing at the top of the stairs. The butler had just reached the bottom and was crossing the hall.

"Of all the cork-brained notions! Why did you tell her such a thing?" came Sidney's irate voice.

"Well, I was that shocked, Sidney, I couldn't think of what to—"

"And what, pray, will you tell her this evening?"

"We may very well find her by then and—"

Moberly reached the door, entered, and closed it firmly behind him. Julia turned away and walked slowly back to her room, her heart thumping. *We may very well find her by then!* What on earth—? Have they *lost* her? Oh, dear God, what can this mean? And where is Redvers? Julia was very, very frightened.

Julia sat shivering in the cold room for some time, trying to think what she should do, but no plan presented itself to her. She gradually became aware that it was most odd that no servant had come with hot water or to light a fire in the cold fireplace, not to speak of unpacking her valise. She shrugged and rose to unpack and hang her gown before it became too creased. Then she removed her bonnet and pelisse, poured some of the cold water she found in the ewer into the basin, and shiveringly washed her face and hands.

Dainty had packed a Norwich silk shawl for evening, country houses were always cold, she had said, and Julia wrapped it gratefully about her shoulders and made her way back to the drawing room. She would have liked to explore some of the rooms upstairs first, but didn't dare do so without knowing the disposition of the other occupants at the moment.

She made her way back downstairs to the drawing room where she found Mrs. Knox-Gore alone, still seated before the fire. She greeted Julia eagerly.

"My dear, how glad I am you've come down. The house is so quiet it quite makes my flesh crawl."

"Your son has gone out?"

"Ah—yes—yes, he has. Some errand in the village."

"I was wondering, Mrs. Knox-Gore, do you have trouble staffing such a large house?"

"Oh, no—that is—yes—at least, we live very simply here, Mrs. Daventry. I try to make do with Moberly and Cook—and a girl to clean from the village," she added with more hope than truth at the moment. "But you would like some refreshments, I'm sure. If you would just pull the bell rope there—so difficult for me to get out of the chair."

Julia obligingly rose to pull the bell and seated herself again. They waited for some time, speaking sporadically of the weather and other trivialities, Mrs. Knox-Gore eyeing the door nervously.

"Well, I do wonder what can have happened to Moberly, he is usually so prompt. Mr. Knox-Gore set great store on promptness in servants. He could become quite cross if kept waiting, so I have always tried—" She rattled on in this vein for quite some time, but Moberly did not come.

Though she hoped he had gone into the village to hire some staff, he was actually at that moment lying fully dressed on his bed, nursing a monumental headache and moaning from time to time. He was also cursing himself with the most vile imprecations at his command for not having done something about those two in the cellar last night as he had meant to do. The truth was, he had helped himself a little too liberally to old Mr. Devereaux's best brandy last night in celebration of his success so far, and to aid his thought processes as he pondered exactly what it would be best to do with them. Several glasses later the prospect of further exertion began to seem less and less appealing, until at last he had persuaded himself it was not necessary at all. As a consequence he had it all to do tonight, and his brain absolutely refused to function as to the practicalities of the situation, and there was the added danger of that coachman and his mistress to be watched out for.

Presently he heaved himself into a sitting position and with trembling hands put his shoes on again. When he returned to the kitchen he found Bob Coachman cosily ensconced at the servants' table with a pot of tea and a plate of cakes. Cook, quite above herself at having this large, good-looking man to keep her company, was chattering away at him as she moved about the kitchen preparing dinner. Bob rolled his eyes expressively at Moberly to share his resignation at the woman's clacking tongue, but Moberly only scowled and turned away to scrub his hands at the sink.

The bell rang and Cook turned. "You'd best get along up there. She's been ringing this hour and more. In a rare taking with you, most like by now."

Moberly continued scrubbing at fastidious length before reaching for a towel and giving the drying of his fingers equal care. He then adjusted his sleeves, pulled down his waistcoat, and strolled out of the kitchen. He was of half a mind not to answer the bell at all. The stupid old besom had no right to continue treating him as a servant. Weren't they equal partners now, and she and that soft son of hers no better than he? At least they would be after tonight, for they'd have no choice, the heiress not being available for marriage. He smirked at his own humour, but then frowned, remembering that he must first get rid of the girl before he would be truly safe. With this in mind he went along to answer the bell, promising himself that tomorrow he'd teach both the Knox-Gores a new tune to sing. He opened the drawing-room door and stood waiting wordlessly.

"Oh—Moberly—there you are. Where·on earth—well, never mind that now. Bring Mrs. Daventry some wine and biscuits. And tell Cook we will have our dinner at six as usual." He withdrew and she turned to Julia. "We eat our mutton early in the country, Mrs. Daventry, but I'm sure you will be sharp-set by then, for the air here is good for one's appetite. We won't wait for Caroline. If she has not appeared before then, I'll have Cook set something aside for her. I've never held with delaying one's meals. Indeed, dear Mr. Knox-Gore was quite adamant about it, as was dear Chandos."

The remainder of the afternoon was spent by the two ladies together, Julia listening for the most part while Mrs. Knox-Gore rambled on inexhaustibly. Julia discovered little was required of her beyond a smile of agreement from time to time, but that it took an almost gargantuan effort of will to force herself to sit patiently when she longed to be doing *something* about Caroline. She was positive beyond any doubt that Caroline was not visiting the Debenhams, whoever they might be, after what she had overheard. She longed to find Caroline's room and look for any clues it might hold, for it was clear she had disappeared and the Knox-Gores themselves had no idea where she was. Julia could only think that Caroline had run away, though it was hardly creditable she would do such a thing. The only alternative, that she had been abducted, was even less acceptable, and until forced Julia did not intend to dwell upon it.

Sidney came in late in the afternoon and Julia was so weary by then of Mrs. Knox-Gore's inconsequential reminiscing of her departed husband, who sounded to have been the world's most irascible tartar, that she greeted Sidney with equally as much enthusiasm as did his mother.

He bent over Julia's fingers and went to drop a kiss on his mother's fat cheek. "You ladies look very cosy, I must say. No sign of our wandering girl?"

"No, Sidney, and indeed I fear—"

He cut her off hastily. "Having too good a time, no doubt. Perhaps young Debenham has come down from Oxford to pay her compliments. Young girls are always partial to compliments."

Julia only raised an eyebrow, but Mrs. Knox-Gore opened her mouth to speak, a worried look on her face. Sidney, seeing it, continued heartily, "Well, ladies, if we don't look sharp we shan't be ready for dinner. Come along and I shall give you both an arm up the stairs."

He bustled them out of the room and if Julia had been capable of amusement she would have found the pair of them comic indeed in their obviousness. She hurriedly changed into her dinner gown, mentally thanking Dainty for packing one with sleeves. She took down her hair, brushed it vigourously, and skillfully piled it into a knot on top, pulling forward wisps of shorter hair to frame her face in loose curls. Then pinning her shawl around her shoulders, she hurried back to the drawing-room fire where she held her icy hands over the flames and wondered how Mrs. Knox-Gore could possibly contrive without maids, at least an abigail, for dressing and undressing must present dreadful difficulties for a lady of so much bulk.

However, when the lady came in on Sidney's arm, it was clear she had solved the problem by changing her cap for one even frothier and throwing a lace shawl over her black silk gown.

"Well, Mrs. Daventry," said Sidney gaily, "one of our problems has resolved itself. Caroline has sent word she will dine and spend the night at the Debenhams's, so we may sit down to our dinner with a clear conscience. Come along, ladies, an arm each and forward."

Mrs. Knox-Gore tittered nervously and cast an uneasy glance at Julia, who smiled back, determined to give a perfect performance tonight of a lady with nothing more pressing on her mind than her eagerness to see Caroline again. There were a great many things she would like to take up with Sidney, but she had decided that she must not rouse any suspicion that she was aware of their lies, for it was vital that she get into Caroline's room tonight and she could only do so when they had gone to sleep, confident they had pulled the wool over her eyes. What lies they might make up tomorrow she would deal with then.

She was happy to see Mrs. Knox-Gore suppressing yawns even before the tea tray was brought in or before Sidney had rejoined them. When these had both arrived and tea was poured Julia allowed herself to be caught yawning behind her fan and presently Sidney suggested they would all be better for an early night.

Once in her room she eyed the unaired bed with misgivings, sure it must be damp and wondering if opening it would be to any avail since the room itself felt dank with cold. She threw the covers back anyway, for what good it might do. Sure enough, the sheets felt damp.

She fetched the lapel watch she carried in her valise and saw that it was near ten. She would give them an hour to fall asleep and then take a chance. She had reasoned that Caroline's room must be one of two on this hall. Mrs. Knox-Gore occupied the bedroom directly at the top of the stairs to the right and had confided that the one opposite had previously been that of Chandos Devereaux, and that it was just as he had left it, and indeed she could not bear to enter it at all. Julia had the one next to this room. Next to her was an unoccupied room. Directly across from it was the room she'd watched Sidney enter when he brought them up to dress for dinner. Between his room and his mother's was another apparently unoccupied, and this was Julia's first choice for being Caroline's, since she would hardly be put into old Devereaux's room, nor was it likely she would be given the one on this side and furthest from Mrs. Knox-Gore, whom she was supposedly nursing.

Julia wondered if she should change into her bed gown and wrapper for appearance's sake, but decided she didn't fancy wandering around in this cold house dressed so. She would have preferred changing back into her claret merino traveling dress, but if she were caught in the halls it would be hard to explain, whereas if she remained as she was she could always say she was in search of a book or something. She next debated taking her candle. On the one hand it would look odd if she didn't and were seen, and on the other there was much less chance of being caught if she didn't.

She remembered now that the moon was very bright tonight and was rising on the other side of the house. She went to the window to confirm this and was reassured by the shadow of the mansion thrown hugely across the park. It would be pouring into the room across the hall. That decided it—no candle.

When the tiny hand on her watch had dragged its slow way around to eleven she approached her door on tiptoe and eased it open. It was very still. She suddenly wondered with a thrill of fear where that dreadful butler slept, then pushed the thought away. After all, it could not be on this floor. Blessing Chandos Devereaux for the luxurious carpet that made her steps soundless, she crossed the hall and with infinite patience turned the knob of the door and pushed it open with no sound. She slipped inside, leaving it slightly ajar so she wouldn't have the task of opening it again.

She stood still, heart pounding, and slowly looked around. Faintly now she heard a low rhythmic rumbling from her left that she identified as Mrs. Knox-Gore snoring. She wished she could hear the same from the other side, but it was silent.

She moved to the dressing table which was bare of any iden-tifying object. She remembered that even at home Caroline always put away brushes and hairpins tidily in the drawers. Julia didn't feel she could take the chance of pulling out the drawers, for she had never known a drawer to open silently. She moved on to the bed and put her hand beneath the pillow. There was something! A flat box—the pearls, of course. She pulled it out and opened it and they gleamed in the moonlight. So there was no longer any doubt—this was Caroline's room.

Julia moved on to the wardrobe and eased it open. Yes, here were Caroline's gowns. Julia remembered each one very well from the day she had chosen them and helped Dainty pack them. Yes, they were all here but the green merino. Now for the outer garments. Here was the amber pelisse, and the dark blue velvet fur-lined cape which they had decided could do for evening if there were occasion to go out, as well as for warmth for walks during the day. That was all—no—wait—the cashmere shawl! She searched, but it was not there. So! Was it possible she had gone to the Debenhams—or anywhere else in this weather with only a cash-mere shawl? Ah, yes, a bonnet. She lifted down onto the bed the large hat box, which when opened revealed both of the bonnets Caroline had brought with her, one with a sadly broken white plume drooping over the brim. Julia stood quite still, eyes riveted on the broken feather, feeling an icy hand clutch her heart. She was filled with such sickening dread that the brightly moonlit room darkened and tilted. She crumpled down in a heap onto the bed and lay there until the faintness passed. Then she slowly rose, covered the box without looking into it again, and replaced it on the wardrobe shelf. She left the room and with infinite patience eased the door closed again.

The hall was very dark after the brightly lit room, but after a few moments her eyes adjusted and the blackness took on gradations. She stood for a moment more, irresolute, before, putting back her shoulders determinedly, she made her way down the hall to the other unoccupied room. Without the advantage of moonlight it was more difficult to see anything properly, but there was enough light to show her that the room was empty of any sign of human occupation. She found herself in the dark hall again, with a further decision to make. However, with courage born of her success so far, she moved off toward the back stairs.

These stairs were uncarpeted and she was forced to test every step before trusting it with her full weight. Every creak seemed to rend the air loudly, so absolute was the quiet of the house.

The stairs debouched into another long hall leading to the front of the house. To her right was the back door and a few steps brought her to the opening into the kitchen, filled with light from the moon. She passed on around a corner and made out a door, closed, and when she tried it, found it locked. She stood before it uncertainly. This must be the cellar door, and she would very much like to explore there, but without the least notion of where the key was kept it would be impossible tonight. Tomorrow, however, if nothing came of tonight's exploration, she would have to do something about that, though what possible excuse she could give for wanting to go down there beggared her imagination, and what she might find she dared not speculate upon. Though she was convinced the Knox-Gores did not know Caroline's whereabouts, and she hoped very much the child had gone away for some inexplicable reason, Julia could not ignore the evidence revealed by

Caroline's closet. She could not have gone out in this cold without her bonnet and an outer garment. Therefore, she had not gone out. The inescapable conclusion was that she was still here, perhaps the victim of an undiscovered accident, such as a fall down these cellar steps, Julia thought with sudden inspiration, turning back to try the door again. It remained adamantly locked.

She stood there for a moment considering the possibility of going to Sidney at once with her idea and enlisting his aid in finding the key. Then she wondered why, if, as seemed true, the Knox-Gores didn't know where Caroline was, they continued to pretend they did and make up tarradiddles about a fictitious visit to the Debenhams? Unless—was it possible that only Mrs. Knox-Gore was in the dark about Caroline's whereabouts? Could it be that Sidney, for some demented reason, had abducted Caroline himself, for some unspeakable purpose of his own, perhaps to do with the dreadful degeneracy he had revealed while drunk to Redvers?

She was so rapt in contemplation of this horrible thought that the hand which suddenly seized her shoulder shocked her almost out of her skin. She leapt into the air, emitting an ear-splitting shriek!

A large, bony hand clamped over Julia's mouth and cut off the shriek, but she promptly bit it and the hand was jerked away with an oath. She immediately screamed again and lashed out wildly, but her hand was caught and twisted behind her back. Screaming and struggling she was pushed and shoved up the hallway by a snarling Moberly, who finally clamped a long arm across her to hold both arms against her body so that kicking was the only effective retaliative measure she could take. But from the grunts of pain and the muttered oaths, she could take some satisfaction that punishment was being dealt on her part.

They erupted, still struggling, into the front hall which was lit fitfully now by the candles held by Sidney and Mrs. Knox-Gore in their nightclothes halfway down the stairs. They stopped in shock when they saw Julia in Moberly's clutch, her smoky dark hair loosened from its pins, tumbling down her back, her eyes shooting sparks of rage.

"Good God, Moberly! *What* is going on?" Sidney yelled.

Mrs. Knox-Gore's mouth was acock but she made only gobbling, terrified sounds as her fat jaws wobbled in agitation and her usually red face turned a lardy gray in colour.

"Found 'er roaming around down here trying doors," retorted Moberly defensively.

"You—but—Mrs. Daventry, what can I possibly say?" began Sidney, completely at sea.

"You can begin by telling him to let go of me," snapped Julia indignantly.

"Oh—of course—let go of her, Moberly, at once. Have you taken leave of your senses? How dare you maul our guest about in such a way?"

"What's she doin' then, creeping about in the dark?" demanded Moberly, releasing Julia reluctantly.

"Well, I'm sure she"—he stopped and eyed Julia—"er—actually, Mrs. Daventry, it is somewhat—er—unusual. Perhaps you wouldn't mind—"

Julia hesitated only a moment before tossing aside any attempt to fob him off with a trumped-up story of looking for reading matter. She drew herself up and threw down her gage. "I was looking for Caroline," she announced challengingly.

"Looking for—! But, my dear Mrs. Daventry, we have—ah—told you where she is."

"Yes, yes, I've heard all about the Debenhams. The friendless daughter, the son with the eye for the ladies. However, I don't believe in them. At least, I don't believe Caroline is with them!"

Sidney and his mother began expostulating at once, but Julia cut through contemptuously.

"She would not go visiting dressed only in a shawl in this weather. Also she would not leave the house under any circumstances without a bonnet."

"But how can you know—" Sidney began in amazement.

"I looked in her room. The only things missing are her green merino gown and her cashmere shawl. I helped choose the clothes she brought with her, so I know every article."

Sidney turned slowly to look at his mother. "You *idiot!*" he ground out from clenched teeth.

"But, Sidney, it never occurred to me—" she began.

"Is everything all right here, missus?" came from the top of the stairs. All eyes swung up in surprise, and there stood a tousled Bob Coachman, his hair standing in spikes from encounter with his pillow, his trousers pulled on hastily and shirtless.

"Bob!" Julia cried with heartfelt welcome at this unexpected ally. "Where have you come from?"

"I was give a room up top, missus. Heard some screeching. Thought I'd best come along and see if you wanted me."

"Yes, I certainly do. The first thing you can do is come down here and—and—plant a facer on this—this *ape!*"

Bob hitched up his braces and obligingly started down the stairs. Suddenly Julia felt herself clamped in Moberly's arm again, hard against his bony chest, and in his other hand, as if by magic, appeared a long and very wicked-looking knife, glinting evilly in the candlelight. It deliberately approached her throat. She stopped struggling instantly and stared at it with wide, mesmerized eyes.

All other movement in the hall ceased also: Bob in midstep, Sidney with mouth open to speak, and Mrs. Knox-Gore clutching her bosom, her eyes in danger of starting from their sockets. With his audience assured, Moberly took command.

"Now, enough of this. I'm in charge from here on in and you'll all mind yer steps or you'll have none to mind."

"Where is Miss Devereaux?" Julia whispered forcefully, still not daring to move, though defiant.

"Shut yer mouth. She's dead and so's that young toff what come nosing around this morning."

"Good God! Lord Redvers," gasped Julia in horror.

"That's right, and you'll be joining them presently," said Moberly.

"I hardly think so," came a hard voice. "Drop the knife at once or I shall take infinite pleasure in blowing a hole through the back of your skull. Then take your filthy hands off the lady and turn around very slowly."

The razor clattered to the floor. Moberly released Julia and turned. Julia whirled around, a sob of relief rising in her throat for she had recognized the voice. "Oh, *Neville!*"

At the same moment both Knox-Gores began speaking at once, while Bob skipped down the stairs and retrieved the knife, which he pocketed.

"Quiet, both of you," Neville ordered, looking up at the Knox-

Gores, his eyes hard as stones. "Good man," this to Bob. "Now fetch something to tie his hands."

Bob slipped past into the drawing room and returned in a few seconds with a tasseled gold cord from the draperies and competently bound Moberly's wrists together behind his back.

"Neville, he says they are dead, Caroline and Redvers," whispered Julia, the full import of Moberly's words only now hitting her after the shock of Neville's entrance.

"I heard," he replied, and in his eyes she caught a brief flash of the soul-sick grief and guilt he was experiencing.

"Oh—no—you must not—!" she exclaimed involuntarily, but stopped at once at the futility of her protest.

"Where are they?" he demanded of Moberly.

"You'll get naught from me," muttered Moberly sullenly.

"Where are the bodies, man, and quick about it! Nothing could give me greater pleasure than to take you apart, piece by piece, so you'd best answer at once!" His voice was flat and so menacing Julia felt a chill of horror shake her. Moberly glared at him, then looked away, not speaking. "Very well. You"—he turned to Bob—"ride to the village and fetch the authorities. I think I will prefer to watch him hang. Meanwhile, Knox-Gore, you and I will search. Julia, Mrs. Knox-Gore looks somewhat pale. You will take her upstairs and stay with her after you light these candles."

He indicated a ten-candle branch on the hall table and Julia hastened to fetch Mrs. Knox-Gore's candle to light it with. While she was doing so Moberly swung around to stare up at the Knox-Gores. "You'd best fix this," he said threateningly.

The stared back aghast, then both pair of eyes swiveled around to Neville.

"Don't expect them to be able to help you, murderer," he snapped.

"They'd best if they know where the butter's to be found on their bread," snarled Moberly. "They're in deep as me."

"Why—why—what are you talking about, you cur? How dare you implicate us in your madness?" cried Sidney, outraged.

"Yes, yes, the man has obviously lost all hold on reason, Mr. Devereaux. We found him mistreating Mrs. Daventry dreadfully.

Oh, those screams! They will haunt me for the rest of my life,'' declared Mrs. Knox-Gore with a shudder.

"I think the best plan would be to tie up his feet as well and let Bob here drive him directly to the Authorities," suggested Sidney.

"The very thing," cried Mrs. Knox-Gore enthusiastically. "Why, he might murder us all. I won't feel safe until the man is out of the house!"

"Oh, no you don't! I'm not leaving you to have it all yer own way. 'Twas her scheme, the fat old besom, and she'll pay for it same as me," yelled Moberly swinging around to Neville. "They'll both pay!"

"What scheme?" shouted Neville, overriding a chorus of outraged protest from the Knox-Gores.

"They're after the old man's money and they hid the will. We was splitting three ways but then they got a better idea. He was to marry the girl and get the money that way—and after, they'd just happen to find the will again—"

"But since that left you out you decided to scotch their scheme by murdering the girl," interrupted Neville grimly. "How was hiding the will in the first place to avail any of you?"

"I've a friend handy with pen and ink who was to make out a new one in Sidney's favour."

"This is the most ridiculous farrago of nonsense I've ever heard!" Sidney shouted. "How dare you implicate my mother and me in such a thing?"

"As if we would be a party to such wickedness!" exclaimed Mrs. Knox-Gore, weighing in. "Mr. Devereaux, I demand that you have this monster removed from the house at once!"

"Ah, stop yer bawling, old woman. I've got you fair and square. If you'll just reach into my vest pocket, Mr. Devereaux, you'll find that which proves my story."

Neville raised his chin at Bob who moved over and dipped a finger into Moberly's vest pocket. He removed a much-folded square of paper which he opened and handed to Neville. Neville scanned it, handed it to Julia, and turned implacable eyes up to the Knox-Gores on the stairs. "Where is the will?" he asked stonily. They stared back silently. "Mrs. Knox-Gore, my patience is very nearly at an end. Fetch the will at once or I shall be forced to take measures—and they won't be pretty, I assure you. I shall break every bone in Sidney's body before your eyes, one for each moment I'm kept waiting.''

The words were spoken very softly and slowly, but there was that in them to cause Sidney to turn pale. "Give it to him, Mama,'' he managed to choke out in a strangled whisper. She hesitated and he shrieked, "Give it to him, you cloth-headed fool!''

Mrs. Knox-Gore slowly reached into the front of her gown and fumbled out from the voluminous folds of flesh there a thickly folded paper. At another sign from Neville, Bob fetched it for him. One glance showed him all he needed to know. He turned sick, hurt eyes upon Julia again for a brief look and her heart turned over with pity for him even in the midst of her own grief.

"I hold you responsible, Mrs. Knox-Gore,'' Neville said dully, "you and Sidney, just as much as this madman here. None of this would have come about if it had not been for your greed. He will hang, but I'll see the pair of you imprisoned for the rest of your lives.''

Mrs. Knox-Gore moaned and Sidney reached for the banister rail as though faint. Moberly sneered at them and then turned cunning eyes on Neville.

"If I was to tell yer something you'd like what would yer do for me?''

"Nothing,'' replied Neville shortly.

"Oh, Neville, wait! He knows where the—where they are—'' Julia protested faintly.

"Then he'll tell us or I'll do to him what I promised Sidney— and with even more relish! Speak up! Where are the bodies?''

Moberly pursed his mouth and glared defiantly. Neville waited for a moment and then turned to Bob.

"Ah—what is your name, young man?''

"'Tis Bob, yer honour.''

"Very well, Bob. You will come here and hold the pistol. You know how to shoot?''

"That I do, sir.''

"Good. Then hold it trained on this animal while I proceed. Julia, you might not want to stay for this. I'll start with the left ankle, I believe, and work up.'' he advanced purposefully upon

Moberly, pushing him sharply so that he sat down quite suddenly, and then reached for his ankle.

"Awright then, awright! They're not dead!" screeched Moberly, kicking his feet out of Neville's reach.

"Oh, dear God," whispered Julia, the beginning of hope rekindling her huge, dark eyes.

"Where are they?" Neville demanded.

"First I want to know what you'll do fer me, then I'll tell you," persisted Moberly, too stupid to realize he had played his last trump.

"Never mind, Neville. *I* know," gasped Julia in an awed voice. "They are in the cellar—and I know where the door is. I had such a positive feeling at that door. But it is locked."

"The key," Neville demanded, reaching for Moberly's ankle.

"In the other pocket, for God's sake, no need to get on yer high horse," cried Moberly, all the fight going out of him in an instant.

Neville fished it out. Julia snatched up a candle from the hall table and led the way at a run. They unlocked the door and hurried down the stairs into the Stygian blackness. They unbolted the first door and as it swung open Neville stepped forward. Sensing a rustle of movement to his right, he raised his arm just in time to deflect a blow that jarred against his arm with such force it nearly knocked him off his feet. Julia cried out and raised the candle to reveal Redvers preparing to deliver another of the same.

"Wait!" she shrieked. "Redvers, it is Neville! Don't hit him!"

Wild-eyed, one arm drawn back, Redvers froze, staring at them in disbelief. From the darkness within Caroline stepped forward—and there they were! Dirty, tousled, wide-eyed—but very much alive. Julia sprang forward with a glad cry and swept Caroline into her arms, sobs mingling with exclamations of joy. Neville, grinning, stepped forward and clapped Redvers on the shoulder, and the two stood laughing rather awkwardly together as men will do when overcome by unmanly emotion.

"Are you hurt, my darling?" Julia asked anxiously, pulling away slightly to look into Caroline's face.

"Not really—only a little hungry," Caroline said, silent tears cleaning tracks through the grime on her face.

Julia hugged her again impulsively before turning to Redvers.

As she released her hold on Caroline, the girl sagged at the knees with only a small sigh and would have fallen had not Neville leaped forward to catch her. Sweeping her up he turned and left the dank room, saying, "Not another word. We'll attend to you two first. Redvers, do not hesitate to lean on Julia if you feel any faintness. She is very strong."

Julia gave his departing back a dazed look of pleasure at this praise, while Redvers looked rather indignant. Both, however, followed meekly. Neville led the way upstairs, and as they passed the goggle-eyed group in the hallway, Mrs. Knox-Gore cried out at the sight of Caroline's limp form. Julia darted into the dining room and returned carrying a bottle of brandy, to follow the rest into the drawing room, closing the door firmly behind her.

Neville deposited Caroline on the sofa, raised her head on his arm, and attempted to administer the brandy, while Julia dropped to her knees beside the sofa and chafed Caroline's cold hands. Redvers briefly explained that he had arrived the day before about five, been set upon by Moberly, and returned to his senses to find himself in the cellar with Caroline who had been there since breakfast. She had also been painfully bound and gagged for at least eight hours, and had now been without food or water for over forty-eight hours.

Julia jumped to her feet and sped out of the room. She returned shortly with a basin of water and a cloth and gently began applying cold compresses to Caroline's temples. In another moment the eyelids fluttered open and Caroline gazed uncomprehendingly at the three anxious faces hovering over her.

"Oh—what—?" She struggled to rise, but Neville put his arm about her, and holding her head firmly against his shoulder, forced her to take a few sips of the brandy. When she weakly pushed the glass away, he lowered her again and Julia tenderly washed her face and hands.

"What she needs is food, and at once," declared Neville. "Is there a cook or servant besides Moberly on the premises?"

"There is a cook, but it will take too long to waken her and get her down. The fire in the stove is only banked for the night. I can have it going in a moment and fix something myself," said Julia getting to her feet.

Neville and Redvers looked astonished at this, neither of them ever having numbered among their female acquaintances one who knew about kitchen ovens or cooking. Julia hurried away, and Redvers, after a brief, reassuring glance at Caroline, went after her, muttering that perhaps he could be of help. In the kitchen, Julia handed him the candle while she administered wood shavings and then kindling to the glowing embers in the stove. While she rummaged in the pantry, he assembled a tray and silver, glasses and china. Julia emerged with a tureen of soup which she emptied into a sauce pan and set on the stove, then returned to the pantry for bread, a York ham, and cheese. In less than fifteen minutes she led Redvers, carrying the laden tray, back to the drawing room. Neville quickly drew a side table up to the sofa to hold the tray and Redvers left the room again. He came back carrying two bottles of claret.

"Noticed your uncle's well-stocked wine cellar before. Did himself very well, your old relative, Neville." He pulled up a chair and attacked the ham and bread, while Julia helped Caroline to the soup. Everyone had a glass of the excellent claret. Caroline finally fell back from the table with a sigh and asked if someone would tell her now what was going forward? Neville replied they would begin with her, since she was the first to arrive. She obligingly related her story, which was quite brief in the telling, for nothing untoward, she declared, had occurred until she had been set upon by Moberly.

Redvers took up the story, repeated his part, and they all turned to Julia. She explained about Margaret's visit, and her own growing uneasiness which set her off in pursuit of Redvers. She tactfully omitted all mention of her urging of Neville to come himself, and went on to relate the unsettling conversation she had overheard between the Knox-Gores on first arriving, her discoveries and conclusions in Caroline's room, and her search and capture on the lower floor.

"But you"—she turned to Neville—"how did you happen to come out of this room? I was so grateful to see you and then everything happened so fast afterward I didn't have time to wonder at it until now."

"I was sent after *you* by Mrs. Dainty, and I'll admit I came re-

idiot I have been! At any rate, I was coming up the drive on horseback. The house was dark and I assumed everyone safely tucked into their beds, and feeling very much put upon, when I heard the most horrendous scream I could ever imagine. By the time I got my horse under control I saw a faint light through the fan over the door. In view of the continued screaming I thought a bit of caution was called for. I must congratulate you, madame, on a very fine pair of lungs," he said, grinning at Julia.

"My theatrical training, sir," she replied modestly.

"Well, to continue, I took a pistol from my saddlebag and headed for these French windows"—he pointed across the room— "I'd remembered them from my previous visit. Fortunately, they were not locked. And that is all."

"What is all?" Caroline asked rather plaintively. "What did you do? I understand you rescued Julia from that beast, but what of the Knox-Gores? Has he murdered them?"

"No, my love," offered Redvers, "they are perfectly safe. Both are outside on the stairs. Oh—" He stopped, a comical look of complete bewilderment crossing his features. "—I never thought—why *are* they out there on the stairs, Neville?"

Julia and Neville looked at each other in dismay and resignation: so much still to explain, so much still to do, their looks said. Neville shrugged and began an abbreviated account to a fascinated Redvers and an only partially comprehending Caroline of the plot and counterplot cooked up by the Knox-Gores and Moberly.

"Now"—Neville rose briskly—"we must make our dispositions for the night. Julia, you must take this child to bed at once. Redvers, you must allow Julia to attend that cut on your head and then find a bed for yourself."

"It is nothing much, I can tend it. But what of—?" He jerked his head at the hallway.

"I'm going to ask Bob to continue to hold them while I ride in to the village and fetch a constable to turn them over to."

"Oh, Neville, surely it can wait until morning," protested Julia, "Mrs. Knox-Gore—"

"I feel no pity for Mrs. Knox-Gore, Julia. It is no thanks to her this pair is still alive. She devised the original scheme to cheat Caroline of her inheritance. But for that, none of this would have been possible. When I think—" He stopped and turned away, overcome by the realization of how nearly the story had come to another ending, and how much of the responsibility would have been his own had it done so.

"You are right, Neville. I was not thinking clearly," Julia said firmly.

"I agree," Redvers said. "Why, she planned to marry that—that degenerate son of hers to Caroline just to get her hands on the money! Damned if I can forgive that!"

Neville turned back with a smile. "Thank you, friends. Very well, then, you three go along upstairs. I'll have Bob take them all into the dining room, and I'll set off at once."

He led the way to the door. Suddenly Redvers stopped and smote his brow. "My cattle! Good Lord, I wonder what that beast has done with them." He flung open the door and advanced upon Moberly, still seated on the floor under Bob's watchful eye. "Here, you blackguard, where are my horses?"

"In the woods, back of the stables," muttered Moberly, not looking up.

"What!" Redvers raised balled fists threateningly, beside himself with rage. After a second, however, he turned away abruptly. "Where is a lantern?" he barked at Sidney.

"In the stables. I'll come—" offered Sidney ingratiatingly, half rising from the step where he sat with his mother.

Redvers stared at him contemptuously and Bob raised the pistol. Sidney sank down again. Redvers went out the front door without another word.

"All right, now, you two will come down here. Bob, get them all into the dining room and watch them carefully. I'm going for a constable. I'll be as quick as I can. Then we can all get some sleep for what is left of the night."

Mrs. Knox-Gore began to wail hopelessly as Sidney hauled her to her feet and led her down. Julia and Caroline, eyes averted, waited until they had all been herded into the dining room followed by Bob. With a brief wave of his hand to the two women Neville went out the door, and as they slowly made their way up the staircase, they heard hoofbeats galloping away down the drive.

"Julia, did I understand aright? Has Great-Uncle Chandos left his money to me truly?"

"It seems so, my love."

"Is it a great deal of money?"

"Enough to set that lot down there to plotting and squabbling," replied Julia dryly.

"It is all truly dreadful of them, I know, but I hope Neville will relent about Mrs. Knox-Gore. I understand she was wicked, but I feel very sorry for her. She only wanted it for her son, after all."

"Nonsense. She is self-indulgent to excess. I'm sure if she had succeeded in getting her hands on the money, she would have made Sidney dance to her tune for every penny she allowed him to have. Neville is right!"

Caroline made no comment until Julia had put her to bed in her room. As she tucked the sheets around Caroline's shoulders and bent to kiss her cheek, Caroline smiled impishly. "Well, I know someone who will be made very happy to learn I'm an heiress."

"Who is that, darling?"

"Lady Wrexham."

While Julia stared at her in astonishment, Caroline's eyelids fluttered down over the dark green eyes and Caroline fell asleep as abruptly and profoundly as a baby, the traces of a smile still curving up her lips at the corners.

=== 18 ===

THERE WAS LITTLE sleep for any of the rest of the party that night. Julia, in spite of exhaustion, could only bring herself to lie down, fully clothed, for short periods before restlessness drove her to her feet again. Her mind whirled with all the emotions she had experienced this evening, but one emotion stayed solidly in place: her love for Neville that now blazed out of her control, fed by the image of his pain-filled eyes turning to her when he had thought Caroline and Redvers dead. That he had allowed her to share the pain he could not bear alone had caused all that she felt for him to solidify in that moment. She could no longer push it down or douse it with anger. How she was to reconcile her feelings with his probable intentions regarding her was a situation she was too exhausted to face tonight, but which would not allow her to sleep.

She finally gave up altogether and went downstairs to build up the fire in the kitchen again, thinking Neville might welcome a hot drink after his ride. Then, without any conscious decision, she fixed a tray and carried tea to the four in the dining room. Mrs. Knox-Gore raised swimming, red-rimmed eyes in gratitude and Julia, moved by pity, went to fetch her a shawl. While she was in the old woman's room, she packed a hat box with a few essentials and carried that down to Mrs. Knox-Gore also.

Shortly after this Neville returned with a constable and the villains of the night's drama were carried away. Neville then lit Julia to her room. Outside her door they stood silently for a moment. Then he put his hand on her shoulder and pressed it gently, she smiled up at him and turned away into her room.

She dozed only sporadically until dawn came, when she rose, packed her valise in readiness, and slipped out of the house for a walk, determined to think through her problem and reach a decision. When she returned an hour later she found Cook in the kitchen grumbling about people messing about with her pots during the night. Julia gave her a simple version of the night's events, which roused Cook to some tongue-clucking and head-shaking, but little else. She really had no time for such things now, what with breakfast to prepare, she declared, clearly hinting that she had no time for Julia either.

The day accelerated sharply after that. After breakfast two gentlemen from the constabulary presented themselves and began taking statements from every one concerned. The only reluctant witness was Caroline, who was adamant in her refusal to speak against the Knox-Gores.

"*They* did me no harm, and I don't for one moment believe they ever would have," she declared.

"The woman unlawfully withheld a legal document, Miss Devereaux. That is a criminal offense and punishable thereby," replied the representative of the law in a lofty manner.

"No harm came to me from it, and as for punishment, I'm sure the night she has just spent is punishment enough."

She remained firm on this stand and would not be swayed by Neville's argument that Mrs. Knox-Gore's scheme produced the climate in which Moberly's truly criminal acts were made possible, nor by Redvers's indignation that the woman could dare contemplate marrying her son to Caroline.

"But that would never have worked, Redvers," Caroline replied soothingly. "Nothing could ever have persuaded me to marry *Sidney*."

Since she refused to lay charges against them, and she was the only one would could, the charges had to be dropped. She was reluctant to see them, however, and Neville volunteered to do so in her stead. His interview with them in the rarely used front parlour of the constable's home was short and grim. Mrs. Knox-Gore, a quivering pudding of tears and nerves was, for once, too overcome to speak and Sidney merely pouted.

"You will bear in mind that I still hold your undertaking to Moberly with your signature. If you ever presume to approach Miss Devereaux in the future, I shall make it my business to turn your letter over to the authorities and do everything in my power to have action taken against you. You are now free to go."

"My—my clothes—" whimpered Mrs. Knox-Gore.

"I will have everything packed and sent to you as soon as you notify Mr. Thistlewaite of an address."

"All very well, but how are we to live, I should like to know," demanded Sidney pettishly.

"Here is fifty pounds. You will soon be receiving the legacy left to you by Chandos. You won't starve," replied Neville in a hard, final voice. It would be a long time before Neville would be able to be more forgiving toward the Knox-Gores, not least of the reasons being the fact that he had allowed himself to be taken in by them in the first place.

When all these unpleasant tasks had been accomplished, the party set forth for London, the ladies in Redvers's carriage, which he drove, Bob following with Julia's carriage, and Neville on horseback. Forced to remain seated for the trip, Julia, after a very short time, subsided into the corner and dozed uneasily, while Caroline, entirely restored by her night's sleep, sat contentedly surveying the sights as they passed.

The moment the carriage pulled up before the house in Mount Street, the door flew open and Mrs. Dainty, obviously on the watch for them, came rushing down the steps even before Redvers or Neville could alight to open the carriage doors. She received Caroline into her large embrace and Caroline laughed and kissed her cheek exuberantly before moving aside to allow Julia to step down. Mrs. Dainty gave Julia's drawn face a searching look before enfolding her tenderly. Julia stood passively accepting the comfort of resting her head on Dainty's well-padded shoulder.

"Well, Mrs. Dainty, we've brought back your lambs," said Neville lightly in an attempt to relieve the emotion-packed moment.

"And not a moment too soon, by the looks of Miss Julia," retorted Dainty, indignation at Julia's exhausted condition overriding her incipient tears. "You'll make your good-byes right here on the doorstep, Miss Julia, for you're going straight up to a bath and your bed and no more company this day," she ordered firmly.

Julia stood back and attempted to protest. "Nonsense, Dainty, it is Caroline who suffered—"

"Don't try to gammon me, missy, as though I'd no eyes to see Miss Caroline all pink-cheeked and bouncing and you completely done-up. You'll come to your bed and no more arguing!"

Julia meekly turned and gave her hand to Redvers and then to Neville. He pressed hers between his own, looking anxiously into her eyes. Julia smiled reassuringly, returned the pressure of his fingers, and turned away to Dainty, who swept her into the house.

Caroline held out her hand to Neville, assured him that of course she would be able to receive Mr. Thistlewaite the next morning, then turned to say good-bye to Redvers. He looked at her with adoration and she gave him such a blinding smile he was struck speechless. With a gay little wave she ran into the house. As she mounted the staircase after the retreating backs of Julia and Mrs. Dainty she looked up and there, leaning over the railing with a grin that threatened to split her face in two, was Margaret.

The next day brought Neville and Mr. Thistlewaite immediately after breakfast. He eyed Caroline approvingly, cleared his throat, and settled down to hear the story. When Neville had related how the will had been retrieved Mr. Thistlewaite allowed himself a small smile and said wryly, "As I told you, sir, lost wills have a way of surfacing when it is to someone's advantage. I should say it was—ahem—very much to Mr. Knox-Gore's advantage at the moment it—ah—did so." He covered his lapse into humour with a dry cough and begged Neville to proceed.

"I think you've now heard the entire story, Mr. Thistlewaite. Here is the will and Miss Devereaux hopes you will handle all her affairs in the future."

Mr. Thistlewaite positively beamed with gratification, becoming quite courtly as he told Caroline nothing could give him more pleasure than to be of service to so beautiful a young woman. He twitted her on the hearts she would be breaking in London and encouraged her to indulge herself with as many new bonnets and gewgaws as she fancied and leave all her worries safely in his hands.

The gentlemen took their leave, Neville pausing to inquire after Julia. When Caroline told him she was very well this morning but being closeted with her hairdresser had not been able to come down, he asked that she carry his best wishes to Julia, and went away.

Julia, much restored by eighteen hours sleep, was viewing the handiwork of her hairdresser when Caroline came upstairs to convey Neville's greeting, and she carefully guarded herself from allowing any reaction to be revealed to Dainty, who raised her head alertly at Neville's name. Julia turned the conversation to a discussion of new costumes for spring, but inside she was experiencing disappointment and puzzlement at the brevity of Neville's message, and what seemed to her evidence of a lack of eagerness to see her on his part. Before she could fall into brooding over this, Belding arrived to announce that Lord Wrexham was calling to see both ladies and had been shown into the drawing room.

Caroline's cheeks turned pink with pleasure and her green eyes deepened and sparkled. She fairly danced out of the room ahead of Julia, who smiled indulgently and a little sadly at Caroline's open eagerness to greet her lover. How easy for the young, she thought, remembering her own rapturous love for Edward at seventeen when obstacles had not even been perceived. Why must it grow more difficult as one grows older, she thought. Shouldn't the reverse be true, considering one had had experience?

Redvers bowed over Julia's hand and presented her with a note from his mama before turning to Caroline. The note from Lady Wrexham was a summons, more in the nature of a command, for Mrs. Daventry and Miss Devereaux to come to call upon her at once. Wrexham, she wrote, would escort them in Lady Wrexham's own carriage. Both son and carriage would wait for as long as necessary.

Julia laughed aloud as she read the note. "Your mama is not taking any chances, Redvers! It seems you are ordered to wait here until we are prepared to come home with you. Caroline, Lady Wrexham has—er—invited us to call."

"Oh, dear!" Caroline's hand flew to her curls, her glance to the plain round gown she wore, and without another word she flew out of the room. Julia followed, leaving Redvers to make himself comfortable with the newspapers.

Thirty minutes later Caroline in her amber and Julia in deep blue velvet returned and were handed into Lady Wrexham's large, old-fashioned carriage which conveyed them at a stately pace to the Wrexham town house.

Lady Wrexham did not rise to come forward when they entered, but she did, for once, say how-do-you-do to each of them, proving that she did observe the amenities upon occasion. She asked them to be seated, remarked on the fineness of the weather, and embarked on a bland series of queries and remarks, clearly impressing upon her guests her own sense of the occasion; a formal, an even solemn one, to judge by her manner.

A frail old butler tottered in, followed by a stout young footman bearing a vast, loaded tea tray. While this was being served in a serious silence, Neville came into the room.

"I told your servant I could find my own way up, dear lady, when he told me you were here."

"You were not invited, sir. What are you doing here?" replied Lady Wrexham bluntly, giving him a severe look.

Undaunted, Neville advanced and took her pudgy, beringed hand. "Why to see how you do, Lady Wrexham—and how Redvers does after his knock on the head."

"I do very well, sir, and my son, as you can see, is in very good health," she replied firmly. Redvers, hovering beside Caroline's chair, only grinned at him. Neville turned to Julia.

"Mrs. Daventry, I am happy to see that you have recovered from your ordeal."

"My ordeal was small compared to that of the others, Mr. Devereaux," she replied a little stiffly. "I only needed sleep." She attempted to withdraw her hand from his, but he did not release it. She looked up to find him smiling down quizzically at her. She could not help smiling back.

Lady Wrexham cut ruthlessly into this scene. "It is as well you have come, actually, Neville. I had not meant to advance matters so rapidly, but I see no reason not to take advantage of your presence and move ahead."

"Move ahead?" he asked politely, releasing Julia's hand reluctantly and turning back to his hostess.

"To the engagement," replied Lady Wrexham.

"The—ah—oh, to be sure, the engagement. How stupid of me.

Please proceed, dear lady,'' Neville said gravely, his lips twitching only slightly.

"Wrexham has announced his intention to ask you for Miss Devereaux's hand in marriage, though I see no need for such niffy-naffy roundaboutation. After all, you are not the girl's legal guardian and she is free to do as she pleases. Apart from that, having spent a night alone with her in the same room, Wrexham is bound to offer to marry her and she could not honourably refuse.''

Three pairs of astonished eyes gazed at Lady Wrexham, while the fourth pair, Redvers's, stared with great interest at the carpet as a wave of colour rose up his neck.

Neville spoke first. "My dear Lady Wrexham, would it not have been better—I mean to say—Caroline might not—''

"That is quite all right, Cousin Neville," Caroline interrupted, "I am in complete agreement with Lady Wrexham. It is silly to go through all the flummery when we are all in agreement already.''

"Caroline!" cried Redvers. He pulled her to her feet. "You will then? Marry me, I mean?''

"Well, of course I will, Redvers," she replied, looking straightly into his eyes,.

He exploded with joy, pulling her up into his arms and waltzing about the drawing room with her, her feet swinging off the floor. She laughed joyously but said she was becoming dizzy, so he promptly stopped whirling and kissed the rosy mouth so near his own.

"Well, really, Wrexham, you show a sad want of conduct, I must say," remarked Lady Wrexham mildly, approval writ clearly in her face despite her chiding words.

After congratulations had been exchanged Julia said she thought it was time they were leaving, but Lady Wrexham proclaimed a desire to become better acquainted with her new daughter-to-be.

"Caroline will stay to dine with us and Wrexham will bring her home afterward. Neville, you may see Mrs. Daventry home," she added dictatorially. Since no one cared to argue with her, this plan was followed.

Neville handed Julia into the Wrexham coach and then seated himself beside her. They were silent for a few moments, neither able to think of how to begin the conversation.

Julia finally said brightly, "Lady Wrexham is full of surprises, is she not? Though, now I come to think of it, I believe she has planned this to happen all along. Why, she seemed to approve from the night of the Knowltons' ball!"

"No doubt because I happened to mention that I believed Caroline to be Chandos's heir," replied Neville in amusement.

"You did?" She turned to him. "But how could you know that when the will was missing?"

"Because Mr. Thistlewaite told me what was in it."

"Oh. I should have guessed something of the sort. She would never have approved unless she knew Caroline would have money."

"Do you know, I think Redvers would not have cared about her approval, thank the Lord. I think it is always a mistake to wait for a nod from anyone before doing what your heart tells you is right."

Julia could think of nothing to reply to this and another silence ensued. Finally Neville spoke again.

"Actually, I came to call on you after I'd finished with Mr. Thistlewaite. When I learned where you were I followed."

"Did you?" she said, studying her gloves with great interest.

"Yes, and I think you must know why," he said, looking hopefully at her.

Now he wants to ask me, she thought, but he hopes that I will save him the trouble of putting it into words. If I am brave enough to accept such a proposal out of love, then he must have the courage to state what he wants clearly, for otherwise it will be a shameful thing he is asking of me. So, "Perhaps," was all she replied, noncommittally.

"Julia, there is something I would ask you. Do you know what it is?"

He cannot say it, she thought sadly. Well, I have already made my decision, and as Caroline said, it is silly to go through all this flummery when we are both in agreement already. She raised her head and regarded him steadily for a long moment. "Yes," she said at last, "I believe I do. And the answer is yes."

"Julia!" he breathed softly, reaching for her hands. "Julia, is it possible you can care for me after all you have seen of my bad temper and—and pigheadedness?"

"Yes," she said, her emotions so near the surface she could not trust herself to say more.

He raised her hands and kissed each one of them tenderly and slowly. "Thank you, my dearest girl. If only there were better words to express my feelings with. But I will think of them—sometime in the next hundred years or so. How soon will you marry me?"

"M-m-marry you?"

"Well, of course, isn't that what we are talking about?"

"I—didn't know."

"But what did you think I meant when I said there was something I wanted to ask you?"

"I thought you—I was sure you meant—" She stopped in shame, biting her lip, and the hot colour flooded her face.

He studied her speechlessly for a moment. "Do you mean to say you thought—you thought I was going to offer you a—a *carte blanche?*" His voice was awed.

She forced herself to look into his eyes. "Yes—I did," she admitted bravely.

"And you were willing to—you would have said yes?" She could only nod. "Oh, my God!" He swept her into his arms, crushing her so tightly she could barely breathe. "You *do* love me, oh my darling girl, you *do* love me!"

"Yes, Neville," she gasped with a laugh, "but I *should* like to hear you say—"

Before she could finish the sentence a great many protestations of love and endearments were showered upon her, along with kisses planted indiscriminately over her face until his hungry lips finally possessed themselves of hers, much to the interest and amusement and occasional outrage of passersby who were unused to seeing a beautiful young woman being made violent love to by a gentleman in a carriage being driven along a London street in broad daylight.